The Secret Diary of a BROODY BENGALI

HALIMA KHATUN

This isn't your average romcom...

Thank you for buying my book and joining me on this author adventure. As a token of my appreciation, I'd love to give you more... so read on to the end for how you can be a part of this very unique series.

5th May, I want a baby

Okay, I think it's time to have a baby.

It's not that I'm massively broody. My ovaries don't do a jig when I see a newborn. Yet, some factors bring me to this decision.

I'm nearly 31, which isn't old by anyone's standards, except a Bengali mum's.

"Do you want to see Hass-" The phone falls dead. "Hello?... Hell-"

"Mum, are you in the kitchen? You never get reception there."

"*Dooro!* This phone! Can never speak in back of house. That's where I always be!"

"Just move to the front room."

"Okay-okay! *Doh-no* what *baghe dora* with the kitchen. Can never talk properly. Let me get my tea cup."

Must ask mum for a proper translation of that phrase before I use it on my mother-in-law. Isn't *bagh* a tiger? So a tiger's got her phone? How does that even make sense?

Mum is busy muttering between the cutting silences while she navigates her way towards a better reception.

"What was I asking? *Dooro!* I forgot now."

"You said about seeing someone. Was it Hassna?"

"Ah. Oh yes. Do you want to see Hassna baby next weekend, if you got no other programme?"

"I don't mind. We were thinking of coming up, anyway," I reply.

"Good, good. And if you get time, could you buy gift?"

"A gift? From me? Or from all of us?" I don't know why I bother asking. Though I can't see her face, I can picture mum doing her upside down lip grimace.

"*Eh*, if you can pick a few things, that would be good. Babygrow, maybe *lit-ool* cardigan, bibs. Usual thing you gift baby. I no able to go shop on own. Your father no go, he complain backache."

"*Eh-heh*... who you talk to?" I hear dad ask in the background. It sounds as if he's quite close to the phone. Uncomfortably close for mum's liking, I'm sure.

"Your daughter, of course!" mum shouts. "The one who do all the driving, even though she no live here! I tell you, we must sort bus pass out."

"*Acha*. She do it when she come home? When she coming home? Today?" Dad sounds hopeful.

"How she come today? She not work? Not everybody free like you."

"Erm... mum, should I call you back?"

"No, no. It just your father asking when you coming."

"I know. I can hear the whole conversation. And it's kind of annoying so either talk to him or talk to me but not both at the same time."

"*Eh-heh* what she say? She be okay?" asks dad. "Did she want talk?"

"You want talk to your dad?"

"Not now, mum. I'll be meeting him soon."

M and I have been married long enough that I don't need to explain who 'him' is. There is no other man I would be meeting after work. "So if there's nothing else, I'll buy the clothes for the baby."

"But I give you money!"

"There's no need, mum. I can get the gifts on behalf of all of us."

"*Dooro! Na, na, na.* Why you pay for everything? I give you money when you come. And buy from good shop. We don't want them saying we cheap."

As always, mum is trying to keep up with the Mahmoods, our almost perfect cousins. God forbid I buy basic clothing for the new baby.

"Mum, when have I ever bought cheap? I might buy things in the sale, but they're from good shops."

"No no! Not from sale. Her *maa* will go online straight away to see if we bought it reduced."

"Auntie Jusna knows how to shop online?"

"She get her daughters to look. The other day, she wore cashmere cardigan! She think she posh? I want to remind her she live in Droylsden! Nothing posh there, ever! Anyway, come to our house early Saturday. I know you be tired, but try wake up early and come quickly. I want to get to their house for 11 o'clock. Then we can leave before lunch. Otherwise, it will be tricky as they have to pretend to offer food and we have to pretend we no hungry."

"I take it I'm driving you all there, then?" I ask.

"Yes! Who else drive?"

"So we're still ignoring the fact that your youngest has passed her driving test?"

"You know how she is. Scaredy chicken! Too scared to drive on motorway. She never as independent as you."

Mum knows exactly how to get me. Lacing a favour with enough praise that I temporarily lose my grudge about still having to carry out domestic duties, like shopping and driving, despite living 200 miles away in London.

"Well, I'm glad Hassna's found someone," I say. "Especially after her engagement broke off."

"Yes, and her sister divorce. That family always had some *shorom*. Now your auntie back to being proud peacock. Saying how great her son-in-law is. And how happy she is for another grandchild so soon."

"It is soon. She's been married less than a year."

"I tell you..." Mum's voice lowers to a whisper, which leads me to think that dad must still be within earshot while she's talking about his side of the family. "I had to get calendar out to check if baby be made before or after wedding. But we be glad for her. As she be getting old now. So had to start quickly."

"Mum! She's the same age as me!"

"That be true. Make me wonder, when will your life begin?"

I love how mum thinks I must be dead all this time and only a child will bring me to life. There was a time when getting married was the main goal in life. It seems that the ultimate achievement is a moving target.

It's the first time in my years of marriage that mum has probed into my plans for parenthood. I guess even for a modern-minded minx like her, being nearly 31, married and childless is testing her forward thinking nature. I must bring her up to speed.

"Mum, it's not like I've been doing nothing these last few years. Straight after marriage, I moved to a new city and had to get used to living with a husband. I relocated offices. Then, just as I got used to this new life, I got made redundant and had to build a career as a freelancer to make sure I had enough money to pay bills and rent. London is not cheap, you know? And after that, I spent the last couple of years... well, why do I have to explain? We've been enjoying our life. And why not make the most of it before kids? Just because everyone else gets knocked up straight after marriage, it doesn't mean I have to."

"No, no. I no saying you have to. It's good that you be independent and do things different. But not too different. No leave it too long. You never know if you have problem having children."

"You mean like you did?"

"*Dooro!*"

"Mum, you said it took a long time for you to have us girls. Remember? That's why there are such big age gaps between us."

"Okay, enough," mum shouts down the line. "So you get clothes?"

"Yes, mum. I'll buy the clothes. I'll go to Oxford Street after work."

"Very good. Also, you definitely drive us? Then I tell your auntie to expect visit."

"Yes, mum," I say, yet again. "I'll do the buying and the driving."

"*Acha*! No need be cheeky with me! It not be like I always asking you to do things."

To avoid a phone argument with my mum, which would interrupt my serene walk towards London Bridge to meet M after work, I decline to mention that I have been chief carpool for every wedding, family function and supermarket trip for the last eight years. It's just not worth the tension. Instead, I will keep score of this latest taxi request to serve as ammunition for a future fallout.

"I'm sorry to say we'll have to jaunt around Oxford Street this weekend." I'm bracing myself for M's response.

"That's nothing to be sorry about. I never turn down an opportunity to go to the shops."

"I thought you might be sick of it, as we've been the last two weekends." Yet again, M is proving to be an exemplary husband, happily going shopping with his wife. The last two trips weren't even for errands. We just found ourselves free on both Saturday afternoons.

"Nah. I don't mind checking out the Ralph Lauren and Barbour stores. You never know when they might have a sale."

I admire M's eternal glass half full nature. We're between every conceivable season that would warrant a sale but it doesn't stop him hoping.

"What's the occasion?" he asks.

"It's my cousin, Hassna. She's had a baby."

"Ah, okay."

We head into a coffee shop just off London Bridge. The one with the art deco walls, colourful tables and loud music. The one we always go to when we have an evening walk around here. We don't even need to ask each other anymore. We follow our noses and walk in.

It's busy as usual, with commuters queuing up for their caffeine hit after a hard day's work. The tables are all taken up by trendy, hipster sorts that look way too casual for a corporate job. AirPods plugged in, faces locked into their laptops. There is a table of four next to us, each occupied by a different screen user. There is a curly-haired girl with oversized headphones and her face buried in her phone. A guy with floppy, pop star hair is on his tablet. The other two occupants are swiping left, furiously. I can't even tell if they're friends or strangers. That's the problem with phones, they get in the way of human connection. Plus it's London. So there's that.

"What do you fancy?" M asks, as he's the default buyer on our coffee dates. And dinner dates. And meals out. And shopping trips. Though, for this weekend's expedition, I might pick up the tab as it's gifts for my side of the family. Otherwise, it might be taking the piss.

"I'll just have my usual." I know full well that I needn't elaborate.

"What about a cake?" he asks.

I stare down at my belly, which is protruding under my cream faux silk shirt. My stomach always looks more prominent when I'm not wearing a padded bra. It's all relative, you see.

I then examine the sweet treats behind the glass counter. There's a chocolate fudge brownie calling out to me. It would be rude not to respond. It is a Tuesday, after all.

We leave the coffee shop, with my usual fruit cooler and M's usual frothy coffee and the addition of my fudge brownie.

Suddenly, my husband stops in his tracks. "Wait, isn't Hassna the girl who just got married?"

"Yeah. We went to her wedding last summer."

"Bloody hell. They didn't hang about, did they?"

"No. Zero messing around. Unlike us, with lots of messing around."

M pokes me in the ribs. "To be honest with ya, I think that's the best way to do it. I'm glad we haven't rushed into having kids. I never understand why people do. Think about it, when we got married we barely knew each other. I mean, obviously, we wanted to get married. We were sure enough about that but we hadn't lived together. We were still figuring out things about each other."

"True," I say. "I remember Hassna's sister, Rashda, telling me that having kids straight away meant her and her hubby barely got to know each other. It added a huge strain. Then again, maybe that's why Hassna hurried things along. Maybe she wanted to get married and get onto the next stage, what with seeing her sister's divorce and her own previous engagement fall apart."

"To be honest with ya, you'd think that would put her off having a kid so soon. It would make more sense to get to know the fella first."

M makes a good point but I've got a better one. "Unless, they had a whoopsie. Who's to say it was even planned?" I slurp on my iced drink. "Sorry. That was a bit louder than expected."

"Don't worry about it," he says. "We've been married nearly four years. Formalities have well and truly gone out of the window. Anyway, onto more important things. What shall we do tonight? With us being kid-free, we can do whatever we want."

I think for a minute. "Well... We had Nando's last night. So maybe pizza?"

"We could do..." says M, though his hesitation suggests he's not so keen. "I had pizza at lunch today. I don't fancy it again."

"Pizza at lunchtime? It's not even Friday."

M looks sheepish "What it was *was*..." Here comes the excuse. "It was Kamran's birthday. So the choice was go for pizza at lunchtime or go to the pub with him and the boys later and watch everyone get pissed."

"You don't need to explain. We can both get back on it next month."

I've lost count of the number of times M and I have pledged to get back on the health wagon before swiftly falling off again. That's the trouble with central London living. There are too many food options and if you don't go out to eat, are you even living in London?

As I take another slurp of my cold drink, M says: "Babe, can we hurry up a bit? I've been brewing a poo all afternoon."

"Oh. Why didn't you go at work?"

"I tried. Twice. Sat there for half an hour on the toilet. Nothing happened, just a few trumps."

M was right. There are certainly no formalities in this relationship.

When we get home and M finishes his business, we decide to dine on a takeaway of burger and chips. Don't judge us.

Dinner is eaten on our laps, in front of the TV, as is custom. But the TV is proving to be disappointing as we've already watched all the decent shows.

"Shall we try this?" I say to M as the screen presents us with a romcom about a married couple.

"Let's have a read of the blurb, shall we?" M replies. "A middle-aged couple navigate the mundane nature of everyday life as empty nesters."

M and I smirk at each other.

"Best not watch that," I say. "We're not there yet."

M continues to flick through the channels, with each one presenting a less desirable option than the last. Then we land upon some kind of Scandinavian crime drama.

"Oh yeah, Jam used to love this programme," says M. "He was always banging on about how we should watch it. How it's a grower and you need to get through three episodes before it gets really interesting."

"Shall we give it a go?"

"Why not?" M starts punching into the remote.

"Do you miss him?"

"Who?" asks M.

"Jam?"

M sighs. "I do a bit. But, on the plus side, we have a well-stocked fridge that doesn't get emptied every few days." He offers a wry smile.

It's only been a couple of weeks but despite my best efforts (and, dare I say, stellar sense of humour), I cannot fulfil the role of wife *and* best friend.

We both return our attention to the TV.

This programme must be a grower as the first 10 minutes offer nothing of note.

I want to break the silence and ask M something that's been hovering about the periphery of my mind for a while.

"Sometimes..." I want to put this delicately, "do you get a bit bored?"

M doesn't even flinch. "Yeah. Sometimes."

"Do you think... Do you think we should consider it?"

"Consider what?"

"Having a baby. Or at least trying for one."

"As a cure for boredom?" M laughs. I don't blame him. It does sound silly saying it out loud.

"Well, not just that. I mean, we've always said we will give it two years before we think about kids. Then two years came, and we said let's give it another two years. We're running out of years!"

"We're not! You're only 30."

"I know, I know. We don't know how long it'll take, though."

M puts his burger down. He's going to say something serious. "Remember how I keep telling you not to worry? Don't worry about that stuff. When it's meant to be, it's meant to be. It'll happen."

He takes another bite of his burger, and slithers of mayo-laden lettuce fall to the glass coffee table, missing the plate.

"I think there's a bit more to it than that. We have to actively try. It won't be a divine intervention."

"Okay, well, we'll see. There's no rush."

That's M's answer to most things. There's no rush to buy a flat. There's no rush to have kids. His life runs at the most relaxed of paces. My lovable snail.

As we go to bed, M turns to me, his bald head bathed in the golden glow from the broken bedside lamp that we never got round to fixing or throwing away. "I don't think we have to actively try but we could see how it goes?"

"What? Kids?" Now it's my turn to be surprised.

"Yeah, kids. We could kind of not stop it from happening."

I think that means M is on board with having a baby.

Shit. What have I started?

8th May, Imposter syndrome

"You have two options. You can have the one day face-to-face session with me, which will be £400. Or, you can do my online course, which has a flexible payment system of £50 per month over a four-month period. Then you'll have access to all the videos, files and takeaway worksheets. Or, of course, I am available for private consultation on a monthly retainer." I pause for effect, then say: "I know which one I would go for!"

I do my best posh laugh. My audience of eight women offer me small, tight smiles. Except for Joy, who sports her usual face of confusion and surprise, as though she's smelt a fart but can't locate the source.

Do I detect discomfort? Have I been too pushy? I can't read the room.

After scribbling in her teal leather notebook, Angela says: "Could you talk me through your course again?"

"Gladly."

One area of my life which is going exactly how I wanted is my career. Perhaps my old colleague, Bryony, was right, being made redundant has given me the freedom to spread my wings and do something I wouldn't have otherwise – be my own boss. It's been liberating and scary. Expecting people to pay top dollar for my PR magic is the most nerve-wracking thing I have ever had to do. I don't have the safety net of a big company behind me. I don't have the blanket of a grown-up boss who could pick up the baton if nerves got the better of me. I don't have the unquestionable justification that comes with being part of a public listed company to explain why my fees are high. I just have... me. And it turns out I am enough.

After bagging a contract with Bernadette, I jump-started my solopreneur career and today I juggle a small clientele made up of business coaches and independent companies. I am loving it. I am loving being my own boss. I am loving working to my own pace. I am loving sending invoices with my name at the top.

However, I also have the biggest bout of imposter syndrome. I keep thinking the bubble is going to burst and I'll be outed as a little girl who knows nothing of the words she speaks. Outed as the brown girl from the first-generation immigrant family, whose dad is a retired restaurant owner and mum is a housewife. I fear that I will be outed for all the hang-ups I carry on my shoulders.

Every time I land a new client, or am reminded that I am good and competent, I feel an invisible tap on my shoulder. It's that monkey. It's telling me: *"Come on now, the game is up. They're onto you."*

I wonder if I'm the only one that feels like that. Are there others like me? Is it a woman thing? Is it something we carry through generation upon generation of expectation that a woman's place is in the home? I don't know. But it hits me hard. No matter how many invoices I bill each month, there's always that little voice of doubt that never quite goes away. Perhaps it never will. Perhaps it's there to keep me in my place and keep me in check.

Just as I'm drowning in a pool of self-doubt, Heather reaches for a form. Belinda does the same. Then Joy, who looks satisfied that the origins of the phantom fart doesn't trace back to me, follows suit. They're doing it. They're doing it! They're signing up for my online course! Bloody hell, they're even filling out the bank details. I was expecting some quibbles on that front and some protestations about data security, privacy and the like. This room of women, who have congregated at my request of signing up to my premium course, are now actually signing up to my premium course.

Do they know it's just me? Do they know it's just me sat behind a camera talking about PR?

The boost of confidence is massaged with moments of panic. What if they don't like the course? What if they all take me up on my rather generous, no questions asked, 30-day money-back guarantee?

Glass half full. Glass half full. I've got this. They know me. I've been networking with them, going every month without fail to have lunch and talk shop for the past year. They know my worth. I need to know my worth. I am good at this. I'm a competent professional. I'm so very, very good at my job. After all, I hired out this makeshift office in the basement of an old man's pub for this meeting. It's got a big mahogany table with eight chairs and a projector. I used the projector for my presentation! It wasn't just there for vanity purposes. I even brought muffins to sweeten the deal. I mean business.

"Great!" I say in response to absolutely nothing. "You won't be disappointed. I should also mention that there is a

30-day money-back guarantee, should the course not be for you."

Oh, shut up. Just shut the hell up. That's the thing you say *before* the sale, not afterwards.

Before anyone has a chance to poke any holes in my self-conscious veneer, I pack away the blueberry muffins, to signify that this free PR session, which led to the inevitable hard sell, is done.

I love central London. I love the bustle. I love that there's always a new nook and cranny to discover. Today, I spotted a cobbled alleyway which houses quaint, picture-postcard shops and cafes, with doors painted in pastel pinks and baby blues.

What I don't love so much is when public transport decides to screw me over. I'm currently waiting for the number 25 bus. It comes promptly and without issue when I'm leaving Aldgate to go into town, yet is painfully late and infrequent on the way home. It doesn't make any sense.

I'll check my phone. Maybe M's messaged me with questions and suggestions about dinner. I fancy a taco.

No messages from M. But there is one from Bushra:

How did you survive this arranged marriage process? I'm currently doing the biodata bit and can't take it seriously. Can I add going out drinking in my hobbies section?

That's just the distraction I need. I won't text her back. I'll give her a call.

"No, you can't put getting pissed as a hobby," I begin. "This isn't Tinder. You're not meeting the next hook up. You're trying to snag a husband. So no talk of drinking, shagging or anything else you wouldn't want a nice Pakistani boy to hear about."

"I dunno, mate. I just don't feel like I'm being myself. I feel like I'm lying."

"Don't think of it as lying. Just see it as putting your best face forward," I say.

The one that's not snogging some random in a bar or shoved down a toilet, expelling vomit, I think.

"Look at it this way, when you go for a job interview and they ask you what's your worst quality, you never say: *'I'm work-shy,'* do you? You spew some bullshit like *'I work too hard'* or, *'I'm a perfectionist and I can't rest until the job is done to the best of my ability'*. It's the same as dating. Whether you meet someone through your family, friends, or online, you're not going to start by telling them all your bad points. Not that I'm saying you've got any bad points," I quickly add.

"Do you reckon I should say anything about... the real me?"

I ponder Bushra's point. How much does one have to share with a prospective husband? I remember Julia playing down the number of boyfriends she slept with when she began dating Josh, the one before the one. I'm sure she's fiddled the numbers for Miles, too. Reena point blank denies having dated anyone when she meets prospective guys, despite having been in a two-year relationship at uni.

It's not restricted to relationship history, either. Generally, when you meet someone, you present your best self. You don't pick your nose, or burp. You don't tell them about any weird habits, like squeezing out the ingrown hairs on your legs. That stuff is saved for later. You let them find out the hard way, when it's too late as they've committed to you.

Come to think of it, is there anything I censored with M? It's not like I had a relationship history to speak of but I'm sure there are certain bits of information I withheld, like the picking ingrown hairs bit. I suspect he did the same with me.

"You don't need to get all your skeletons out in the first meeting. Especially not in front of your families."

"What do you mean?" asks Bushra.

"He'll be coming round your house on the first meet, right?"

"Nah, man. We don't do that. There ain't none of this serving tea bullshit. I'll just go for dinner with the lucky guy, or get a coffee somewhere. Do you guys still do that? Hosting a guy and his 50 relatives at your house?"

I'm glad we're on a call and Bushra can't see me squirm at the thought of being outed for being different, yet again.

"Not quite 50 relatives but we do have the guy come to our house. If we like each other, we can meet on our own afterwards," I say, reminded of all the times I've had to justify, over explain or put a positive spin on the way we do things. The irony is, usually I'd have to PR the arranged marriage process to white colleagues or friends, not another Muslim girl.

"Fair play. That's what my mum did. She told me how she had to serve tea to my dad when they first met. It sounded proper cringe. She had to cover her hair and bend down in front of him to place a tray of tea and biscuits on the coffee table. If I did that, a boob would probably pop out!" Bushra snorts as she laughs.

"Then it's a good thing your lot have moved on from the tea parties. Though having said that, us Bengalis never did the whole serving tea thing. I didn't serve anyone. I just had to sit there, while my mum and sisters ferried around the boy and his family. Anyway, I'm glad it's done now and my sitting pretty and looking coy days are over."

"Lucky you." This time Bushra's laugh is dry and laced with a hint of envy.

"Come on now, there's no need for the pity party. You'll meet someone in no time."

My words sound so false. It's what I heard so many times when I was single and looking. Words uttered by another settled and sorted person. A person who throws out that casual piece of hope, though we all know they have no intention of backing it up.

I remember at uni, I was the eternally single one and so was my friend Sonali. Reena was practically in a live-in relationship as well as most of the girls I knew but it didn't matter. I had Sonali and she had me. We were each other's dates to the end-of-year ball, we'd go to the freshers fairs long after we were freshers, just to get the free pens and pasta sauce. We had each other when the bitchy girls would make snide remarks about us being among the few that lived away from home that didn't have boyfriends. We could shield ourselves from such comments. We could shield one another.

Then, one day, I made a friend in the marketing module of my degree. His name was Ritesh. We had been paired with a bunch of randoms to work on a project. Being people-pleasing and conscientious, Ritesh and I were the first in our group to arrive at the library to meet the randoms.

That's when he asked: "You know your friend, the one that I saw you with the other day?"

"You mean Sonali? What about her?"

"Is she single?"

I hadn't even thought about pairing them up but now the potential opportunity was there, I could see that they'd work together. Both Hindu, vegetarians (these things matter, chicken-loving Reena warned me) and they were even a similar height, both being short.

"She is, I think…"

"You think?" Ritesh naturally thought it strange that I didn't know about my friend's relationship status.

"No I… I mean, we don't really talk about relationships but I'm pretty sure she's single."

"Would you put in a good word for me?"

I looked at Ritesh, all spiky hair, stubble and charcoal black eyes full of hope.

"Sure. I'll put in a good word for you."

I didn't put in a good word. I never mentioned anything to Sonali. I couldn't. I couldn't risk losing my one single friend at uni and being the only one on campus that wasn't attached to another person. It was hard enough being one of two singletons. I couldn't risk being the last.

Single people are hard-wired not to ask. Not to follow up. Not to sound desperate. I should know, most of my life I've been one. So at our next group meeting, Ritesh looked at me with eager eyes, hoping I'd have news. That I'd have spoken to Sonali. I hadn't, and I didn't bring it up. The hope faded from his eyes and he never, ever brought it up again, either.

I haven't told anyone this. Not even M. Especially not M. I was ashamed at having sabotaged an opportunity to play matchmaker. I was ashamed that in order to preserve my happiness, I potentially jeopardised hers. That may seem a bit dramatic. We were just 19 but in this world, where it's damn hard to find a partner and many people meet the man of their dreams at uni, who knows where it could've led? That's the thing, I couldn't risk it. I couldn't risk it leading somewhere, not until I was settled myself.

M never really understood the significance of being single at uni. He would always say: "Uni is the time you want to be single. You've got your whole life to settle down. I don't get why anyone would waste their time getting in a relationship."

I'm not like M.

Ritesh and I stopped talking once he was on a different module. Sonali and I lost touch after uni. Life got in the way. But of course, with the wonder of Facebook, everyone can nosey at everyone's stuff. Social media tells me that Ritesh is married. His profile picture is of a wedding photo, as is mine. The last time I looked, Sonali's status was very much single.

Jealousy is an ugly thing.

Finally, the bus arrives and I can shake off the feelings of guilt by people watching. Around a dozen people clamber onto the number 15. I'm poked by the handle of an unnecessary umbrella. A man that's about 6ft tall and 4ft wide barges into me, making me wobble in my kitten heels. I wish I'd brought ballet shoes for the journey. I feel unsteady, uncomfortable and warm. But I'm also grateful. Grateful for the distraction from the feelings of guilt for the wrongdoings of my younger self.

"I was just thinking," I say to M, as we settle in for our usual TV night after work. "You know my mate, Bushra?"

"The one you used to work with?"

"Yeah, before I got made redundant. Anyway, she's still single. Do you think you might know anyone for her?"

"Dunno, really. Is she Pakistani?" M gets down to the core criteria.

"She is."

M dips a double chocolate chip cookie into his tea. "The only guy I know that's Pakistani and single is Kamran but he lives in London. Plus he's a bit of a lad."

"That's okay. Bushra is a bit of a party-loving ladette. They could be made for each other."

"Shame that he's in London and she's up north."

"Yeah, that's true," I say.

As I grab a biscuit from the packet, it occurs to me that I moved to London for M. Who's to say she won't do the same? That's it. That's me prejudging. Dismissing an option out of hand. That's what people do. They assume for someone else, without even asking the concerned party. They may be great for each other. He might be her person. I'm not sure why I didn't think of Kamran sooner.

I put down my biscuit, while M readies himself for a lecture. He knows me too well.

"In the path of true love, geography isn't an issue. I'll speak to Bushra about him and see what she thinks."

"Cool. I'll ask Kamran if he's looking. Obviously, I'll probe him on the sly, as I wouldn't want to embarrass him in front of our work lot. Now, can we get back to the programme? You always have a breakthrough when it's my show."

"Your programme? It's Jam's. And so far, it's pretty rubbish."

M smirks. "It's growing on me. Anyway, we could both watch whatever we want if we bought another telly."

"No more TVs!" I say. "I've already told you, a TV has no place in the bedroom. We're not at that stage in our marriage where we both have to be in separate rooms, watching our own programmes."

M takes another biscuit, not that I'm keeping count. If he helps me matchmake, he can have the lot. I'll be happy that I can atone for the wrong I've done to Sonali, by finding Bushra a man. In turn, I will be blessed with fertility at a time of my choosing.

15th May, Families are annoying

"Do you think she be Bengali?" asks mum.

Judging by the smirk on the cashier's face as mum speaks mother tongue, I'm guessing this girl is from Bangladesh. No doubt mum deduced this from the girl's darker complexion and black headscarf.

"Ask her." Mum elbows me while the girl scans the baby sleep suits, bibs and socks.

"I'm not asking," I mumble back. "You ask if you care so much."

Another smirk from the cashier. Mum is so embarrassing. As am I, by association.

"Okay, that will be £29.20."

"*Yalla!* That much?" Mum gasps.

"You chose them, mum. I don't know why you're not satisfied with what I bought from London."

"Your clothes look too cheap but now this be too expensive! You check if that's okay? Ask girl, is that right price or mistake?"

"No, mum. I'm not asking. There's a queue."

There's an agitated couple behind us. The woman, with a blunt fringe and jaw-length silver hair, whispers something to her burly companion. He replies: "They're everywhere now."

Who is everywhere? I look around the store. Between the clothes racks, there are a few hijabis. It's hardly a brown melting pot, though.

"Things so expensive these days," says mum, as she rifles through her purse and pulls out two £10 notes. "You take card?"

"I'm sure the department store takes card, mum." I could offer to use my card and save the whole embarrassment, but it's a point of principle now.

"Yes, khala, we do," says the cashier.

I guess that confirms things. The girl has made my mum a maternal aunt, in a way only Bengalis know how.

"Okay, sister. I thought you were Bengali when I saw you. Where do you live?"

What the hell? Is mum tapping her up for a proposal for her imaginary son?

The girl laughs nervously. "*Jee*, uh... Longsight."

"Aha. Longsight got lots of our people. Her father once owned restaurant there. Hey, where your father?"

I scan the store to see dad rifling through the men's briefs. Oh dear.

"Erm, you need to put your pin in now, khala." The girl points to the card machine which remains untouched by mum.

"Oh, yes. Yes, let me think... What is this one... That's why I call your father. Will you get your father? Actually, I think I know. Err... 1...4..."

"Mum! You're not supposed to say your pin out loud."

"Shh! This be only way I remember. 1...4...3...2."

I dare to look again at the queue behind us. The line of shoppers has snaked onto the main floor. One woman is huffing and puffing, while her daughter dangles around her legs. Behind her, a man sports a bright red face. I'm not sure if it's due to frustration, impatience or warmth. Maybe it's a bit of everything?

"Right, that's all done now, khala." The cashier hands mum the big, brown paper bag.

"*Acha,* stay well." Mum cocks her head and smiles at the girl with more enthusiasm than she has ever shown me.

We head towards dad, who is holding a pair of long Johns against his short legs. "Do you think this be my size?"

"No, but we can fix it at tailor. You need to get new unders, too. All your pant holey. So embarrassing."

"So I buy?"

"Yes," says mum.

Dad puts his hand in his coat pocket. "*Eh heh*... I only have £5."

"No worry. I got card on me," says mum proudly. "We go to nice cashier girl at till. She be Bengali."

Oh, my life.

Families are annoying.

By that I mean extended family. The cousins, aunties and uncles who you're connected to by a thin line of blood but you'd rather you weren't. I guess direct family members are annoying, too (as my shopping trip would attest), yet you love them unconditionally and take them as they are. Most of the time.

We are currently at dad's sister's house. It's not fun. I would rather spend my weekend up north meeting Bushra and telling her about Kamran, or going into town with my little sis. Or even cleaning the toilets at home. Basically, anything but this.

"Children just make house warm, no?" Auntie Jusna beams at her latest grandchild.

Surely central heating does the same job?

Hassna, the girl who birthed this baby, sports a different expression on her face that suggests she doesn't quite agree with her mum. Her eyes are the puffiest I've ever seen. Her hair has strands of grey. Since when did she turn grey? She's my age! And her tunic is creased, still more presentable than the ones I wear at home, but lower than her usual standard of dress.

"How are you?" I ask.

Hassna looks at me and takes a deep breath. "I'm okay."

"Why she not be okay?" Auntie Jusna, who claims she's losing her hearing, manages to pick up on her daughter's hushed words. "She got her mum doing everything for her! I even took baby last night for four hours!" She holds up four fingers, just in case I couldn't count. "I gave him bottle! I tell her, people who say breast is best no done it themselves. How you breastfeed all day, when you got house to run! Anyway, she got her mum to take care of all these things. Take these silly ideas out of her head, like don't give a dummy! You show me the child that goes to sleep without a dummy, then you show me the mother. No you can't, because the mother be dead! Without a dummy, whole house getting no sleep!"

My mum is in the middle of auntie Jusna's viewpoint. She firmly believes breast is best but also thinks a pacifier is a huge saviour. During this discussion she sips her tea, expressionless. Probably for the best.

"And what of you?" Auntie Jusna turns her attention to me.

It was only a matter of time. I've already been here ten minutes. I've even had a biscuit. These days, there's no such thing as a free lunch or tea. Every meal you're invited to is loaded with questions about conceiving. "Do you like to be blessed with children?"

"*Insha Allah*, one day." That's the only right thing to say, isn't it?

I look at Hassna. She doesn't look blessed. She looks burdened with bulging, heavy boobs.

Satisfied with my answer, auntie Jusna goes into the kitchen, followed by mum, who looks sad to leave her cup of tea behind.

"Don't rush having kids," Hassna says, once the coast is clear. "Take your time. Go on holidays. Because when you have one, everything changes."

"Is it that hard?" I ask.

Hassna looks down at her baby. She doesn't have the look of love you see in magazines and books and on the faces of smug mums whose children probably sleep. It's the look of resignation. "It's harder."

Hassna's sister Rashda walks in munching crisps. She's wearing a maxi dress. Not the trendy summer kind but the type you wear to bed. The Rashda of old would have had a tray of tea and samosas in hand, which she would have placed delicately in front of us. Now, post-divorce, she's more relaxed and free to show the world that she really couldn't care less to serve tea.

"I always hear people saying amazing things about motherhood, like it's this magical rite of passage," I say.

I'm really hoping Rashda, who's older, wiser and been through it all, will verify some of the salient points for me.

"Whoever says that is lying."

I guess Rashda won't provide a ringing endorsement of motherhood, then.

She shrugs. "We're expected to say good things, because it feels like the right thing to say. The truth is, you're constantly exhausted, everything aches, and nobody seems to understand that. Even those that should be the most understanding..."

And just like that, auntie Jusna walks in. "What you ladies talking about? You got plenty help with children!"

"I'm not saying I didn't get help." Rashda looks away from her mum and fixes her gaze on Hassna's baby. "I'm just saying it's hard. It's even harder on your relationship with your husband. Because I'll tell you, no matter how modern and supportive your man is, it's you that gets lumbered with all the work. *All* the work."

Mum comes in from the kitchen with a saucer of samosas in hand. One of the pluses of auntie Jusna's formal, outdated attitude is that she still believes in plying guests with homemade fried snacks.

"Oh, I didn't know you were here," mum says upon seeing Rashda.

"I'm always here now, auntie. Whether I like it or not," she mumbles.

"Ah, of course. And where are the children?"

Rashda looks down into her packet of crisps, seemingly heartbroken as she is nearing the end. "They're with their dad. It's his turn."

To that, mum has nothing to say. It's new territory for us, conversing about co-parenting.

Auntie Jusna's face darkens. I think it's a new normal she'd rather not discuss.

As I dip a second samosa in ketchup, auntie Jusna winces. What's her problem? It's not like I've got sauce around my mouth. Then she says: "You stay for dinner?"

"*Nah, nah*. We couldn't! We ate before we came," says mum.

That's a lie and everybody knows it. We got here at noon. Nobody in the history of the Bengali speaking world eats lunch so early.

"What you talking about?" Auntie Jusna's usual harsh tone is laced with good intentions. "You eat here!"

I can smell lamb curry in the kitchen. I will say nothing and let the elders do this whole to-eat-or-not-to-eat dance. It makes for great entertainment.

Mum: "*Nah, nah, nah*! No talk silly! We've already eaten, I say!"

Auntie Jusna: "What you eat so early?"

Mum (doing a lip grimace thing as she realises she's been rumbled): "We ate big breakfast."

Auntie Jusna: "Breakfast! That be whole other meal! *They ate breakfast*, she say. Hmm."

She looks to her uninterested audience of daughters. Rashda is still munching crisps and Hassna is holding a full bottle of milk at the lips of her sleeping baby.

Auntie Jusna: "Cereal no make you full."

Mum: "Oh no, we didn't have cereal. I did bread squares fried in oil and egg. Very filling."

Another lie. We had Weetabix.

Mum: "You should try it. You just chop onion and fry -"

Auntie Jusna: "Try it? I taught you to make it, remember? Just like I showed you spring roll pastry samosas. Before you were rolling dough. I bring you to modern world."

Mum points her lip grimace at me this time, which I take to mean she's not sure what to do. For what it's worth, I would happily eat here. Mum didn't have a chance to cook as we were busy shopping for extra baby clothes, so there will be a tin of sardines waiting for us as that's the default option when we haven't defrosted any meat or chicken.

"You have to go to in-laws?" mum asks me.

"Not until later. He'll pick me up around eight." That's my code for there's plenty of time to eat auntie Jusna's meat curry.

"Well then, you lunch here!" Auntie Jusna declares. "You lucky you got in-laws who no mind you still doing jobs for your mum, like driving around."

Oh yeah, I forgot that after marriage I'm supposed to cut my family off like they're a tumour. Weird auntie Jusna with her archaic views.

Auntie Jusna then says: "But if you need go, that's okay."

That was a quick gear change.

Mum: "*Nah, nah,* it be fine. Her in-laws be very good. She lucky to have them."

Okay, so are we staying for lunch or not?

Mum doesn't move. Neither does auntie Jusna. It's like they're locked in a game of chess.

Auntie Jusna laughs nervously, though I'm not sure what the joke is. "Hmm... Hmm, *acha.*"

She looks at her eldest daughter. Rashda shrugs. If I was a body language expert, I would say that means: *"Well... you offered."*

Auntie Jusna reluctantly rises from her comfy chair and walks towards the kitchen. She looks back at Rashda, who fails to return her gaze and instead dusts off the last of her crisps and licks her index finger.

"*Acha*! That baby sleepy enough! You put her down now or she think you be bed! You can help me in kitchen."

Hassna's face spells anguish. I'm not sure if it's at the thought of leaving her cute baby or going with her mum. Both options sound horrible.

"No, you sit," says mum. "New mum need rest. We come help you." Mum includes me in this little recce of the kitchen.

After decades of what seems to be a fraught relationship, mum still has this veil of respect and, dare I say, a misguided affection for auntie Jusna. Even though they're related by marriage, here we are visiting her without dad, her own brother. He decided he was too tired after this morning's shopping expedition to join us. Plus, with uncle not around, he reasoned it was best us women meet and discuss 'lady things'. It's like after getting married, he passed on the relationship baton to mum. She fulfils this obligation by helping out, just as she did when she came to the UK as a married teenager to live with dad at Auntie Jusna's house. It's an unwritten rule. Even if auntie Jusna serves up biscuits, mum will bring the plate to the table. I'm not sure if it's the same rule the other way round. I'll have to pay attention next time auntie Jusna visits.

My feelings of good fortune, having been spared tinned sardines, quickly changes to misfortune, as the curry I could smell was an illusion. Yes, there is lamb curry but it's dried into the corner of a small pot. It looks dated. I would put it at two days old. Maybe three. And there's not enough to feed mum and me, let alone the rest of them.

Auntie Jusna can't hide her resentment at having to make an impromptu meal. I don't get it. Why would she insist if she didn't have anything in the house? My mum does this, though with less force. Mum asks gently enough so that she feels like she's offered, yet holds back a little so the person knows full well that she has nothing to give them. It's still weird. I feel no such obligations when I have people round in London. If they're not invited for dinner, it's biscuits on the menu. With the exception of Jam, of course. He'd always end up staying for food, regardless of what was on offer.

The downside of this unintended meal is that I have to sit for longer in the kitchen than I would have liked, in the company of the family I would rather not be with.

Auntie Jusna's kitchen invokes a pang of jealousy and inspiration. It's a feeling that has been passed down from my mother to me. The feeling that no matter how hard you try, there is one particular family that will always be a few steps ahead.

This is the second kitchen they've lived in. The first one was a small L-shape in a two-bedroom terraced house. It's the house that mum stayed in for a few years. This one, which has been the heart of auntie Jusna's home for the last two decades, is quite the upgrade. It's big, square and plays host to an island, way before kitchen islands became a thing. Mum tries to compete, but our house, the only house mum and dad ever owned, just doesn't have the dimensions for an island. I've never got the point of them, anyway. Yes, they look great but is it just something that you lean on when you're having a conversation? I don't see what other purpose they serve, apart from a deterrent for small children to run around the kitchen willy-nilly.

"Hassna will be moving to new house now," says auntie Jusna, placing some eggs in a pan of water.

That's it, then. We'll be having egg curry. The default, along with tinned sardines, when you don't have time to defrost meat and people decide to stay for lunch after you fake insisted.

"I tell her good! Of course you must have own house. Who live with in-laws these days?" Auntie Jusna laughs. "Also, he paying all mortgage. She need break after children. May not bother working. Only if she choose. But only for her own money, not for house. I say, buy house. Have mortgage. Don't rent and pay somebody else mortgage."

Mum looks at me through the corner of her eye. I say nothing.

"Renting is foolish! If man cannot afford home, why marry?"

I still say nothing.

"Are you still renting?" auntie Jusna asks the inevitable.

"Yes," I say. "We haven't decided whether we want to buy in London, or if we would come back up north."

Mum furrows her brow. I think it's code for: *Don't say too much. Don't give your nosey auntie any ammunition to stir shit. Don't fall for attempts at disparaging your life to elevate her daughters.*

I can't help it, though. I can't let sly digs wash over me. Especially when they're digging at my pride. The pride I take in my own home. If I owned my own home which, as auntie Jusna happily highlighted, I don't.

She fries some onions in a wok, whilst mum gets to work peeling the hard-boiled eggs. A piece of eggshell flies across the counter, landing in the corner near the microwave. Mum smiles. So do I. The kitchen could do with being lived in.

There aren't any crumbs. I don't see dust on the worktop. No spots of oil, or grease, or water stains. There aren't any hairs on the laminate floor. Why are there no hairs on the floor? They've all got good manes. I didn't even see any shoes in the hallway, any coats on the coat rack. Where do they store all their shit? How do they manage to keep things so pristine? Are some people just like that? Are some people genetically predisposed to be good at home-making? Mum's placemats are never without biscuit crumbs. My windowsills in London gather black dust from the constant building work outside. A week doesn't go without a new high rise going up, and we pay for it in debris.

"The work is going good?" auntie Jusna asks, while stirring her sautéed onions. I'm assuming that's aimed at me, as I am the only one in paid employment here.

"Yeah, it's going well. I just signed a new business."

Another glare from mum. Oh yeah, she muttered something on the journey here about not mentioning that I'm self-employed. I never understood why. I must take that up with her later.

"You work very hard. Too hard. You must tell your husband, he need work harder so you can take break! One day he'll need take lead, no?"

"And where is Iqbal living now?" asks mum.

Auntie Jusna, who's about to spice up the onions, drops some turmeric onto the counter. "Ah, well... he is now in... I think... Birmingham? Somewhere like that."

Now it's mum's turn to look smug. "That be very far away. Why Birmingham?" Then she fires her missile. "Isn't that near his in-laws?"

Auntie Jusna's face reddens. "Yes, but he moved for work. Do you know with doctors, when training they need to move from place to place?"

"Well, it be handy to be near his mother-in-law. To get home-cooked food every day. But you must miss him?" Mum hands over the peeled eggs.

Auntie Jusna scores the eggs with a knife, tosses them in the turmeric and throws them into a separate frying pan. That's a stage of the process that mum often skips and I don't blame her. I've never seen the point in dyeing eggs yellow before adding them to golden yellow onions.

There's a much-needed moment of silence. Mum's sucker punch landed firmly on auntie Jusna's throat and managed to muffle any further digs around me, my work or my husband.

As I have added precisely no value to the afternoon's cooking, apart from fending off questions, I head back to the living room.

Rashda's gone, leaving Hassna sat there with her baby. It looks like she's struggling to get him on her breast. He's retching, gagging and crying as he moves his head away from her nipple.

"I told mum. I told her I didn't want to start giving the bottle so soon. Now I'll never get him back on me." Hassna sighs.

"So how is it? Really? How is it having a baby?"

"It's weird. I don't know how else to describe it. It's so strange that something you love so much can be so hard. Or something that gives you so much joy can also be a bit of a nightmare, really. I can't imagine life before him. Though I can imagine sleeping. I don't fully remember what sleep was like now it's gone but I think it was good. Sleep is good, right?" She laughs. "Do you want to hold him?"

It would seem rude to say no, so I oblige. I take the tiny parcel in my hands and look at him closely. Eyelids heavy, eyelashes long and black hair full and spiky. He's like a little hedgehog. I don't have the same melting moment I had when I saw middle sis' newborn. Maybe when it's your direct family, you see cuteness more than you would with any other child. Having said that, even with my nephews and nieces, I was more than happy to hand them back. I didn't feel a pull. I didn't feel a longing. I'm not yearning to have one of my own. Should I feel like that? Am I just thinking about trying because of time? Should I be broody? I just don't know.

"Anyone who tells you they were broody before having kids is a bloody liar!" is middle sis' rather broad sweeping state-ment.

"Weren't you?" I ask.

"As if. I love my kids but I wasn't dying for them before they were born. You just have them. It's like the next stage of your life. You get on with it."

"I'm kind of thinking of getting on with it," I say.

"I suppose if you're sure..."

Even though we're speaking on the phone, middle sis couldn't make it any more obvious that she's not really inter-ested in my revelation.

"That's the thing. I'm not really sure it's just... it's proba-bly about time."

"Go for it, then! But first things first, you need to get off the pill."

"Yeah. I'm a bit scared to do that. What if I get pregnant straight away?"

"That's the risk but it's just one of those things. You can't decide one day you wanna get pregnant, jump off the pill and then expect to get pregnant straight away. It might happen, or it might take a bit longer. For me it was quick. Remember, I told you about my whoopsies, because I forgot to take the pill?"

"Yeah, I remember you telling me how incredibly fertile you are."

"Don't worry. It'll probably take you longer as you're over 30. That's expected."

Middle sis' final statement has done the opposite of what was intended and I am indeed now worried.

"Oh, I don't know, lady," says big sis.

Yes, I decided to call both my older sisters to consult them on the subject. I've got time before M picks me up and little sis isn't in my old bedroom so I'm making the most of it. A problem shared and all that.

"What's there not to know?"

"You've got such a lovely little life over there. You got your career, your little job, your life with your hubby."

"But I have to think about it at some point, don't I? I am getting on," I say.

"That's true. Though everything changes after kids. And you know you're not going to have any support while you're in London."

Big sis makes a good point. We have no family there apart from uncle Tariq and auntie Rukhsana and I doubt they'll be able to do much. I couldn't expect them to. You can't expect that of anyone that's not your mum, right?

"Plus, you really ought to be getting settled before you think about kids." I can tell from the tone of that remark that big sis is about to get preachy.

"I'm already married. How much more settled do I need to be?"

"As in laying roots. Getting a house. You don't want to raise a baby while you're still renting a flat, do you?"

"If I wait for that time to come, I'll be waiting forever."

"Oh dear."

"What do you mean, *oh dear*? Everyone rents in London. It was different for you. Easier. You got to live rent free with mum and dad after you got married as your hubby was fresh from Bangladesh and couldn't provide for you. You had years to save up, while we were all squeezed in at home to make space for you."

Big sis doesn't say anything.

I know I went a bit below the belt, but she just gets to me with her little points. Perhaps a change of subject will help shift gears.

"Anyway, what are you having for dinner today?" I ask.

"You'd know if you bothered to check your messages."

I think for a minute. When did she message about dinner? Then I remember. It was a group text. "You do know you sent that aubergine emoji in completely the wrong context, don't you?"

"What do you mean?"

"Why do you think none of us replied?"

"Because all my sisters are too busy to care about my aubergine *bazee*?"

"No, it's because your exact message said: *I can't wait to dive into some...* followed by an aubergine emoji."

"What's wrong with that? I haven't had aubergine for ages."

"Never mind."

16th May, He's a good husband

He's a good husband. He's a good husband. I have a good life. I have a great life. We have our own space in London. Away from meddling family. Just near our friends. Just how I like it. I love the city life. I love all it has to offer. I have a good life. I have a great life.

I chant these words in my mind like a mantra. It's a soothing reminder that my life in London, without a care in the world (minus bills and the usual), is indeed good. That is my main life. This is a temporary change of scene that occurs once a month, when I roll up my sleeves and swap press releases for curry. Yes, that's right, I'm currently at my in-laws. I've peeled and chopped five onions and shed many a tear in the process. I've washed and scored some chicken thighs and legs. And now I'm at the business end of the cooking session – I'm descaling the fish.

Years into my marriage, I've still not got used to the jarring juxtaposition of my life down south and time up north. Here, I'm wearing a pale pink salwar kameez, which I don't hate, to be honest. I love ethnic wear. However, I'm less enthused about the accompanying smell of fried onions and spices that permeate my skin, my hair and even my coat that is hung up on the far end of the next room. That stench gets everywhere.

M's sister-in-law has managed to excuse herself. Again. This time she is wiping her son's arse. I thought kids could clean their own faeces by the age of seven. Oh well, what do I know?

It seems that, along with joy and fulfilment, having children provides a get-out-of-cooking card. I used to think my career in the corporate sector was a good enough reason not to get my hands stained by turmeric. It certainly has got me out of deep frying duties during Ramadan, as my mother-in-law worries about me getting splashed with hot oil.

"You got office job. Can't have burns on work hands," she'd often say.

I quite enjoy getting out of that one.

However, kids are the real Ace in the pack.

While we've been in this olive green kitchen, M's sister-in-law has excused herself to clean a bum, help with spelling homework, and braid some hair.

"Shall we do some chicken kebab? You eat kebab?" asks my mother-in-law.

I would love to eat kebabs, I just don't want to make them.

"Yes, we can do. If you want," I reluctantly reply.

My mother-in-law is like a whippet. Before I finish speaking, she's already rifling through one of her many cupboards in search of the blender.

Must come up with an excuse to excuse myself. Even for five minutes.

"I just need to make a call. It's for work."

"Work? On weekend?"

I smile at her. "When you're your own boss, you sometimes work on the weekend."

M's mum retrieves her big, industrial looking blender and hefts it onto the table. "What your job?"

Not this again. I should have been a doctor or lawyer, as there's no explanation needed. "I will tell you later, mum. I just need to go and quickly make this call."

While M's mum pulls a face I can't decipher, I run upstairs.

"Oh, sorry. I didn't realise you're in here," I say to my sister-in-law upon finding her in the spare room where M and I sleep.

"Don't worry," she replies, stretching her arms out on the bed as though it's a sun lounger. "I tell you a little secret. Between cooking, give yourself small breaks. Come upstairs and read prayers, then you can relax a bit."

I knew it! She is skiving on the job. She is not tending to any children, as I can hear them jumping on the mattress in the master bedroom. And as the prayer mat is folded in the corner, it looks like she's done on that front, too.

"I can't pray at the moment, as it's that time of the month," I say.

She shakes her head. "Unlucky."

"To be honest, I find myself rushing my prayers to get on with things."

"You shouldn't. Treat it as your time. It's a break from everything. Just like meditation. English people used to think it's strange that we pray five times a day. But now, meditation is all the rage. And what's the other thing, the manistation?"

"Manifestation."

"Yes, that. Is that not basically when you wish for what you want at the end of your namaz?" She sniggers as she flattens out the creases on the multicoloured floral duvet. "Funny how these things are trendy now. We've been doing it for centuries."

She's right. I never thought about prayer that way. And truthfully, I'm not very efficient with my five-a-day prayers. M isn't, either. We're bad influences on each other. I try my best but I let the excuse of life get in the way. I want to finish a programme in the evening with M. Or, I'm tired after a day's work. I see prayer as something to do. A chore. I've never considered it an escape from the real world. I write affirmations in my journal. I observe mindfulness, though my mind is constantly busy with thoughts. I see these tasks as a sanctuary. Not prayer. Maybe I should adjust my mindset. I should definitely start taking my time when praying at my mother-in-law's. For a break and for the spiritual reward, of course.

M's niece bursts into the room and clambers onto the bed. "Mama, I'm hungry."

"That's why I told you to have more breakfast!" M's sister-in-law looks at me. "She doesn't like cereal. How many nine-year-olds do you know that don't like cereal?"

"I don't know many nine-year-olds." Hang on, is my nephew nine? I lose count these days.

The little girl nuzzles into her mummy, something that I thought kids stop doing after the age of five. It's sweet.

Her mum tenderly strokes her hair. "Okay, go downstairs and have some Nutella on toast. *Dadu* bought some especially for you."

"And there are chicken kebabs coming later," I add.

"Thanks, sasee." M's niece skips out of the room and shouts to her brother: "We're gonna have kebabs for day dinner!"

Sasee. The name you call a paternal uncle's wife. It sounds so grown-up. Perhaps it's because the only sasees I saw growing up were so matronly. Wearing cotton sarees and hair in a low bun with a parting down the middle.

M's sister-in-law looks into the full-length, dusty mirror and adjusts her maroon headscarf. She pulls down her grey, cotton dress. I think that's a normal knee length dress from the High Street, with chinos underneath to make it desi. Whatever works.

"How have you managed to stay so slim after two kids?"

"Trust me, when you've got kids, you won't need the gym. You'll be slim from running after them. Plus, a baby will give you plenty of breaks from cooking." She winks at me.

I offer nothing in return.

"Are you trying?"

Bloody hell! I didn't see that coming. Do I tell her? No, I've not even told my family.

"Not really. It's just, I worry about the future. I'm still working. I don't know how I'd manage with kids."

"Once you have kids, you might not even want to work. You don't know how you'll feel."

I'm highly doubtful that my career hunger will be swapped with maternal instinct. "I do love my job," I say.

"Work isn't everything. Also, the bigger worry is your age and leaving it too late." M's sister-in-law doesn't flinch as she continues placing pins in her scarf.

I, however, am winded. That was abrupt. Is it the being from Bangladesh thing? Was her sentiment lost in translation because English isn't her first language? I can't tell and judging by her poker face, I don't think she meant any harm.

Am I really that old?

"Whatever will be, will be," she says. "Shall we go downstairs?"

I follow M's sister-in-law down the steep stairs. I don't say a word, because I don't have any words to say.

M's dad is in the living room, watching the Bangla channel. He must've just returned from the mosque, as he's wearing a crisp white jhubba. He's immersed in the programme he's watching, which looks to be some sort of debate about rising energy bills. We don't disturb him.

In the kitchen, M's older brother is toasting a bagel. The kettle is on, too. It's 1pm. Closer to lunch than breakfast.

"What time will lunch be ready?" he asks his wife.

"Ask the boss," she mumbles with a smirk.

M's big brother looks to his mum, who is busy shaping chicken mince into round patties.

"It looks like it will be a while," he says. "I'm just going to Asif's house."

M's sister-in-law rolls her eyes. "If you go there, don't eat. I know what they're like. They'll offer you food. And I know you'll take it."

"It's rude to say no, especially if they're already eating."

"*It's rude to say no,*" M's sister-in-law mimics him. "You hear this?" she asks me as I look away, not wanting to get involved. "If you eat there, don't eat a second lunch here. Look how big your belly is getting."

M's brother slopes away, having been granted permission to leave. My mother-in-law continues with her kebab making, lowering patties into the oil.

I'll tell you what, M's sister-in-law is brave. And brazen. Perhaps she's earned her stripes having been married so many years. I wouldn't talk to M like that in front of his mum.

The rice begins to bubble.

"Shall I tip it, mum?" I ask.

"No, you might burn yourself. Worker hands."

M's sister-in-law swoops in. "Here. I'll do it."

She secures the lid on the heavy pot and lifts it across to the sink. She places a colander over the plughole and expertly tips the pot on its side, pouring out the steaming hot, starchy water. She continues to hold it like this, with the pot teetering dangerously on the edge, until the stream of water slows down to a drip. Then she returns the pot to a low heat on the cooker.

In all the years I've been married, this is one job I have managed to avoid. Worker hands, you see.

M comes into the kitchen to see what's cooking and grins upon seeing the pile of kebabs that is getting higher by the minute.

"I was thinking, seeing as it's our weekend tradition, we'll have this for lunch and order takeaway in the evening. Do you fancy pizza?"

"Yes!" M's sister-in-law and I both reply.

31st July, New office

I'm currently staring at the last packet of pills as I sit on the toilet in our windowless bathroom. The extractor fan, which turns on with the light switch, is distracting my thoughts.

Should I bin these pills? That would be a really dramatic statement. It would be me putting out to the universe that I am done with this for now. But then... what if I change my mind? I am indecisive like that. What if M changes his mind? What if we both decide that kids can wait? It will be a nightmare to get a GPs appointment for another packet of pills. What if they don't give it on repeat prescription? That would mess up my hormones big style.

No, no, no. M and I have agreed that after my birthday I would go off the pill. It felt quite symbolic.

I guess I will chuck them. There's only about two weeks' worth left, anyway. Or, should I wait and complete a full month cycle? Would that be better? I never thought to ask the doctor about this. Perhaps I should have.

God. I just need to decide. To take the pill or not to take the pill... Forget it. It's not a big deal. I'll come off it, be a raging ball of hormones and then be back to my usual highly-strung self.

It feels weird not doing something I've done for years. Popping a morning pill has been part of my daily routine, akin to brushing my teeth. What if I get pregnant straight away? That would be way earlier than I'd have planned for.

Not that I've planned, but you get what I mean. I know I can't control these things but I'm hoping to have at least three months between coming off the pill and falling pregnant. That way, I'd have a full year before I have to deal with a small person. God, when I think about it like that, even a year seems too short. Will there ever be a right time for this?

It's fine. It'll take as long as it takes, which hopefully won't be too long or too soon.

Half an hour later, I'm still thinking about it.

I hope it doesn't take too long to get pregnant. I don't fancy going down the road Sophia mentioned, of pissing on sticks and monitoring my ovaries. That seems like a slippery slope.

Right, enough about that. I'm on my way somewhere exciting – my new office space. Granted, I could continue to work from home, given that we now have a two-bedroom flat and the spare room has turned into my communications hub. However, truth be told, I'm feeling a little lonely. I miss having a team. Yes, I network like a fiend, getting myself to different parts of London every few days but when I'm working at home, toiling away writing press releases, media statements and client profiles, I get bored. I so desperately crave company that I find myself waffling when on the phone to a journalist, which is the one thing you're not supposed to do when pitching a story.

Before I start to sound like a changed woman who's been touched by London money, I will have you know that this office space rental is only part time and at a slap-down price. For £100 a month, I get to rent a seat one day a week. This means I can brag that I've got a swanky St Paul's address on my business website and casually mention this in meetings.

I only had a brief recce of the place when I first met the office manager, Graham, so I'm looking forward to seeing it with fresh eyes.

I have two choices. I could walk 25 minutes to my new office, or I could get the number 25 bus, which will take me there in around 20 minutes, depending on the traffic. I'm taking the bus.

I hotfoot to Whitechapel High Street, shuffling past a line of schoolgirls in black hijabs, walking in pairs, holding hands. They must be going to the nearby Islamic school.

Some Asian men unload a van full of fruit and veg, selected for the market stalls up the road. Suddenly, my skinny jeans feel a little too skinny and I'm regretting pairing them with a pussy bow blouse. I wish I'd opted for a longer top.

All my life, I wanted to live in a Bengali area. Now I live in the most Bengali part of the UK, the novelty is wearing off. It's not that I don't like it. I love the convenience of having several halal butchers within walking distance. It's great eating out without worrying if the pasta sauce has been cooked in wine. The world food market is amazing, with an abundance of stalls vying for my attention, plying me with free samples as I survey their wares. It's also handy that Whitechapel High Street has an abundance of saree shops, so I am never short of outfit options when invited to a last minute wedding. Of course, all our weddings are last minute. I've said it before and I'll say it again, we don't do long engagements. Oh, and perhaps the best bit about living in Bangla town is that I get my eyebrows threaded for £3. Yes, that's £3. Cheaper than Manchester, yet they say it's more expensive living down south.

However, having lived in a non-Asian area my entire life, I've become conditioned. I'm used to speaking mother tongue in hushed, barely audible tones in public. I'm used to wearing what I want, within modest reason. I'm not used to... this.

Am I turning into that person? Am I becoming a self-hating Asian? I hope not. I'll hate myself for it.

A man shouts into his phone in Bengali: "I told that son of a bitch if I see him again, I'll sacrifice him!" I don't think he means that in the religious sacrificial sense. "He can't keep money! Not one taka! It goes through his fingers like water."

I love eavesdropping.

This man's coarse tones are punctuated with the odd drag of a cigarette and spit onto the street. There are a few more dirty swear words, including the one I was told is the worst possible Bengali expletive. Something that translates into son of a prostitute, I think. I hope he's not getting the bus.

Damn, he is. He squats down on the bus shelter seating that looks more like a handrail. I'm not sure it can withstand the pressure.

Also at the bus shelter is a petite girl who looks to be in her early 20s. She's sat with her earbuds firmly on and face down, blocking out the world. Her long auburn hair, falling in loose waves over her eyes, is adding an additional screen.

I often wonder what the white people in the area think of this unapologetic Bengali-ness around them. I've never heard any blatantly outward racism, or name-calling (I guess they wouldn't dare, as they'd be outnumbered many times over). However, I'm intrigued as to how they feel, really deep down in the core, about being a minority in their land. I shouldn't call it *their* land but I can't help it. I was raised to believe that I was a foreigner here and that the girl at the bus stop has a greater equity on the part of London on which she stands, than I do. I wonder if she thinks that? It's not something anybody talks about, is it? You know, those deep-seated feelings that are a bit racist. I wonder if she's sick of this loud shouting in a foreign tongue, the smell of herbs and spices and onions and the call to prayer from East London Mosque. I would love to know what she really, truly thinks of it all.

A Bengali lady, wearing a green hijab and black coat, stands near me with her toddler in a pram. She's probably about my age, so I shouldn't call her a lady. She's a girl. *I'm* a girl, aren't I? While this girl doesn't look much older, she *seems* older. I guess it's because she's a mum.

I offer a smile in her direction. She returns it back, look-ing weirded out by the gesture. I forget, Londoners don't make eye contact or speak on public transport. Silly me. I should have got the memo by now.

Ironically, living at the heart of Bangla town, I am yet to make a Bengali friend. They are hard to come by. It's not like I can just rock up to one of the many women I pass in the street on my day-to-day business. I can't just talk to some-one out of the blue, can I? As demonstrated by my awkwardly requited smile at the girl/lady at the bus stop, it's not the done thing here. You need a segue, a path to an introduction. I don't have that. Usually people make friends in work or, as my older sisters often tell me, on the school run. My work is transient right now, and even when I was in a standard 9-to-5 in the corporate sector, there wasn't another Bengali among us. Here in Aldgate, I either see girls in their teens or early 20s, with whom I'll have nothing in common, or women like this lady at the bus stop, who's currently offering her son a lollipop as a pacifier. In this Tower Hamlets bubble, that is both deprived and gentrified, I'm yet to meet anyone like me. As a married but childless 31-year-old woman, I am an anomaly. That seems to be my default position in life. I've always been the odd one out. Why would it be different now? Maybe that's how it is. Maybe the way you start out in life is the way you'll always be.

As the bus chugs along, it stops frequently, letting off more brown passengers to make way for white. That's not deliberate, of course. It's just what happens the further we travel in from the east end. Pretty soon, I'm a minority again.

As I get off the number 25 bus and manoeuvre my way between many men in suits, I feel like the odd one out with my casual attire. I didn't have any client meetings, so didn't feel the need to dress for the occasion.

That's interesting. From the outside, the building looks a lot smaller than when I last checked it out. It's got a dilapidated vibe to it. Actually, scratch that, let's not call it dilapidated. I'd say it's got character. Bags of character. It's an old building, likely to have been someone's house at some point before London got so crazy expensive that every townhouse turned into a flat. The cobbled street, just off the main thoroughfare of Cheapside, houses many buildings like this. Though it seems to be the only one that has a front door that could do with a lick of paint. The sign above the buzzer says it's not working. Okay, I guess I'll just knock on.

"Hey, good to see you again," says Graham, upon answering the door. "Come in. Welcome to your new base. I can't remember if you had much of a tour the last time, so I'll show you around now."

This office definitely has more of an edgy, East London vibe to it. There is a row of whiteboards covered in scribble. I spot some bulletin boards with laminate posters featuring a series of faces, all looking caught out by the camera flash. Maybe it's their grunge way of taking headshots. I'm guessing they're the senior members of the team.

A guy wearing a red jumper and dad jeans is holding court at the head of a long picnic table. I hear glimpses of conversation. Something about this being the next Tinder, perhaps bigger. That's a rather lofty claim. I admire his ambition. His eager audience, that look more like students than working professionals, listen and nod. A girl, sporting black and grey cornrows, looks terribly bored. She's even chewing gum. Gosh, there really are no rules when you don't work for a corporate. I hear a few eastern European accents, and I think one guy is French. He's talking about metadata, and SEO. I know snippets of this because, on the down low, I have started to blog about my life adventures so far – finding a husband, getting married, negotiating life with a man, in-laws and a new city – into a blog. To keep it light, I'm throwing in lifestyle content, too. I'm not sure where I'll go with it but I have contemplated turning it into an award-winning book. Okay, I guess dad jeans guy isn't the only one with lofty ambitions.

"Can I get you some water?" Graham interrupts my thoughts.

"Yeah, that would be great."

Graham grabs a finger-stained tumbler glass and runs it under the tap. Wait, what? He's giving me unfiltered water? I haven't drank London tap water in years! It's nasty. I only drink from the tap up north, where I guzzle it down as I've missed the taste. Not here. Not in these parts. I'm all about the filter jug.

"Some people are a bit funny about this office. They come here expecting all the mod cons, like a filter tap. Or a water cooler. We're just not set up that way. And it's reflected in the fees." I guess Graham read my mind. I can't argue, my decision to rent this office space was a fiscal one.

I take a polite sip of the lukewarm hard water and leave it on the counter.

It doesn't go unnoticed as Graham gives a subtle hint of side eye to a guy wearing a black turban and a broad, gappy smile.

"You might want to speak to Jasdeep. He is one of our founders."

Graham gestures towards smiley Jasdeep, who puts out his hand. "Welcome to Bedroom to Boardroom."

Though the name of the space summarises my situation perfectly, it sounds totally wrong.

"What do you do?" asks Jasdeep.

"I run a PR consultancy." I return an equally broad smile, prepared to talk shop about my biggest achievement.

"Brilliant! I'd love to know more about it. Maybe I can grab a chat with you later?" Jasdeep takes a step closer and I notice he is more gums than teeth.

"Sounds great," I reply.

I've only been here a few minutes and I've already bagged a potential client. This is perhaps the best business investment I've made.

"Right, you can sit over here, if you like," says Graham, as he leads me to a row of chairs where it looks like I'll be the only woman seated, let alone the only minority.

A couple of faces glance up, before looking back at their desks. The guy next to me is a little more forthcoming.

"This is Benedict." Graham gestures towards my new workmate.

I've never met a real life Benedict.

"Nice to meet you," says Benedict in a voice as posh as his name suggests.

"You too. What do you do?" I say, a little too keen to get into client hunting mode.

"I've got a logistics company. I work with small businesses to get them better deals when delivering items to the post office." Benedict chuckles. "Not the most exciting work."

He lost me at logistics.

"What about you?"

Oh Benedict, I thought you'd never ask...

I launch into subtle saleswoman mode and talk about how I get small businesses, just like his (wink, wink) in the media, by writing kick-ass press releases and pitching to journalists.

Benedict smiles politely and listens patiently, before concluding: "That sounds more interesting than what I do. Anyway, it's good to meet you." He looks back at his computer screen.

Never mind. I'll get Jasdeep later.

I open my laptop and decide that the first order of business is to matchmake Bushra with Kamran. Very important work. I begin drafting an email. Should I send a screenshot of Kamran's Facebook page? I go to his profile. Of course, his profile isn't private. Of course, it says interested in women. Of course, it has a picture of him in a tight white vest flexing his overly large, overly built arms while on holiday in some exotic destination. Of course, he is pictured next to a sad, submissive looking tiger that's probably been injected to reduce the fury. Kamran, I barely know you, yet I know you so well.

Wait, will he know I've looked at his profile? How does this stalking business work? Damn, best logout and get off his page. And stop fixating on his arms. You're a married woman, after all.

I know... I'll screenshot his LinkedIn photo. That seems much more appropriate. Then, if Bushra decides she wants to look up his credentials, it'll be all the easier for her.

I head over to LinkedIn to find that I have a profile view from Jasdeep. He doesn't hang about. I wish I used a more professional photo, instead of uploading the same one I used on the Muslim dating website, with my loose hair and sparkly earrings. Must change that soon.

Kamran, on the other hand, has a much more respectable, suit-wearing photo on his LinkedIn. Just as well, I don't want Bushra's imagination running wild.

Send.

Bushra is surprisingly quick at replying to my email, given that it was sent to her personal address. Does that girl ever work?

She says: *Where did you find him? He is yum.*

This is followed by two emojis, a face with heart eyes and another with its tongue hanging out. I get the picture. I might have just made a match. And therefore redeemed myself of the guilt I'd felt about doing the opposite of matchmaking for my friend Sonali.

In my left ear there is a piercing voice in an accent I can't quite decipher. It's coming from the adjacent desk which seats a group of four. I'm not sure if they're all one team.

"My name is Loren and I work for QuickTime Solutions. I'm calling to tell you about our services. We've been featured in the Financial Times, the Guardian and the Daily Express. Have you seen us in any of those?"

As a PR person, I can see right through that spiel. I'm assuming QuickTime Solutions has been featured all but once in each of these publications. What are the odds that the person she's calling has read every single story, every single day, in those newspapers to catch the humble QuickTime Solutions? Not likely. Still, I'm sure it sounds impressive to a layman's ears.

"Okay, let me explain to you what we do," says Loren. "We're an email marketing company and the first to market as we offer solutions in such a unique way..."

Loren launches into more sales speak without actually divulging what is unique about the business. Another tactic. Muzzle the client with words so they don't question anything.

"Right, I'll check in with you in a couple of weeks, if that's okay?" And with that, Loren hangs up, having received what is likely to be a hard no from her potential client.

Barely 10 second later, I hear: "My name is Loren and I work for QuickTime Solutions. I'm calling to tell you about our services. We've been featured in the Financial Times, the Guardian and the Daily Express. Have you seen us in any of those?"

It's going to be a long morning.

"Hey, would you be free to chat now," asks Jasdeep, just as I was thinking of calling it a day.

This is it. My chance to secure a new client in this office space. How brilliant would that be? I would be so proud if I booked someone on my first day here. It's probably unheard of.

"The lift is broken, so we'll take the stairs."

"No problem," I say.

I follow Jasdeep up two flights of scuffed red carpet. I'm tired already, and I haven't even launched into my pitch. The office is empty now, with only a couple of desks occupied by budding entrepreneurs. It's 6.30pm. I hope this won't be a long meeting. I'll try to stay on point. Jasdeep walks into one of the meeting rooms, which is occupied by a large oak table and a whiteboard covered in pie charts. The dark green leather-effect chairs have that metal button detail that would be more suited to a fancy dining set. This place is nothing if not eclectic. It does seem like it's the lovechild of an eccentric millionaire and IKEA. Gaudy, minimal and rundown at the same time. I never knew you could have such a combination.

Jasdeep says: "This is where I have all my meetings. I've been doing this for a while, so you're sitting in the seat of history."

The seat is missing a metal button, and the faux leather is covered in cracks.

"I've funded some people that have gone on to six and seven-figure businesses."

He's got some cash, then.

"Yeah, it's really good." Jasdeep nods, as if in agreement, though I've yet to say anything. "I've got properties as well and not just in the UK. I have an apartment in Dubai...some stuff back in India..."

He smiles. Where have I seen that gummy, gap-toothed smile before?

I smile back, listening on while occasionally glancing at my watch.

"And I've got two houses here. One I live in, and the other one I've not bothered renting out. I just park my car there before I get the Tube in to work."

"Where is it that you live?"

"Wembley. I've got an apartment in Earl's Court as well."

"Mm." I mean, what else can I say?

"I've got a call centre in the works, too. It's in India but I'll be running it from here."

"Wow, you are busy!" Again, struggling to drum up the necessary responses to this onslaught of bragging.

"I like to keep my fingers in lots of pies." Jasdeep smiles again.

I look at my watch in the hope of getting the conversation moving. It's 6.45pm. I'm meant to be meeting M for dinner at 7pm.

"I'm really sorry, I must get going soon. So if there wasn't anything…"

"It's just that with the call centre I'm setting up, I could really do with a strong marketing brain to keep the team in check."

"That's not how marketing works…"

"No but it would be a role that has a lot of opportunity to be shaped. You could shoehorn your marketing expertise into the management role."

Is he talking in riddles?

"My discipline is more on the PR side of things. It's more about media management, rather than people management," I say.

"There'll definitely be lots of media opportunities, too."

"What is the role? Is it for PR, or is it for management?"

"Both."

This guy is clearly off his rocker, offering me everything yet nothing. There is a small part of me that sees an opportunity. I can't help myself. I'm a business owner and I need to pay my share of the rent every month. I'll indulge him a bit.

"How many hours would you require?"

"As many hours as the job needs."

"O-kay... I'm quite busy with my actual business of running a PR consultancy."

"That's fine. That's no problem at all. If you can make it work around your business, you can work the hours that suit you. You could even do it from home if you wanted. In your pyjamas."

"You mean manage a team in India, from the comfort of my own home in London, in my pyjamas?"

"Yeah, yeah. It's a small world. People can work remotely now. You don't need to be in an office."

"And is there a salary for this? Or a day rate?"

Jasdeep scratches his earlobe. "Oh yeah, big salary. I could meet the market rate."

Now he's got my interest. "Have you ring-fenced budget for this?"

"Not yet. It's only just starting out. So we have absolutely no budget."

And... he's lost my interest again.

"Right, well I better be going, as I'm meeting my husband shortly..."

"Yeah that's fine. But do think about my proposal. It'd be really good to work with you. And before you go, I just want share a bit more about my vision. Did I mention I've got a flat in Earl's Court?"

"And it went on like that for ages," I tell M and Jam.

Oh yeah, Jam invited himself over for dinner last minute as he was in London for work. As it's his first trip back here since he started contracting in Bristol, M felt he couldn't refuse. Or at least that's what he told me by text when I was en route.

M's belly is undoubtedly rumbling, having waited 45 minutes for me to arrive but I have to finish my story.

"The worst thing is, I don't even know what he was talking about. He kept banging on about all his different flats and houses. He even mentioned that he's got a care home. But then he was wearing a bobbly jumper. Hardly the image of a high-flying entrepreneur."

"It's obvious he fancied you," says Jam, seemingly forgetting that my husband is sitting with us.

M only shows the slightest sense of discomfort in the form of a shuffle on the wooden bench. Bloody Shoreditch, with its fashion over function seating.

"I doubt it was that. I think he was just... I don't know. Is it weird?" I didn't sense that Jasdeep was hitting on me, and I did namedrop my husband enough times. He didn't reciprocate about his personal life, though I assume he's married. After all, who'll be living with him in all these properties?

"Trust me, men are like that." Jam shakes his head in disapproval. "Why would he talk to you for that long after hours when everyone else had gone home?"

M sits up in his seat, rolling his shoulders back. "Who is this bloke, anyway?"

"Apparently one of the founders of the office space," I reply.

"He sounds like a proper weirdo," says Jam, who, after noticing my smile, adds: "I bet you've missed my honesty."

"Yes. It's not been the same since you left. He's felt it the most." I gesture towards M.

"It's true," says M. "Bristol's gain is our loss. I miss having someone to watch the footy with, man."

Jam looks embarrassed, almost emotional. "Have you seen City recently? Absolute joke. They can't even defend. I was going to watch it the other night, then I realised it was on those pay-per-view thingies that I normally watch at yours."

I can't help but smirk at Jam's thrifty ways.

"What are you smiling about? I'm not paying for that. Especially when I've got it for free at your place. Anyway, I realised I didn't have it and I don't know anyone there yet. I was tempted to just take out a package to watch that game. I looked into it and there was a way around it where you can pay to see a single match if you wanted. I've even bought a dodgy box so I can watch programmes without having to pay for streaming. Not that there's ever anything good to watch these days."

"You're telling us. We haven't found a decent programme in ages," says M.

"It's not even that. There is some good stuff, it's just that a lot of it I've already seen. There was a rerun of the cop program. The reality one? It's kind of like a documentary. It's about people that are in police custody. There was one the other night where the guy was accused of fingering this woman after he met her on a night out. Then her story didn't stick 'cause she was drunk. But then he looked really fishy as well, as he was saying they barely spoke. So how did they go from not speaking to going to the toilet together? Sorry if that's a bit vulgar." Jam looks in my direction briefly before carrying on. "Anyway, it's quite interesting. I think I'll watch that again but there's not much else on TV. What was I talking about?"

"How you watch football at our place because it's free? And now you can't as you don't live here?" I say.

"No, I still live here. I've still got my flat here. I just sublet it now. We don't let the landlord know. Not that you'd ever meet him but, say you did, don't mention it."

"How does that work? Are you sharing the bed at different times?" M asks.

"Nah man. Abdul takes the sofa. And he's got a Mrs in some other part of London. Hackney, I think. He stays there when I need to come over in the week. It's been working out okay, so far. He's not particularly messy or anything, though the other day I did find -"

"Excuse me, are you ready to order?" A waitress comes over to us.

"Do you need more time to look at the menu?" M asks me.

"No, it's fine. I've kept you waiting long enough. I'll just have the chicken fried rice."

"Cool. Jam? What you having, man?"

"I'll just have a bit of what you two are having. I left my card back at the flat, and I don't have any cash on me."

M and I look at each other. Standard Jam.

"You didn't mind what I said earlier about that guy, Jasdeep, did you?" I ask M before we go to sleep.

"Why would I mind?"

"I mean, did it make you uncomfortable?"

M laughs. "Yeah, I was getting jealous and worried that my wife had an affair with the guy with the made up life and made up properties."

"To be fair, there were a lot of made up properties," I say, glad that I didn't incite any envy. "As if I'm going to believe all that crap. I guess all the other people in the office do. If he's a founder, they must listen to his shit every day. I still don't get it, though. I wasn't looking for a job or anything? People are weird, right?"

M doesn't respond. Then, I hear a dull, nasally snore.

I switch my phone to night mode, rendering the white screen red, in the hope of not disturbing M's sleep.

I'm going to look up this Jasdeep guy. His LinkedIn profile has him as an entrepreneur and CEO. CEO of what? I'll check out his Facebook for more info. A quick scan doesn't give much away. It does say he's married. I would love to see a picture of his wife, just to be nosey as I'm too awake to sleep now. There are no pictures of his wife but lots of pictures of him. There's also one where he's wearing a red turban and it looks like he's at a wedding or something. Wait a minute... I've seen that photo before. Where have I seen it?

"Bloody hell!"

"Huh? What happened?" M lifts his head, startled.

"Oh, nothing. Doesn't matter."

"You sure?" M has one eye still closed.

"Yeah. I'm okay. Don't worry, go back to sleep. I'm going to do the same."

It's best not to mention to M that this Jasdeep is the Sikh guy that was on the Muslim dating site back when I was single and looking. He messaged me and I blocked him. Did he recognise me? Was he married when he was looking on the wrong dating site?

A look through his Facebook feed reveals more. There is a memory photo that shows what looks like his wedding day. He's wearing a cream sherwani, brandishing a silver, diamanté encrusted sword. Again, no picture of his bride. It's time stamped at 10 years ago. The maths makes sense, as he looks to be in his early 40s. He was married when he was on the dating site. What was his game? Was he just hoping to have a bit on the side with a girl from a different religion?

Bloody hell, it goes to show, anyone can be anyone on the internet.

I best keep this to myself, as I don't want to turn M's casual coolness into raging jealousy and jeopardise my place in the office. I'll never find a cheaper rental. I also really ought to avoid Jasdeep like the plague.

31st August, the light hits different

"It's my mother-in-law. She's being a right pain in the backside," says Sophia.

"Really? I always thought you had great in-laws."

I remember when Sophia mentioned how her mother-in-law waits on her hand and foot when she visits. That's something of an anomaly in Asian culture as it's usually the other way round.

"Not really, hon. I wanted to go away with Adnan. Just the two of us for a weekend. Maybe a spa somewhere in the UK. She usually has Imran every other weekend. Except the one time I actually want to make plans to do something, she can't do it."

"Did she say why?"

Sophia sighs. "Something about how she's not getting any younger and she's not as strong as she used to be. And you won't believe this," she pauses, "as a consolation, she suggested going along with us on a spa date. That way, she reckons she can watch Imran while we do our own thing. I thought, it's not quite a romantic weekend when you've got a third and fourth wheel with you, is it?"

"Yeah, that could be a bit much," I say. "It's great that you had the help while she was able."

"Hon, she should be still able. She's not even that old or unfit. She talks about how she's only got about 20 years left to live, while I'm thinking, 20 years is a bloody long time!"

I think about my future... what will happen when M and I have kids? I always thought I wouldn't want to burden my mum with babysitting, as she's done enough over the years. But then, where is my refuge? Who would I turn to when I need a break? My mother-in-law doesn't seem in the best of health. She's not seriously unwell but, with an achy hip, a slight limp to her walk and diabetes, I know I wouldn't be able to expect too much of her. Just like my own parents, she's not getting any younger. In fact, now I'm no longer living at home, they all seem to be ageing quicker. With each visit, I notice another grey hair, more lines, more naps and less enthusiasm to go for walks. So, what's the answer? I certainly don't have it.

One thing's for sure, I don't know what Sophia's complaining about. However, I decide to change the subject. Sophia is not one to take the high road on a debate, while I'm all for an easy life, so I'm not going there.

It's time to share my plans.

"You're trying for a baby?" Sophia's squeal is so loud that she really didn't need to call me. I would've heard her all the way from Manchester.

"Well, kind of... but not really. As in, it's business as usual. I'm not trying extra hard or anything." I'm not sure if I'm getting into TMI territory here.

"But you're off the pill?" Sophia asks.

"I am."

Sophia is the first person to hear about M and I trying but not. I'm a bit too scared to mention it to anyone else, not least my family. They would be the worst people to confide in.

Even sharing with Sophia is scary. There's that monkey on my shoulder again. The one that warns me that I shouldn't get my hopes up. That this happiness is fleeting. That I've got the husband, the life in London, the freedom, the career. That I've got more than I expected so I should be super grateful about my happiness as my luck has run out. This is as good as it will get. There will be a catch somewhere. I'm trying to be glass half full but it's hard. I'm trying to undo decades of low expectations born from a lifelong fear of jinxing myself. So Sophia's probing isn't helpful.

"Okay, but even if you're not really trying, give yourself the best chance. Remember, we spoke all those years ago about what to do? Have you got some ovulation sticks?"

Not this again. "No, I haven't. I'm not quite ready to pee on a stick."

"Right. Maybe get yourself some, anyway. Just in case. Do you want my pregnancy books?"

"Erm... I think I'll hold off for now. I don't want to get into full-on trying to conceive mode."

Sophia laughs. "Fair enough but remember, whenever you need them, I've got stacks of books. And I want regular updates."

"Okay." I'd now rather change the subject back to Sophia. "What else is going on with you, besides needing a weekend babysitter?"

"I'm good." She pauses, again. "I wasn't going to say anything because it's quite early, but since we're on the subject... I'm pregnant again!" Another squeal from Sophia.

That was unexpected. I always thought Sophia and Adnan were done after one.

"That's amazing! I'm so glad. I know it's been hard for you…"

"You're right. I didn't think I'd ever be a mum. Never mind having two! I just feel blessed. But now I've got to think about work. Not that I'm complaining but it's like I've finally got myself some normalcy after being in the mum brain fog. So diving right back into it… it'll take some getting used to."

"You're great at what you do, so I doubt mum brain will be a major problem."

"Here's hoping. How will it work for you when you have kids? What with you having your own business and all?" Sophia asks.

"I've not given it loads of thought." That's a lie. How I'd get paid is one of the first things I looked into when considering whether to try for a baby. "But having a limited company means I get maternity pay…"

"That's good. Is it minimum wage?"

"Pretty much." My voice, and enthusiasm, is lowered with the revelation. It's not the most lucrative package. I imagine Sophia will be more cushioned when she goes off on leave.

"OMG! I'm only five weeks down the line. What if we end up pregnant together?"

"Whoa, whoa! Let's not get too ahead of ourselves. Like I said, I'm trying but not really."

"You know what they say though, hon. It only takes the one time to make a baby."

I don't know who says that but one thing I'm sure wishing is that I hadn't been so forthcoming with Sophia.

"Right, I better go. I'm just about to head into the event now," I say, glad to be putting this conversation to bed.

"No worries. Ooh, just an idea... maybe you could start a blog about trying to conceive. There's a lot of interest in that. I was reading all of them when I was trying for baby Imran."

I think that confirms Sophia hasn't got the memo about me keeping this whole thing on the down low. The last thing I want to do is blast out my personal details on the web.

Anyway, just in case I do get pregnant quite soon, I better fit in all the blogger events while I can.

Shit. Am I really old?

No sooner have I arrived at the ridiculously chic looking meeting room in this rainbow-coloured building, I am greeted with an onslaught of gen Z phraseology. There's a bunch of people talking about finding their truth, needing to feel seen, and how the light in the room just hits different. Hits what?

I decide to do what's best in this situation, raid the free food. There is a giant oval table in the middle of this vast room, playing host to cans of fizzy drink, crisps and biscuits. It's not quite dinner, but I'll take it as a win.

"What are you going for?" a lady, who, thankfully, looks older than me, asks. Unlike the other women here, who are preened and polished, she has hair that looks unbrushed and a camo outfit that looks more safari than catwalk. I feel better about myself, with my humidity ravaged hair. Why is it that I can never achieve a sleek, blow-dried style? Oh yeah, it's because I never blow dry my hair.

"I think I'll have a can of Coke," I say.

"Shall we share one?" asks the waste-conscious woman.

Is it rude to say *I'd rather not*? I decide it is. "Yeah, sure."

"So what's your platform?"

I tell her about my burgeoning blog, where I anonymously talk about the pursuit of a man and other real life struggles such as whether you can pull off red lipstick when sporting a hint of moustache. It's all riveting, groundbreaking stuff. Then I have a moment of concern... everything I've done so far has been anonymous. I don't use my real name. I don't show my picture. The times I have to show off something, like a swatch of lipstick, I use my arm instead of my face. I'm not sure if I'm blowing my cover by sharing too much with this woman.

"That sounds really interesting." She raises her hand. "I'm Jennie, by the way. I write about how to encourage biodiversity to combat climate change."

Now my blog sounds shallow. I want to ask her how she monetises her platform, though that would make me sound even more shallow.

"How did you get into it?" I ask.

"I was just looking for interesting topics and I came upon this area. It's a great niche to be in. Advertisers love it. The other day I had a sponsored post with Unilever as they're trying to be more environmentally friendly. You'll be surprised how many big brands are getting on the bandwagon."

I guess everyone has a price.

"Anyway, I'll see you later." Eco-warrior Jennie walks away and sidles up towards her next networking project.

Over my shoulder, I can hear bits of a conversation.

"Influencers shouldn't be underestimated. Everyone laughed at first. Take me, a 45-year-old bloke saying his job is doing funny videos on Instagram. Now I earn more than I did in my old job. Who's laughing now?"

I turn around to see who is indeed laughing. It's a guy with an early 2000s, greying Mohican hairdo, a black Punk rock T-shirt and jeans with more chains than pockets.

I need someone to talk to. Anyone. Otherwise, I'll be the only saddo in the room that's not with the in-crowd and perhaps invited by accident.

I do that thing, where I slowly walk towards a group and start smiling, inching my way into the conversation. I approach some girls who are talking about viral trends.

"I was going to video myself shopping at Whole Foods and going through their stuff," says a girl who looks like she's just left the office, as she's in an all black outfit of blazer, skirt and tights.

I don't know who would want to watch that.

"So what do you do, when you're not in Whole Foods?" I ask.

"I just work in an office. But I'm tired of it. I'd rather do this full time."

"And what is it that you do?"

"I'm on TikTok, mainly. I do videos around hair care for Afro hair. It's been good. I've been gifted silk hair wraps and stuff like that. But whenever I try to do something different, like talking about healthy food or sharing a funny video, it doesn't get the numbers. I've put myself in a niche."

"Awww," I say. "What do you do in your day job?" That was my real question but I didn't have the heart to say so when she started talking TikTok.

She looks at me like I've asked her how often she brushes her teeth. "Just an office job."

I find it so strange, having prided myself on having a career, that others would do their best to get out of it. And for what? For this? For the predictably unpredictable world of social media, where as soon as a platform peaks, it's taken over by something new? A place where you have no real contracts, no written rights, no redundancy, or paid leave?

"The freebie sounds good. Hair wraps and all that." A girl with black and electric blue braids adds. "I find mainstream brands don't want to work with black girls. Unless it's a token thing, like a Black Lives Matter thing. The real work goes to the blondes, or the light-skinned girls."

I have barely dabbled in this world and am now learning that marginalisation exists in the social media sphere, too. I shouldn't be surprised, really.

"Can I have your attention, please?" A man who looks more investment banker than influencer, takes to the mic. "I'm Neil and I wanted to thank you so, so much for coming over. Especially on a Tuesday evening, as I know some of you have just left work."

There are some groans and grumbles from the audience, including the reluctant office worker next to me. "But I wanted you guys to be the first to hear about this amazing new initiative. It's called *Keeping it reel*. As in r-e-e-l." Neil points to the flatscreen, which displays the word in bright blue capital letters, just in case we were still unsure. "It's all about freeing your truth, taking away the airbrush and being your authentic self. Social media has become so filtered and we want to go back to how it was, when blogs and pages and profiles were about normal people doing normal things. The good. The bad. The ecstasy. The agony. The moments of celebration. The moments of mourning. We want to be there with you. We want you to be there with the world, capturing it all."

"Already on it," a girl near me mumbles to someone else. "I posted about, like, my dog dying last month. I just shared, like, a black-and-white picture of us. I didn't do it for views or nothing. I was just, like, in bits about it. But it went viral."

"I wish I'd done the same." A girl next to her, with her mousey brown hair in a bun that is anything but messy, is regretting not oversharing. "Six months ago, my great uncle died. I wasn't that close to him but I wish I'd posted about it. I was gonna share something, but I was busy posting belated holiday pics from Rome. I should've just done one tribute video, at least."

"Make sure you do it next time," the grieving dog owner says. "You owe it to your audience to, like, share everything. The more you share, the more likely they'll join you on your journey."

I'm not sure about this. Coming from a family where you don't share your private business, this feels like a slippery slope. The end game is, obviously, to bring in a big enough audience that you can start charging for your content. However, if you capitalise on the grief of your dog, should you also make money from the death of a loved one? How far is too far? How much is too much? The line is so blurred, I can't see where being open ends and cynical oversharing begins. I don't know.

Even with my own very modest blog, I have contemplated sharing my face. If readers cannot put a face to the content, it won't resonate with them. I've read about this in numerous online blogs which offer advice followed by a call-to-action to join their paid course, because nothing is really free. If I talk about my life, do I have to include M? Will I be pissing on a stick on camera, holding up the results to see if I'm pregnant or not? Will I record my reaction for the world to see before I've broken the news to my family? Where will this lead? Where does this all end? And after that, when the follower interest inevitably dries up, when things plateau, when the views start to dwindle, where do you go from there? After all, when you've commoditised every aspect of yourself, and there's nothing else to sell, will it all have been worth it?

"And as a token of our appreciation for you attending here tonight," says Neil, "there is a gift bag waiting for all of you. There's loads of goodies, including a skincare set from our lead sponsor, True Beauty and a lipstick duo from NARS."

Well, I do like lipstick so I guess that sweetens the deal.

Looking around, I can't help but feel that this is more of an event for someone like Naila. Nestled among the office girls and middle-aged men in tight jeans, there are pretty girls that look like they've stepped out from a fashion shoot. Their cheekbones are sculpted beyond anything I could ever emulate. Their eyelashes are feathery long. Their lips are full of filler. These girls would be interchangeable were it not for their varying ethnicities. In fact, I think I spy an Asian girl in a bright green, look-at-me coat. Wait a minute... Oh my life... is that? It can't be... Actually, it really is. It really is Naila. What is she doing here? Surely she's not an influencer?

She has the look of embarrassment as our eyes meet. It's the equivalent of spotting someone you know in a club, when neither of you should be there.

She leaves her identical friends and comes over to me. This could be awkward. I haven't seen her since that crap coffee date she took me on in central London, where she probed into my marital status and planted seeds of doubt. Gosh, we're talking one and a half, maybe two years ago? Avoiding her has been quite easy, as she's never at uncle Tariq and auntie Rukhsana's house when I go over. Perhaps courtesy of marrying Darren, she's not been at the few weddings we've attended, either.

"What you doing here, man?" Naila approaches me with an air kiss. "It's been time."

"It has been time," I say. "I'm just here for..." Shit. What do I tell her? I don't want any of my family, no matter how close or distant, to know about my blogging hobby. It's supposed to be a secret. Should I tell her it's about makeup? No, that won't work. She'll definitely want to look at my site, the nosey cow. What should I say? Think, think. "I'm here for work."

"Yeah? Me too! Like, are you even a makeup artist if you're not on Insta? I didn't know you did beauty PR. Otherwise I'd have tapped you up for free publicity long ago."

She laughs and so do I, relieved that she swallowed the lie.

"What kind of content do you post? Just makeup tutorials and stuff like that?" I ask.

Naila hesitates. "Yeah... That sort of stuff. I'll tell you what, you wouldn't catch me dancing or any of that crap I see on there." She laughs. "If I did that, I know I'd go viral and have way more followers but it's not my style, man. And what would my dad say? I'll stick to my shots of brides and selfies. I might diversify, though." Naila moves closer to whisper through the loud chatter around us. "It's just that... I'm preggo, innit?"

She pats her barely there tummy as I give her a look of genuine surprise and offer slightly feigned congratulations.

Why is everyone suddenly getting pregnant all at once? Is there something in the water? Should I be drinking that water?

I am not jealous. I am not jealous. I'm not jealous. Anyway, why would I be jealous? I've got loads of stuff going on. I wouldn't want to be pregnant today, right this moment. I want at least a year, maybe longer, before a baby comes into my life. I've got a good career. A great life with M. All the date nights, all the restaurants. We watched The Lion King at the West End on the weekend. We lie in. We watch TV until 3am because we can. I couldn't do all this if I had a baby. So no, I'm not jealous. Not jealous at all.

But then... what is this feeling? As I sit waiting for the number 15 bus that is taking its sweet time to arrive as per usual, I've got a strangeness in my being. I'm not angry, I'm not frustrated, just... I don't know... something. I can't quite pinpoint what it is. Obviously, I'm not jealous. I've only just started trying but not trying. I'm... weird about it.

If I really try, I can recall similar feelings when I was looking to get married. I felt like everyone else was getting that bit right and securing a suitable husband. Everyone except me. I remember looking at Facebook updates of friends who were celebrating anniversaries, going on holidays with their fella and generally living life. While I, meanwhile, was at home in my single bed next to my baby rhino wheezing sister. I don't feel hard done by at all. I should be happy. Is it just the fear of missing out? Is it like when a small kid sees another small kid with a ball and ultimately decides they have to have it? I've seen my nephews and nieces do this often. I've witnessed a fight over a toy car, a stick, a pebble on the driveway. It's all the more desirable when someone else has got it.

As I've got time to kill, I go on my phone to hunt for Naila on Instagram. Yep, she's using her full name on her profile, so is super easy to find. I couldn't miss those full lips and fluttery eyelashes if I tried.

She doesn't hang about. She's already posted a photo from today's event with the caption:

The light hits different when you share your truth... @Keepingitreel, thank you for having me. It was a mood. And in honour of keeping it reel, I'm sharing some realness of my own. Can you guess what it is? #invite #bump

The accompanying photo is of her with her green trench coat resting on her shoulders, to reveal a fitted black dress. She's resting both hands on her stomach. How is it that she manages to get the camera at exactly the right angle? The photo looks like it's from a magazine.

Maybe it's time I started to show more of myself. Sod this incognito business. It's getting me nowhere. I only got invited to the blogging event as I had reached the bare minimum of 100 views per month. I'm pretty sure most of it's from me constantly refreshing the homepage.

I take a selfie leaning against the fence. I hold the camera upright, as I've seen many others do. Apparently, this is to make your face look slimmer and reduce the number of chins. I do a small smile, not too toothy.

Click.

Examining the photo, I see that I look constipated. What are those dots on my face? Are they age spots? Or freckles? Do brown people get freckles? I have so many short hairs that are poking out from my head. Why do they look like pubes? And it's less a case of the light hits different, more the light is casting shadows in all the wrong places.

I think it's wise to stay incognito for a while longer.

7th September, Playing cupid

Bushra is coming to London and staying at mine. She's wangled a meeting with work, though it's something she totally could've done from up north, over the phone. However, much like I used to use the excuse to work from the northern office, she's doing the same. She has an ulterior motive and I'm all in on it.

My role of matchmaker has proven rather successful after M and I arranged a social media introduction between her and Kamran. They're going on a date.

"This is amazing," says Bushra, as she steps out of the Tube station.

I look at the black bin bags, full of litter, lining the pavement. "Do you think so? My family aren't that impressed when they come here."

I'm all the more aware of the urban-ness of Aldgate when people visit. Especially people that come from up north, where houses with gardens are an affordable luxury. I'd happily walk past dozens of trash bags, not batting an eyelid, in my daily life. But when someone not so accustomed to East London looks on... it's a different story. Even Julia can't hide her surprise when she comes to see me. More often than not, I opt to visit her, or meet somewhere central.

The one thing I am glad about, however, is my cool, newish flat. We moved in last year and it's got a concierge, a large lobby and lift access, which makes up for the fact that

M and I only occupy a tiny space with two bedrooms in the building.

Bushra's eyes widen. "I feel like I'm on holiday."

"That's a bit of a stretch, Bushra."

"No, it feels warmer here. Don't you notice it's warmer than in Manchester?"

"It rains less."

Bushra is certainly dressed for warmer climates. With her sleeveless orange jumpsuit and platform heels, she wouldn't look out of place at a Turkish resort.

We enter my fourth floor flat and the illusion is somewhat ruined as we shuffle in and make space for ourselves, our oversized handbags and Bushra's suitcase, in the square hallway that's not quite a hallway.

"I'm so grateful you're having me over."

"No worries. What's the plan? And don't say funny business."

"Yeah, right." Bushra sniggers.

Phew.

"Nobody born after 1981 calls it funny business."

"Oh."

"Relax, my sweet darling girl." Bushra takes her phone out of her bag. "We're only going for a drink." She then looks up with a grimace like my mum's. "Do you think I'm really bad?"

"No! Why would you think that? I'm not one to judge," I say, knowing full well that I have judged her in the past and am slightly judging now. "It's not my business what you do. I just hope it works out for you."

"Me too. He's *soooo* fit."

I don't want to sound like a mother hen or anything, but where the hell is she? It's half eleven.

"Don't worry about it," says M, before turning in to bed. "He's probably taken her out for a drink and then they're getting some food or something. You're not her mum. She is older than you, isn't she?"

"Maybe by a month or two. That's not the point. Should I check in on her, or is that a bit weird? Maybe I should stay up a bit longer."

"Nah, don't bother. To be honest with ya, she should've told you as a courtesy if she's staying over with him."

"God, what if he's a bit rapey?" I really hadn't factored this in when matchmaking. I've been watching too many Bollywood movies, not to mention the example of my own romance. I thought they'd have a hot chocolate together and he'd chivalrously drop her at my door by nine.

M laughs. "He's not rapey. He's a good-looking guy."

"I don't think it matters how attractive he is."

"No, but what I mean is..." M struggles to explain his theory.

I'll fill in the gaps. "Good-looking men can be predators, too. If it was only the ugly ones, then you wouldn't get these Hollywood actors caught red-handed. Or being handsy."

"Like who?"

I think for a minute. "Fine. I can't name anyone right now but you hear the stories all the time."

"Yet you can't name a single person..." M tickles my shoulder.

"Because you've put me on the spot! And quite frankly, I don't like this chauvinist attitude and it's something we'll have to unpack in the future. But right now, I need to know Bushra is okay. Shall I message her?"

"If you want."

At this point, M will say anything so he can go to sleep.

Oh crap. Crap. Crap. Crap. Crap. What is happening? Is she okay? It's midnight. She has to hurry back before she turns into a pumpkin.

If she's getting laid, I'm going to be seriously annoyed. I mean, how dare she use my house for a booty call. What does she think this place is? On the plus side, at least they both didn't come back here.

Glass half full and all that.

I am an awful friend. Awful. Why did I let her walk into the arms of a monster? Is she my responsibility, as she is living under my roof tonight? Should I call the police? Does someone have to be gone 24 hours before you can file a missing person's report? It's only 2am.

I know, I'll text her one more time:

Hi, checking in again. Hope you're okay and safe. Any problems, let me know and we can get you. Please message me back so I know you're okay.

Must try to get some sleep. Must stop fretting about Bushra.

Oh my God. I've just realised I don't have any contacts for her next of kin. Who would I call if something happened to her? I don't even know her mum's name.

That's weird. M's phone is buzzing. Who's texting him at this time of night? It better not be a girl.

"Do you wanna get that?" I ask.

M is fast asleep so I shove his shoulder. He lifts his head up and raises his arms out, ready for combat. He must think I'm an intruder.

"Relax. It's just me. Do you want to check that?"

"Hmm? What?"

"Your phone. I think someone text you."

M grunts as he checks his phone. "It's Kamran," he says, going from squinty to wide-eyed. "You might want to read it."

He passes me the phone.

Can you tell your wife to stop cock blocking me? She's been messaging all night. We're busy ;)

Dirty bastards.

8th September, Friends are annoying

"Are you annoyed with me?"

That's always a rhetorical question, isn't it? I can't full well say: *"Yes, I am annoyed with you, Bushra. I am annoyed for having stayed up half the night thinking you'd been raped, or murdered, or worse. I'm not sure what's worse than rape or murder but that's beside the point. I'm annoyed that you didn't even bother to tell me you'd be going over to Kamran's. I'm annoyed that you didn't bother to put my mind at ease. I'm also annoyed that you're getting more action than me, and I'm the married one who's trying for a baby. So yes, I am annoyed with you, you thoughtless cow."*

Instead, I say: "No, it's fine. A bit of a heads up would've been nice, to let me know you weren't coming back to ours."

"I know, I know. It's just that I'd had a bit to drink. I think I was tipsy. Then, after we left the bar he suggested going back to his and well, he is fit. He ticks all the boxes." Bushra gazes out of our window, looking wistfully into the opposite tower block. She looks like she's in love. "You are very cute, being concerned for my welfare."

Was I wrong to be worried? Should I not have been concerned, given that she was technically under my care? Am I turning into a mum? Bloody hell, is that it? I don't want to be mothering someone who is my age. Maybe I should have left her to it.

"Do you think I'm really bad?" Bushra's eyes dart nervously from side to side. "Come on. I'm not that bad, am I?"

I lay down the toast in front of her, along with a steaming mug of tea.

"It's none of my business what you do. Like I say, I was just concerned that you were chopped up in Kamran's freezer, or floating down the river Thames."

"Oh, you are cute!" She looks at her breakfast and winces. "I'm alright for food, thanks. I feel a bit sick."

Great. Well, that's just great. She could've told me before I made it for her. Some people are just so inconsiderate.

"Could you do me a favour?" Bushra whispers, though there's no need as M is in the shower so he won't hear anything. "Could you get M to find out what Kamran thinks of me?"

"I would've thought he thinks very highly of you after last night."

"I mean whether he'll want to see me again."

"Fine, I'll find out for you. Though I doubt you need to worry on that front. If he had you round to his, I'm sure he's very keen."

"Mate, you and me both know that doesn't really mean anything." Bushra sighs.

"If that's the case, then why did you -" I stop myself from saying anything that may come across as judgemental.

Bushra looks at me, waiting for me to continue. I don't.

"It's not just about him being fit. There was more to it."

"Like what?"

"You know..."

"Obviously I don't." I am so far out of this game that I haven't a clue what she is on about.

"It's just... I'm the black sheep, aren't I? I'm nothing like the kind of girl a nice Pakistani boy would want to take home. I'm nothing like any other women in my family. They're stuck up, settled cows, who married nice boys from nice families. I have to sit with them at weddings as I'm the only one who is single as fuck. The one who stands out with her shorter hair and tighter salwar kameez. I'm nothing like the other women and I thought there was no one else like me. But it seems like Kamran is. Someone who I can take home to meet my parents but is still a bit of a black sheep, like me. I wouldn't have to hide around him. Or worry what he'd think about my past, or the fact I like to party. I mean, even if he didn't want to after marriage, I'd be fine with it. I'm done with going out. I just wanna have a nice life with a nice man. Like you have with M."

I try to do my best reasoning. "You know I love you, so I'm going to say this from one sister to another, and it's nothing you haven't heard before -"

"I know. I know it." Bushra raises her palms in the air. "You're gonna say the same thing. Don't go to the bars and clubs to meet a guy. Go to museums and photography meet-ups and some other shit. I'd happily do all of that if I had somebody to go with. Why do you think I'm out on Thursday, Friday and Saturday night? All my single friends are. What am I supposed to do, stay at home and wait for a man?"

Bushra and I have more in common than I first thought. I don't mean the obvious, that we are brown and Muslim.

I'm talking about something deeper, the feeling of never fitting in.

"Come on," I say. "You better drink your tea before you get late for work."

Bushra takes a sip. "I envy you. You don't have to rush to work in the morning."

"I do still have to wake up early. I woke up before you, didn't I?"

"Yeah, but still. Being your own boss seems pretty sweet as you can work when you want."

I want to explain to Bushra how it's not that simple. How the amount of work I put into this business directly correlates with what I get out of it. My income is dependent upon the happiness of the clients I service, the press releases I write and the column inches I secure. I have no guaranteed salary. And despite what she, and many others think, this isn't a jolly. I'm building something here. However, looking at her dark under-eyes and smudged, day-old eyeliner, I decide it's not a debate worth having.

I dutifully drop Bushra off at the station, like the mumsy mum I am, bidding her farewell as she goes to the workplace that ousted me a couple of years ago.

"Remember to ask about Kamran, yeah?" says Bushra.

"Don't worry, I will."

I begin the journey to my rented office space near Saint Paul's Cathedral. I hope I don't bump into Jasdeep today. I haven't seen him since he had me on edge with his super awkward meeting. I'm not sure if he's keeping a low profile, or perhaps he's found another victim.

I decide that today is the day I'm going to start peppering talk of my PR course. The one that's going to make me a millionaire. The one that enables me to scale up, without having to work extra hours. It's an absolutely genius idea, getting people to learn by themselves. Training them up online. Why didn't I think of it earlier?

My first victim (sorry, client) is Benedict.

"Have you thought about doing PR for your logistics company?"

Yes, I know that was a rather heavy-handed hint. However, I've got bills to pay. I don't have time to beat around the bush.

"I'd love to. Especially when I'm seeing all the coverage you achieved. I just couldn't afford it right now. I'm not even paying myself a wage. My girlfriend is holding the fort."

"What does your girlfriend do?"

"She's a doctor."

Okay, so the coffers aren't exactly empty. Does the *what's mine is yours and what's yours is mine* rule apply before you're married?

"It is hard when you're starting a new business. That's why so many go bust within the first three years," I say, before realising that's the worst sales pitch ever. Loren would not be impressed. Fortunately, she's too busy repeating the same spiel to notice...

"My name is Loren and I work for QuickTime Solutions. I'm calling to tell you about our services. We've been featured in..."

I need a change of tact. Perhaps I should appeal to Benedict, entrepreneur to entrepreneur. "It's difficult when you're on a shoestring budget. That's why I created my course to help start-ups like us level up with big businesses. That allows people who want to do PR but don't have the budget to hire an agency, do it themselves."

"Sounds good." Benedict swings his chair around to face me. I'm not sure if it's genuine interest or politeness.

"Yeah, it's worked for small businesses like yours." I don't want to be all sell-y, sell-y, so I check myself. After all, if he doesn't want my business, I'd still like us to be mates. He's one of the few people I talk to in this office. Everyone else seems absorbed in their own stuff. Especially Loren, who spouts the same script, 50 times a day. If she were to fall ill, I could pick up the slack as I know the pitch off by heart now.

"I can email you over the details, if you like?" I say, after delivering my promotional message.

"Yeah, that would be good," says Benedict.

At lunchtime, I sit in the communal dining room/meeting room/social area. It seems like the best way to make new acquaintances, business contacts or even friends.

As I pick at my potato salad, I wonder, why is it like being back in school again? Why am I getting déjà vu?

Julia has been my best friend since primary school. Yet, we were separated in high school. Why did they separate us? Didn't we get a choice to be in a class with our friends? I guess not. To be honest, I didn't even think she'd go to the same school. Julia came from money. Not super rich, but money compared to us and most of the other kids in school.

We were both academic and therefore in the same sets for maths, English and science but we were separated in the morning registration before lessons began. Those 20 minutes, where we had to announce our presence, were the longest 20 minutes of my life. I started the school morning in silence, while everyone around me chatted about what they did on the weekend, who they fancied and who they were going to get off with at the disco I wasn't allowed to go to. I'd sit at the table that faced the wall at the front of the class. I felt eyes burning on the back of my head whilst I prayed for every minute to pass quicker.

Two decades later, I have familiar feelings. I still feel like the odd one out. Last time I was here, they had work drinks because one of the founders was leaving. I didn't know what to do with myself with my orange juice in hand, while everyone chugged away at beers. And I was the only brown face there. So far, I've met one Chinese guy and two black girls. Plus Jasdeep, of course. It's hardly diverse.

Today, I hear a few accents from other parts of Europe. I think that's about it.

Oh, I spoke too soon. There's an Indian girl who sounds like she isn't born and bred here. She's selling curries to the start-ups. I put away my home-made salad in favour of something spicy.

"Which ones are halal?" I ask, feeling presumptuous. Though it is central London and I've come to find halal options in the unlikeliest of places.

"Everything is. There is lamb, chicken, goat." The girl waves her hand across the table of Tupperware.

I opt for the chicken curry with rice.

"Excuse me, are these samples?" A skinny ginger haired boy comes over and asks.

"Sorry?" The girl blinks in surprise.

"I mean, are these free?"

She shakes her head. "I'm afraid not. If I was to give away full-sized containers of curry, I wouldn't be able to feed myself."

The boy shrugs and walks over to the sample plates of nuts near the pool table.

She flares her nostrils, making her gold nose stud glisten in the sun-soaked room. "If I had a fiver for every time someone expects something for free.... I'd be a billionaire and wouldn't have to do this anymore. Do you get that in your business?"

"Not so far," I say.

"Maybe I need to do what you do." She laughs and holds out her hand. "I'm Neetu, by the way."

Neetu has a strong handshake and a confidence I wish I had.

We fall into a conversation about work. I share how impostor syndrome impacts me, as to this day I pinch myself when I get a day's work at full rate.

Neetu details her own experience. "I once used a marketing lady. Didn't like her. For what I was paying, I didn't get much return at all. She did some social media and got me in the local paper. That was it. I really expected better. Like a full marketing plan. Some level of accountability so I could quantify what I was getting."

"I guess marketing and PR isn't as simple as that. It's not tangible so we can't guarantee results." I feel like I'm getting a little defensive of my profession, but it's a conversation I've had before, many times.

"That's fine but at least I need to know where I stand. I want to know that you're going to approach this many journalists. I need to know you're going to send out this many tweets." Neetu counts each point on her fingers. "I want to know roughly what to expect in terms of output and outcomes. If I don't, how will I know what is value for money? Especially after all I've paid."

"How much did you pay, if you don't mind me asking?"

"£250."

"Per day?"

"No. For the whole project."

I don't say anything. I'm hoping silence can convey the irony of what she is saying, given her complaint about the enthusiastic entrepreneur wanting a free meal. As it seems that the penny hasn't dropped, I only have one thing to say.

"The curry is lovely, by the way."

Neetu turns her attention to a couple of girls in athleisure.

"I dunno mate, shall I get the korma with a naan bread?" asks a girl who looks like she'll be fine with a few carbs.

"Don't do it, Nat. It's not worth it. No carbs before the fashion show, remember?" her friend warns her.

Nat sighs and looks down at her flat stomach. She's wearing a fitted lycra zip top with matching leggings. There isn't an inch to pinch. "Do you have any salads?"

Neetu looks baffled. "Sorry, the curries come with a flatbread and salad. I don't really sell salad on its own. You could always take a full meal and have the curry later?"

"Deal," says Nat, before turning back to her friend. "Anyway, I just don't get why the sponsors are being so arsey about things. At the end of the day, we're building an empire here. They're getting in early, which means they'll be in with us at a good rate. They dunno how good they got it."

I smile at them, hoping to segue in a conversation. Nat looks at me like I'm weird. Do the rules of no eye contact go beyond public transport? I thought that was a Tube thing.

"Bollocks to them. We'll just rock up tonight, looking amazing in our gear. And if they don't sign up as sponsors, we'll have the free champagne and sack them off. There is a party downtown, anyway. We'll go there."

The girls in lycra leave with their Tupperware. No doubt they'll be walking off the carbs they haven't eaten. Perhaps that's where I go wrong. I'm a skinny girl, but I can't shake off my paunch. I've never had washboard abs. I'm guessing it's my love of rice, bread and pasta that's the cause of it. But honestly, if you don't have any carbs on your plate, is that even a meal?

As I go in for another spoon of chicken curry, I feel squeamish. Did I make a bad choice? The first mouthful was tasty enough. It's like my stomach's turned. Unusually for me, I'm taking issue with this portion size, too. It's too much. I've been feeling like this for a couple of days, but I'd rather not read too much into it. Best preoccupy myself with office chatter. But who to talk to? Neetu is networking like a pro, while I'm friendless. I guess I should get back to my curry, though I don't think I can stomach it anymore. What is up with that?

Oh crap, Jasdeep has just walked in. I now feel vulnerable, too. Oh my life, he's coming over. I look down, hoping to disappear into my curry. I might not be able to eat it but the portion is big enough to drown in. I can still see him, approaching ever so slowly, a silhouette of black turban, shirt and trousers.

Oh man, I could do without this high level creeping at my place of work. This should be a safe space. Come to think of it, is there even a HR person here?

I'm bracing myself for whatever oddness comes next. Maybe I'll call him out on his double life, being both married and hunting for girls on the internet. No, that would be far too brave. I know, I'll be very cold and distant with him. Only offering one-word answers to anything he may ask. That should give him the hint not to bother me, ever again.

Better still, I spy a bleached blonde guy that has come and sat near me. I'll talk to him as a distraction.

I look across and offer a smile.

"Oh hey, I'm Ben."

I exchange the quickest of pleasantries before asking the question that will see off any advances from Jasdeep. "What do you do?"

"I'm a sock entrepreneur."

I think I misheard him. "What was that, sorry?"

"I make socks for individual sizes. Well, technically *I* don't. It gets made in China. But yeah, I've found a lucrative gap in the market. It's literally a pain point for everyone."

Ben looks under the table at my feet, which almost outweirds Jasdeep. He sighs upon realising that I'm not wearing socks. It's a ballet pumps and tights day today. I think this may have poked a hole in his sales patter but he tries, anyway. "Don't you get annoyed that socks never properly fit?"

No. It's never bothered me in the slightest, I think. "All the time," I say.

"Neetu *ji*," Jasdeep shouts with an exaggerated Indian accent for effect which would be racist were he not also brown. "You never fail to bring the good stuff! I could smell your lamb bhuna from outside the office."

Wait, what?

I look up. Jasdeep gives the air an exaggerated sniff. "Mmm. Who needs home cooking when I've got this in the office?"

Hold on. Has he not noticed me? I am here.

Neetu laughs. "You know it. Now, I just need you to buy 25 curries and I'm good for the day."

Jasdeep grabs a slice of cucumber. "Never mind that. I'll give you my investment, which is worth much more than 25 of these containers. Then your boat will have well and truly come in."

"Aren't we supposed to be meeting about that?" she asks.

"Yes *ji*. Full calendar today, then I've got some calls in India about the call centre, funnily enough." He chuckles but nobody else joins him. It was worse than a dad joke. "When I get some clearance in the diary, you'll be the first one I'll be meeting with. For now, my dear, I'm going to need that lamb curry and I'm taking it straight upstairs. Board meeting."

Jasdeep grabs his container. "I don't have any cash. I carry the plastic. I don't suppose you can take Amex." Another chuckle, this time his shoulders are involved, bobbing up and down as he laughs.

Neetu's enthusiastic smile suddenly looks less enthusiastic. "It's on me. You can pay another time."

"What? No! I'll be running up a tab at this rate."

How many free meals has this guy had at the expense of Neetu's struggling start-up? More to the point, why am I unseen?

"It's fine," says Neetu. "You can make it up to me by investing in my business."

"You know it." And with that, Jasdeep disappears upstairs without even a glance in my direction.

What the fuck?

"Here's a sample, by the way." A pair of olive green socks come into my field of vision, having been pushed across the bench by Ben.

"Thank you," I say, stroking the socks out of politeness. To all intents and purposes, they seem like a regular pair of socks.

"Oh sorry, they're not to keep." Ben pulls the socks out of my grasp. "I was just showing you as you're asking but I can sell them to you, if you like. It's £15 for the pair."

I sometimes wonder whether some of the entrepreneurs here have set up their businesses out of a real passion, or because nobody else would hire them.

My phone rings, offering a welcome excuse not to buy a pricey pair of socks I don't need. It's Julia.

"Oh my God! Oh my God! Oh my God!"

"What? What's happened?" I ask.

She sounds like she's hyperventilating. "I have to see you. Are you free after work?"

"Actually, I can be free now if you want? But why? What's happened? Is it Miles? Has he done something? I never liked him."

"What? No! It's nothing bad. It's just I need to see you. I don't know who else to tell. If you're free now, you can come and meet me or I'll come to you. I'll come to Saint Paul's. I don't mind at all. I just really, really need to see you."

"It's fine, I'll come to you." I am happy to leave this mixed bag of co-workers, so head out to see Julia.

"*This* was your emergency?"

I examine Julia's sparkly new ring. It has an oval diamond with more clarity, a clearer colour and definitely more carats than my engagement ring. Though I did get gold and she won't. Must keep reminding myself of that.

"Yes, I was so shocked! I literally started shaking. As my best friend, I had to tell you. I wasn't sure who else to speak to."

"You sounded like you were in distress. A little context would've been nice. I was thinking the worst."

"Distress? I was delighted!" Julia wistfully puts her left hand on her heart. I can tell she's going to be one of those girls who inadvertently shows off her ring at every opportunity.

"Well, now I'm over the worry, I can say congratulations."

I give Julia a hug. She smells of Chanel. She's probably wearing a Chanel suit, for all I know. My knee length red spotty dress from Next is worn over my Tesco leggings. I forgot to spritz any perfume this morning. Luckily, I showered and used roll on. "How did it happen? Don't tell me it was on Millennium Bridge."

"Relax," says Julia. "That is very much your spot and Miles knows it. He proposed at the Shard. We were on the top floor having lunch earlier and then the next thing, he disappears to the bathroom. I didn't know what was going on as he was taking ages."

"I'd have assumed it was a number two."

Julia grimaces. "I don't think Miles does that."

"What? Poos?"

"I don't think he uses public toilets. Unless he's got a really bad stomach from a curry that's too spicy, or something like that. Anyway, he came back as a waitress came over with a chocolate brownie that had a sparkler on top, and then he popped the question, there and then! I nearly choked on my olive." Julia's smile changes to a look of concern. "Erm, also, I'm not sure if I misheard in all the excitement but do you really not like Miles?"

"What?" She's caught me off guard.

"That's what you said on the phone. I'm pretty sure you said you've never liked Miles."

"I did?"

"Yes. Unless I misheard."

"Erm..." I'm not sure what to say.

I don't want to gaslight Julia and it's not that I've never liked Miles. We're just totally different. He talks in polite tones and there's always an air of formality. We've attempted a couple of double dates, but it's usually been Julia and I doing all the talking, while our other halves sit quietly, filling in the odd gaps. One time, I'm pretty sure Miles showed Julia his watch, as one of our dinners ran into 11pm. It was the weekend! We were at Edgware Road, which doesn't come to life until midnight.

Truthfully, I don't blame Miles for clock watching. I don't blame either boy for having little to discuss. They're both so different. M, like me, is a second generation Bengali. His dad used to work in a factory, money was always tight growing up, and he loves football.

Miles is middle-class to the bone. He's only ever lived in a white area and I'm sure ours was the first ethnic house he'd visited. And he hates football. There just isn't much commonality. However, I don't dislike Miles. I don't really know him.

I better say something to Julia, as she's biting her bottom lip with worry.

"Of course I like Miles. More importantly, you like him and he likes you. It doesn't really matter too much what I think. Anyway, have you told your mum?"

"Not yet. She'll kill the mood. You know what she's like. She'll say something like: '*About bloody time!*'"

I remember Julia's mum well. With high standards and high expectations of her daughters, that is probably the kind of thing she would say.

"Are you okay?" Julia examines my face as I start to feel squeamish.

"I'm fine but... I do feel a bit weird. I couldn't even eat my lunch. That's why I've got it with me." I hold up the paper bag containing Neetu's curry.

Do I elaborate? It's far too soon. Then again, Julia shared her biggest news with me before anyone else. Maybe I should share my potentially big news with her? I have to tell someone. I haven't even said anything to M.

"Between you and me, I think I'm a bit late."

Julia gasps. "You're not!"

I don't want to smile. I don't want to smile. I don't want to jinx myself by smiling.

"I don't know. It could be nothing but I do feel kind of weird."

"Have you done a pregnancy test?"

"No, not yet. It's too soon. Plus, I don't want to jinx myself. But I have a feeling."

"A feeling?" Julia's mouth falls open. "That's nuts! Are you okay with this? I mean, was this part of the plan?"

"It's not nuts. And what plan?"

"I don't know, I'm just saying, what with you guys still renting far away from family. I always thought you'd go back up north when you want to have kids."

"We figured we'd go back up north at some point. We just don't know when. I'm not ready yet." I feel a pain in the pit of my stomach. "I'm not ready to leave all this behind."

Julia looks around at the packed out market place. There is a stall where a woman is selling boxes of crisps whose brand I haven't seen in the supermarkets for a long time, alongside bleach, toilet roll and fake plastic flowers. There is a falafel stall, where a girl is standing with a tray of samples in hand. Scores of lawyers are stampeding towards her. Everyone loves a freebie. There is so much hubbub, bustle and general shouting that it all sounds like white noise.

Julia raises an eyebrow. "You don't want to leave all this?"

"You know what I mean. This life."

Julia smiles, except she doesn't know the half of it.

She doesn't know about the life of a Bengali bride when she goes to her in-laws. She doesn't know about the cooking by default, the tripping over long gowns to go in the cellar to fetch some rice. The assumptions. The expectations. I would never tell her. I worked so hard to show Julia that we're not backward brownies. Now, she finally sees that I have a great life with M. I don't want to shatter that illusion so will keep my other life a secret.

"Have you thought about what you guys will do when you have kids?" I ask.

Julia sips her coffee, showing off her ring and on-trend manicure of pale pink nails with red tips. "I came here before I met Miles. Given that he's got his family here, it's likely we'll stay."

"Well at least there'd be some family support," I say.

"I don't know about that. His mum won't be changing nappies. She had a part time nanny for Miles even though she didn't work. She's got such a packed schedule, too. She's always at the gym, or tennis club. I think we'd have to do it all ourselves." Julia sighs. "Anyway, come here." Now it's her turn to pull me in for a squeeze.

"Let's not get over excited. It's nothing. Anyway, I don't want to overshadow your news. And honestly, that diamond is bigger than my eye. And you know I've got big eyes."

"It bloody should be. It took him long enough..."

Julia hastily says goodbye as she remembers that she is a lawyer with a proper job, unlike me who is self-employed and can come and go from work as I please.

As I make my way back to the office, I wonder if this is the beginning of a new chapter. Julia will get married. I might be having a baby. She's right. It is nuts. However, I really, really hope Julia has a long engagement. As I don't want to be heavily pregnant at her wedding.

Before I get to the station, I check my emails. It's become a compulsion of mine. I try my best not to be glued to my phone at all times but the convenience of having emails at the click of a button has become inconvenient.

There is a message from Benedict. Great, I've been waiting, like an eager beaver, for a response ever since I sent that email to him. He might be my first office signup.

It reads:

Hi,

Sorry, when I was talking to you earlier I misunderstood.

I thought you meant that the course was for free. I don't have the budget right now for it, though it does sound great. Best of luck with it!

Regards

Benedict

Neetu was right, you do get a lot of freebie seekers in this self-employed game.

12th September, Don't say a word

Don't say anything to M. You'll only get his hopes up. Don't say anything to M. It will only get his hopes up.

"Did you have a good day?"

"Yeah, it was fine."

He's onto me. My usual answer would be a rambled stream of consciousness during which I forget what he initially asked.

"What did you eat for lunch?" M resumes safe territory.

"I had a shawarma."

"A shawarma? Where from? That doesn't sound very Saint Paul's."

"I ventured a little and found a takeaway near the back end of the Cathedral."

"There's a backend near Saint Paul's Cathedral? Which street?"

"I can't remember the name."

"Is it as if you're going towards home or into town?"

"Well... kind of... I don't know. Because it was a backstreet, it wasn't in an obvious direction. It's like a side street."

"Okay, so if you were walking from your office, would it be in the direction of home? Or as if you're going away from home?"

"It was more sideways. Kind of as if I was walking like a crab."

"A crab?"

"Yeah. It's kind of between work and going sideways towards the Cathedral and there's a little street."

M looks like he's had an epiphany. "Is it near that buffet place? The fill your Tupperware one?"

"Not quite that street but not far from it."

"How do you not know where you ate?" M laughs.

"Why the hell do you bloody care so much?" God, he's annoying at times. "You know how bad I am with directions."

"Alright, chill. I just don't get where you mean. I want to check it out myself, that's all. I had a Thai green today. Speaking of which, what's for dinner?"

I don't say anything.

"Are you okay?" M asks.

"Yeah, I'm fine."

"Have I done something wrong?"

"No. It's not always about you."

"Just checking." M goes to wash his mug, squeezing liquid onto the already foamy sponge. It's a departure from his usual habit of leaving it to soak in the sink.

I feel I want to say something before this turns into an unnecessary fallout. I'm already coming across a little weird and defensive. I just won't mention the potential pregnancy.

"I can make some arabbiata for dinner. Also, the thing is..."

M looks back at me. "Go on..."

Don't mention the potential pregnancy. Don't mention the potential pregnancy. Don't mention the potential pregnancy.

"Well, it's probably nothing but my period hasn't come yet."

Bloody hell, I said it.

M has the goofiest grin.

"Don't get too excited. It doesn't necessarily mean I'm pregnant."

"What does it mean, then?" asks M. "Do you have to be not getting your period for a certain time to be pregnant?"

"That's the way it generally works." I laugh at M's naivety.

"I don't know these things. I didn't learn about periods until I was well into my teens."

"What do you mean? Didn't they teach you in primary school?"

M thinks. "I don't remember them doing that. Maybe I was off that day. Anyway, forget boring arrabbiata. Let's go out. We might have something to celebrate."

I knew it. I knew he'd start getting excited. "No, no, no. We're not celebrating anything. Not yet. Not until I can be sure."

"Then we'll go out in celebration of the fact we don't need to cook."

"I was happy to cook," I say. "Also, is my arrabbiata boring?"

It's weird. My back aches. I feel like I can only walk at a snail's pace. M clasps my hand as we get to Brick Lane.

"Oi! What are you doing? You never hold my hand in Bangla town, or anywhere else, for that matter."

"Extenuating circumstances. Very extenuating circumstances. And a special occasion."

There he goes again. Getting all excited.

It's like I've got period pains. There's a churning in my stomach that's making me gassy. I feel bloated. I don't really know how much I'll be able to eat. As we walk past the various curry houses, the mere thought of spicy food makes me feel sick.

"We don't have to get curry if you don't want to." M reads my mind.

"What does that leave us?" I ask.

M goes through the restaurants on Brick Lane that we are familiar with. "There is the Italian, and if you don't mind walking further, there's that Thai place. Then again…"

"I know, you already had Thai."

"Yeah," says M. "I don't mind having it again though, if you want to. You get to choose today."

I get to choose most days, I think to myself.

"I don't want to be awkward, but there's nothing that really appeals to me here."

"Are you up for walking a bit further?" M asks. "We can go slowly."

I wonder if it's wise to walk so much at this early, delicate stage. If it's a stage, of course. Then again, a walk will probably do me good.

We head into Shoreditch. Just like any night of the week, it's buzzing. Bustling with life. It's a part of East London that would've been very working-class back in the day. Now it's super gentrified, with hipster beards, girls that are way more on-trend than I've ever been, and city workers that have poured in from the Square Mile for an after-work drink.

These men have ditched their blazers on this breezy evening to stand outside pubs, pints in hand.

On the next block, there's a huge storage container-style building with an open hatch serving dessert. Diners are sitting outside on picnic benches in the AstroTurf garden. Some are seated on the floor, as if they're sat on real grass. Suddenly, I fancy ice cream, though it's not really the weather.

"We can go here, if you want," says M.

"Are you sure? It looks like they only serve ice cream here."

"Ice cream before dinner. Is there anything better?" M's eyes light up.

Given my delicate composition, M chivalrously leads me to an unoccupied bench.

"What shall we have?" He looks at the laminated menu which offers every flavour of ice cream and sorbet imaginable.

"Have you ever tried salted caramel?" I ask.

"No, and would never want to. Salt should not be mixed with sweet stuff."

"It's all the rage now but it's probably a fad that'll die down," I say. "I think I'll play it safe and go for a berry sorbet. What do you reckon?"

"I think I'm going to have an Oreo sundae."

"We can mix and match."

"It's alright," says M. "You can have some of mine but I'll only try a spoon of yours. Sorbets are full of sugar."

"Are they? More than ice cream? Maybe I should choose something else."

"No, you go for it. You're allowed as you're eating for two."

I glare at M.

"*Maybe* eating for two," he says.

M goes to order, leaving me to people watch. There are groups of guys and girls sitting on the floor, drinking milkshakes. They look like students, with their grungy clothes. Maybe I'm being judge-y.

A couple on the next bench are chatting animatedly. She's got long, dyed red hair that runs down her back. A white T-shirt is riding up to reveal a jutting spine bone. The boy sat opposite her is wearing a fluffy coat more suited to winter. By the looks of things, I would say it's their second, or third, date. There's familiarity but still a bit of excitement. Not that I'm a love expert or anything.

M returns with a sorbet-filled paper cup for me, and a towering sundae for himself.

"The portions were bigger than expected," he says, sheepishly.

"I'll help you with yours." I slice some cream off the top of his sundae. "What do you want, a boy or a girl?"

"Dunno, to be honest with ya." M pauses and then realises I'm waiting for him to say more words. "Either is fine. What about you?"

"Either is fine for me, too, but I feel like I'm having a girl. I think I'd like it in that order."

"What order are you thinking? And how many?" M looks worried.

"I've not given it a lot of thought." That's a lie. I have a vision board at home, tucked under the spare bed in the office.

"But maybe… girl, then boy, and I don't mind what comes next, but no more than three."

"Definitely no more than three. Two seems like not enough, but then four kids are too many," says M. "I think it'd be nice to have two girls in the equation."

"Really?"

"Yeah. Two little girlies would be cute. Then they'd have each other as besties growing up."

As we sit nestled among the evening noise and bustle of young Londoners out and about, it occurs to me that my time doing this will be fleeting. Perhaps only nine months, if that. I think I'm okay with it. We've been doing this for what feels like an eternity. Going out on a whim whenever we want. Not worrying about curfews or responsibilities. We've done all that and it's been great but I think I'm ready for the next chapter. In fact, I'm more than ready. I'm excited.

13th September, Not flooring it

"I don't want to sleep on the floor," I say.

"Why not?" asks big sis.

"Do I really need a reason? I'm always taking one for the team. I'd like to be in a bed for a change."

"I don't know, lady. How else will we do it? Will the little man have to stay on the floor? He's far too small." Big sis looks at her nine-year-old son, who has grown tall and strong and looks perfectly capable of flooring it.

"I don't mind, mum," he says.

"Don't be silly!" She gives him daggers. "You'll regret it in the middle of the night if you roll off the airbed. And did you do a wee? Make sure you do a wee! It's been ages since we got here and you haven't been. I shouldn't have to keep telling you."

My nephew rolls his eyes as he heads to the bathroom.

"Most kids love to sleep on the floor. It's the done thing when they stay at their grandparents' house. Everyone just decks out in the front room in sleeping bags."

"Well, we're not everyone," says big sis. "We're not English. We can't do stuff like that."

"I don't think it's an exclusively English thing. We used to do that at auntie Rukhsana and uncle Tariq's flat all the time when we were younger. Remember?"

"We never stayed on the floor. They did!" Big sis pulls a face. "But, yes, we would sleep three in a bed, sideways and all sorts. Again, that's different. People that live in flats in London are used to being squeezed in. It's not how we do things."

Big sis looks at me as though I am now one of them, courtesy of living in an apartment in London. She is such a snob.

"So, what are you saying? I'm the host? This isn't my house, either. It's not been my house since I got married."

"You know what I mean! It's more your house than it is mine. When you have kids, it's different. You feel like you're visiting. Whereas for you, lady, being childless, it's just like coming home. Coming and going as you please without any baggage." Big sis smiles at her son, who has returned from his tactical wee, only to be called baggage.

"Anyway, you could've at least brought your own duvets," I say. "It's not that warm now."

"On the train, lady? Golly, you'll be asking us to bring backpacks next, like we're travellers."

I'm beginning to have a love/hate relationship with sleepovers. I love seeing my family. I really do. Big sis and middle sis' visits are confined to the school holidays and I always try to coordinate a visit, flexing my very flexible work situation accordingly. However, as we get older, it all gets harder. Their families have expanded so much that they've taken to alternating visits.

My newlywed specialness wore off very quickly after the wedding. I no longer get a bed and am relegated to the floor. And as big sis reminds me, yet again, being childless means I am one station below her and therefore require fewer privileges. A bed being one of them.

"Can I borrow your phone?" My oldest nephew comes in to ask big sis. His voice is deeper than the last time I heard.

"What for?"

He looks sheepish.

"It better not be that game again. Always on my phone, always wanting to play."

"If you'd let me have my own phone, like everyone else has, I wouldn't need to borrow yours."

"I don't want you glued to a phone all day. That's why you're not having one."

"You're so awkward. I need a phone. Remember the last time I had football after school and you forgot so turned up all panicked? It was well embarrassing."

"Why? I wore English clothes, didn't I? It's not like I was in a salwar kameez."

My nephew huffs. His younger brother giggles. I stay out of it.

Big sis reluctantly hands over the phone and both boys leave us to debate who sleeps where.

"I didn't want to say anything in front of the boys, but there's a reason I don't want to stay on the floor."

"Oh, really? Blimey lady, are you expecting?"

How did big sis jump to such an accurate conclusion? It's like she's a baby witch.

"No... well, maybe. I don't know. I might be."

Big sis clasps her hands together. "Tell me all about it! How are you feeling? Have you been sick? Do you feel bloated? Your face looks a bit puffy. I noticed that when I first saw you. I assumed it was weight gain."

I stroke my cheek. Am I already bloating? "Nah, I think that's just the food. We eat out a lot. Also, no, I'm not feeling any of those things. I do feel a bit nauseous, though."

Big sis has a smile that isn't dissimilar to M's. It's annoying.

"Don't get excited and don't tell mum!"

"I might have to, lady. It's just so surprising. We were all wondering when you'd get yourself sorted. I was hoping you'd have bought a house first." Big sis shakes her head. "But never mind. You can do that later."

"I'm sorry I haven't done things in the correct order for you."

"Oh, lady, I'm only saying. Don't be so sensitive. It's a good thing if you are expecting. After all, you're not getting any younger. Anyway, of course you can have the bed. We'll make it work. This once." She looks down at the well-trodden carpet with dismay, before resting her eyes on my invisible bump. "Right, I'm assuming it's very early days, so be very careful. When you're back in London, try to avoid taking the Tube and don't rush about too much."

We really are sisters. I've already started doing my mindful walking, as though I am carrying a jug full of water inside me, careful not to spill anything.

It's weird. I love mum's curry but right now I don't fancy it. I also can't get used to the 9pm eating time that was such a staple of my upbringing. It feels so late. The meat curry with potatoes is calling me. I should be all over it. But it just looks... bleurgh. Maybe it's the morning sickness kicking in. But then it's not the morning. Is there such a thing as night sickness during pregnancy? I'll have to look it up.

"Did you see the pictures of Kabir's wife?" mum asks big sis.

"No I haven't yet. I was sad to miss the wedding but it was too far to go for the day. It's annoying nowadays, with people having joint weddings and ending up in weird places, like Birmingham."

Mum nods. "I was going to go. His mum was on phone to me, telling and telling but who take me?" She giggles and glances my way.

"You do know you have another daughter who knows how to drive now and has full use of my car while I'm away in London."

"Yes but..."

"But nothing! That's the reason why I didn't bother selling my car in the first place. So that she could use it when I'm not here."

That's not the real reason. Keeping my car up north affords me some much needed freedom when a three-day weekend cooped up at mum's gets too much.

"She not as good as you. This one be wimpy."

Little sis looks up from her plate, crestfallen. I can't help but smile. She isn't as good as me. I am the best daughter. Even now, despite being over 200 miles from home, I'm the best.

"It's 'cause you make me nervous, mum," says little sis. "Whenever I go anywhere, you're praying under your breath. The other day we went supermarket and–"

"Sorry, what was that?" I interrupt.

"I said we went supermarket-"

"You went *to the* supermarket. Talk properly, will you?" I can't help myself. I hate this new way of speaking, dropping essential words from sentences and hoping it works.

Little sis ignores me. "Anyway, I'm trying to get into a parking bay and mum is like: '*Watch out! You're too close to the car.*' I was miles away from it! She bloody makes you panic. Then she's like: '*Just park in disabled bay.*' I'll get done for that!"

Mum does her upside down lip grimace. "No problem. I have arthritis in knee. If you park there, I just do limp."

I'm glad little sis has picked up the baton of being annoyed by mum on a regular basis.

"This why I can never go weddings," mum returns her attention to big sis. "I got sent WhatsApp picture of bride. Hold on, let me get my phone."

"Since when did you use WhatsApp?" I ask.

"I downloaded it for her," says little sis. "I have some uses."

Mum reaches for the chest of drawers which houses everything from washed hand towels, hairbands, combs and, it would seem, mum's phone.

"Hold on... Let me switch on."

The suspense is killing me.

Mum powers up her phone with great difficulty, before attempting to show pictures of the bride of the distant cousin I've met once and really couldn't care for.

"Who can open photo for me?"

"Right now, mum?" I ask. "We're about to eat."

"Food can wait. Look, it still have steam coming from your rice."

I reluctantly open mum's messages to retrieve this fabled photo of the shiny new bride. I'm not bothered to look, so pass the phone straight back to mum.

"Hmm… Very nice. Very pretty. So fair. She look like English lady." Mum passes the phone to big sis, who approves.

"Yes… She is very fair, isn't she?"

She hands the phone to me, like it's a game of pass the parcel with the shittiest prize.

I examine the photo of the bride, who's wearing an unusual orange gown. "Oh, come on!"

"Come on what?" asks mum.

"She's no great beauty, is she?" My comment is bitchy but I'm exasperated at the colour blindness of my family. "You're just saying she's pretty because she's fair. Imagine the same girl, with her close together eyes and hooked nose, with dark skin. You wouldn't be impressed then, would you?"

"I still think she be pretty. She looks like egg. A little big maybe. But okay. So bright looking."

"Exactly, mum! So bright! Fair doesn't always mean beautiful."

Big sis huffs. "Lady, you're so politically correct these days. Let's be honest, if you could have fairer skin, you would, wouldn't you? Anyone would. I would!"

I glower at big sis, with her already fair skin saying she would be fairer if the option was there. It's madness.

Little sis says nothing. I can't tell if she agrees or not. I hope she doesn't get indoctrinated into this.

Somewhere though, deep down, big sis has hit a nerve and she is right. A lifetime of being told I'm dark has made me struggle with my brown skin, especially in light of having fair sisters.

I feel a pang in my stomach. No, it's something more. Something different. I suddenly need the toilet. Is discharge a common symptom in pregnancy? Yuck. I have to leave the table.

"I'll be back in a minute."

"Where you go? Food get cold," says mum.

"Obviously, it's a number two. You could've waited," adds little sis.

I run upstairs to my old bedroom in the hope of finding some pads. A rummage through the top knicker drawer uncovers those light flow ones, reserved for the last day of your period. Perfect. I don't want to waste the night ones with the extra capacity.

"*Heh!* Shall I cover your dinner with microwave lid?" shouts mum from the bottom of the stairs.

"No, I won't be long."

"*Heh?* I can't hear you. You go toilet?"

"Yes. Still there. Won't be long."

I look down to see that I need the heavy pads after all, as I am faced with what is, for all intents and purposes, a regular period.

14th September, It's alright

"It's alright," says M.

That's his answer to most things whenever there is a problem. It's alright. We're alright. It'll be alright.

But it's not always alright, is it? Sometimes it's not alright at all. Sometimes it's crushingly disappointing.

I didn't tell anybody at home about my false alarm. I didn't want to talk about it. What is there to say? I was late for my period and then it came. But it was more than that. I was feeling sick. My back ached. I couldn't physically move at my usual breakneck speed to get from A to B. That was real, wasn't it? Surely that wasn't all in my head? Maybe it was. Maybe I wanted it too much that I conjured it up in my mind. I do possess a very vivid imagination.

Now, I'm here. The last place I would feel comfortable to talk about it. My mother-in-law's kitchen. The house is mercifully empty as both my in-laws are doing their prayers upstairs. As for M's younger brother and sister, I don't know where they are. I also don't care. Today is not a day to query the whereabouts of people. Today is not a day for much, really. Least of all, talking. But M is not done talking.

"Do you think you were actually pregnant?" he asks.

"I don't know."

"Had you done a pregnancy test?"

"No, it was too early. At least, I thought it was."

M's got his thinking face. "So is it like when you have a baby and then you... don't?"

"You mean a miscarriage?"

He surrenders his hands to the air. "I don't know these things. Is that what you call it?"

I look at him, stunned. "You mean you've never heard the word miscarriage?"

"I have but it's not something I hear often. Most of my friends don't have kids. And the ones that do, they don't talk about that stuff."

"Well, maybe you need to start. You can't always hide behind the fact that you're a bloke, as if this doesn't matter to you. Having a baby is as much your job as it is mine."

M goes quiet. "I don't know what you want me to say."

"Nothing. There's nothing you can say."

"What you do?" asks my mother-in-law, smiling as she enters the kitchen. Then, upon seeing us, her expression changes to concern. "What happen? What's going on?"

"*Jee*, nothing," I say.

Her eyes dart between M and I. "Tell me. Something happened? Is it your mum? Everything okay at home?"

"Yes, everything is fine, mum. It's just..." Think of a lie. Think of a lie. Think of a lie. "I've got these trousers for work and they're too long. I need to make them shorter so I brought them here. I'm guessing the tailors are cheaper up north."

This is half true. I have bought new trousers and they are a bit long. I wasn't going to take them up though, I was just planning on wearing extra high heels.

"Why take to tailor? I be tailor!" My mother-in-law rolls her shoulders back, proud. "Leave it on sofa, I fix it for you."

"Okay, mum." I turn to M. "I think it's in your side bag. Can you grab it later?"

M nods, helping verify my story.

"What shall we have for lunch?" I ask.

Another smile from my mother-in-law. "Do you want *seetal maas kofte*."

"Have you already made it?" asks M.

"No but I have *seetal* in ice. Can get it out now to defrost." My mother-in-law tentatively walks over to the chest freezer.

"Leave it! There's no need to cook anything. We'll get something in as there's already last night's meat curry," says M.

That's an incredible amount of restraint from M, considering that fish ball curry is one of his favourite dishes, and one that only his mum can make.

"I don't mind," I tell him.

"No, no need to cook today," he insists.

"Honestly, I don't mind. I could do with the distraction."

My mother-in-law doesn't miss a trick as she flits over to the freezer before I change my mind upon M's insistence.

"You really don't need to make anything. Just take it easy today," he says.

"I want to."

"Do you want me to do anything? Can I help?"

"No, it's fine. I'll just get on with it. Maybe we could grab some food later?"

"You mean get a takeaway? Or eat out?"

The latter is a rarity here and that's on me. I feel guilty about going out when I'm at my mother-in-law's, given that we're not here often. I feel like I should stay in and show face. Today, however, I'll make the exception. It feels like exceptional circumstances.

"Can you come and help get fish? Must be right at bottom of freezer."

M heads towards my mother-in-law. I grab his wrist to stop him. "I'll go. It's fine."

M looks at me like I've lost the plot. It's understandable, considering I'm never so forthcoming in domestic matters.

The family chest freezer is like Doctor Who's TARDIS. It's full of all manner of Bengali treasures. There are freezer bags full of beans, ice blocks containing little silver fishes, and carrier bags full of meat.

"Can you see the *sital maas*?" my mother-in-law asks.

I move several bags out of the way. "What does it look like?"

"*Otho*, you know... like a big fish. Best thing to get all the bags out."

"All of them?"

"Yes, it make for quick work that way."

My mother-in-law sits back in her chair, while I pull out the heavy, fish-filled bags from the bottom of the freezer. Perhaps I should've let M do this.

As I hunch over to reach the last bag, I feel the urge to run to the toilet.

"I'll be back," I say.

My mother-in-law looks at the mess of fish I've left on the floor, dismayed.

"I'll clear all this up," I assure her. "Won't be long."

"What's up?" asks M, as I bolt through the living room. He must've been waiting for me to see if I need support in the kitchen.

"I need to get something." I retrieve my bag from the side of the sofa. "Bloody hell. A bag this big and it doesn't have what I need."

"What do you need?"

"Not to be all too much information but my period has come with a vengeance and I'm extra blobby. But I don't have any pads. I completely forgot to bring any, as I was too busy being sad."

"Do you need me to buy some?" M asks, though his face spells bewilderment. "You have to tell me what I'm looking for, or I'll bring home the wrong thing."

"I kind of need it right now. I could stuff extra tissues in my pants to buy some time -"

I hear the door slam. Then the sound of dainty feet running up the stairs.

I think it, then M says it: "Or... you could ask my sister?"

"I guess that's one way of bonding."

I lightly knock on the door of M's little sister's room. In all the years we've been married, I've probably been in there twice. Even then, it's been to retrieve a glass or plate because there weren't enough to go around at dinner time.

"It's open," she shouts.

What else would it be, locked? Does she have a lock on her bedroom door?

The door creaks open to reveal M's sister, with the same look of surprise she's had since day one, which suggests I've caught her in the act. This time she's painting her nails a deep shade of red.

"It's that time of the month," she says, with a nervous laugh. "Since I can't pray, I'm making the most of it and painting my nails. I'm sure, one day someone is going to invent a nail polish that's permissible to wear whilst praying."

"I'm sure the invention is coming," I say. "And snap. It's my time of the month, too. We must be synced up."

She looks grossed out. Was that too much? Did I cross a line? Maybe that's the Bengali in her, embarrassed to discuss something that afflicts all us women.

"That's why I'm here. Do you have a pad I can borrow? Actually, not borrow. I don't think you want it back."

She giggles, this time with marginally less repulsion.

"Sure." She reaches into the bottom drawer of her dressing table.

There are some obvious perks to being the only daughter. She's got the second biggest room in the house. Her dressing table plays host to a grand, rose gold, triple mirror set so she can admire herself from every angle. Her scroll back chair is devoid of any clothes, unlike the chair-drobe at my mum's. She has a row of expensive perfumes. On the wall, there's a framed black page with the words '*Your vibe is your tribe*' inscribed in gold. There are two double wardrobes to house all her clothes, one of which has an outfit hanging on the door. So that's why she doesn't have a chair-drobe. The outfit in question is a full-length black sequin dress, with short lace sleeves.

"I've got a friend's 21st birthday tonight," she says as she catches me eyeing up her outfit. "Got to make sure I get out the door before dad sees my dress."

"I remember those days. Here's a tip, wear a long coat and take it off once you're out of the house."

"That's a good idea," she laughs and passes over the sanitary towel.

As I grab it, I feel my fingers trembling. I look at the packet and squeeze its green plastic wrapper. The cushion interior bounces back.

Oh no, oh no, oh no. Please don't cry. Don't cry. Not in front of my sister-in-law.

"Are you okay?" she asks.

It's too late. I can feel the tears in free flow.

"Oh... erm... shall I give you some space?" She gets up to leave her own room.

"No, it's fine. I'm just a bit emotional, that's all."

She slowly sits back in her chair. I think she'd have preferred to leave.

"Has something happened? Is it my brother?"

I shake my head, trying to blink away the tears at the same time. "No, it's not him. It's just a lot of other things."

She puts her hand on my shoulder, but keeps her fingers flexed, as she doesn't want her nail polish to smear.

"Marriage seems so hard," she says. "I'm not looking forward to it."

That wasn't exactly the reason for my tears but I indulge anyway, as I can't tell her the truth.

"It can be hard but it's also amazing. These are the best years of my life. And it will be the same for you. You just need to find the right person."

She looks down, giving me a good view of her false eyelashes. "It seems like such a big life change. I don't know how I'd cope, living with another family. At least you guys are away from us so you have your space."

"You don't have to worry about this now, anyway. You're so young!"

"Some of my friends are already engaged. Or they're planning to get married and they've already met someone. Don't tell mum that bit."

The deflection is helping dry up my tears.

"I won't. And I know the feeling, when it seems like everyone else is getting settled. Don't rush because of that. You'll meet the right person when the time is right. I felt like time was passing and I ended up getting married at 27. Now, girls get married in their mid-30s and it's absolutely fine! Your priority should be deciding what career you want. Have you thought much about it?"

She shrugs. "I'm thinking of doing a PGCE. It seems like a good choice. Being a teacher, you get school holidays off, so it's handy when you have kids."

"It's a good option but do it because you want to, not for future kids. You can figure out that bit later. Anyway, I'm just glad you're not going to be an influencer as that's what everyone seems to be doing these days." I'm not sure why I said that.

She blows on her fingernails. "No way. You'd never see me dancing for views. Or doing a blog. I'd rather have a life."

It's a good thing my little hobby blog is a secret.

I never realised scraping the flesh from the inside of a fish could be so soothing.

Less soothing is the constant commentary accompanying this task.

"Scoop more. More! There's more fish you can reach. Get to the bone. You don't want to waste good food." My mother-in-law is next to me, shoulder pressed against mine, observing the process a little too keenly.

I continue scraping, saying nothing, until there's no flesh left on the bone.

"Have you got everything you need for Ramadan?" my mother-in-law asks.

"Erm... yes, I think so." My mind is blank.

"You sure? Everything? Chickpeas? Broken basmati rice?"

"I haven't bought any rice yet but we can get that from Whitechapel."

"Why get from Whitechapel? I've got some. Go look under stairs."

"It's fine. I can always use regular rice."

"What you mean. Use long grain rice for kisuri? How that work? You need broken!"

My mum often uses regular unbroken basmati rice for kisuri but I don't mention that, lest it makes us look like uncultured hicks.

"Okay mum, I'll grab some of your rice after I finish cleaning this fish."

"Get it now! Or you forget. I know what you like. Memory like colander." She giggles.

"There's no point washing my hands only to have to clean the rest of the fish. I'll get it after."

"Hmm okay. Make sure you no forget. Waste money buying double," she mumbles. "And did you plant tomato seeds I gave you?"

What's she on about? "Seeds?"

"*Seeds, she says.*" My mother-in-law mimics my tone. "Remember, I gave you seeds back in summer. I told you, plant them straight away! On the windowsill. It be hot in London. Hotter than here. You'd have a nice tomato plant by summer. No need to ever buy from shop."

"I forgot," I say.

Clearly she did, too. Otherwise, why would she bring it up months later when we're heading into autumn?

"Where are the seeds now?"

I'm scared to say. "I'm... uh... not sure. Probably in the cupboard back in our flat."

"You must look after these things! You plant seeds now, you have food for months."

I don't think M and I could live solely off tomatoes. However, I don't dare argue. It's easier to say nothing. I wish there was some more fish to scrape.

"I give you coriander seeds?"

"Erm... It's too late now, isn't it? Can you plant something in September?"

My mother-in-law sighs. "*Eh-heh*. Too late. I told you to plant these things when I gave them. If you keep waiting and waiting, you miss the season."

I turn to face her. "When was I supposed to do it? I'm not sat at home in London. I work all day. In fact, I work even harder now that I'm working for myself. Then on top of that, keeping the house tidy, making the meals, which is mostly on my head. So tell me, when should I plant the seeds?"

My mother-in-law steps back. "Mmm. *Acha*. You can do in future when life less busy. Anyhow, I think it be time to read namaz. I go now."

She limps away slowly. Her long white scarf is trailing behind her, brushing the kitchen rug as she goes.

Now I'm left to ponder what to do with all this fish flesh.

"Oh shit!" I suddenly remember.

"What is it? Are you okay?" M lunges forward as if he's trying to catch my imaginary fall.

He's been hovering in the other room in overprotective husband mode. I hope he didn't hear me snap at his mum. If he did, I hope he'll understand I didn't mean anything by it. I'm just hurting.

"I'm fine," I say, "but I just remembered I told big sis that I might be pregnant. I better tell her I'm not before she starts blabbing her mouth off."

"You told your sister, yet you told me not to tell anyone?"

"Yeah. I said don't *you* tell anyone. I'm allowed to. It's my pretend pregnancy."

I go to the privacy of our temporary bedroom to call big sis. Her phone rings interminably. She never answers the phone and always takes a day to get back to me. What is she actually doing? It's not like she's busy with a job or anything. The kids are in school. She's got a good six hours to herself. Surely she's not making that many curries?

I'll have to make do with messaging her. How do I convey this?

Hey lady, bad news. I'm not pregnant.

No, that doesn't work. It's not necessarily bad news. It's just news. I'm not devastated. I don't want to sound overdramatic about losing a baby I wasn't pregnant with in the first place.

I'll try again.

Hey lady, I tried to call you but no answer so I'll tell you anyway...

No, scratch that. Why do I have to explain what I'm doing? Surely the fact that I'm messaging her and she'll see a missed call on her phone explains all that.

Let's give it another go.

Hey lady, just to let you know, I'm not actually pregnant. So please can you not mention it to anybody?

No! *'Just to let you know?'* That sounds like I don't even care. It's like 'just to let you know I won't be home later', or 'just to let you know you need to pick up some milk on the way home'. It's not that kind of thing. It's more important.

Hey lady, turns out I'm not pregnant. So don't mention it to anyone as mum will only get overexcited, or worried, or both. You know what she's like.

That'll have to do. I don't care anymore.

"It's nice we can still do this," says M as we sit down at a Thai place in Rusholme. "When we have kids, these dates will be a rarity."

"Or non-existent," I say. "Neither of our mums are getting younger. I can't imagine they'd be up for much babysitting when we come up north to visit. Though I might get out of cooking duties. Like I did today."

I excused myself from the afternoon's domestic chores. After messaging big sis, I stayed upstairs for a little while. Then it became a long while. By the time I returned to the kitchen, my mother-in-law had cooked the fish kofte. She didn't say a word, neither did I.

Now, here I am, sitting in a bougie restaurant with green velvet seating and floor-to-wall black, wondering whether I made the right call. Whether I should have helped finish the dish. Whether I should have come out at all.

Then my papaya salad arrives and I conclude that it was the right decision to eat out tonight.

"Do you think it's really that bad? The sleepless nights?" I ask.

M doesn't flinch. He's so used to my random questions that pop up without any build up.

"I don't know," says M. "Surely, babies sleep at some point, right? I think parents exaggerate, to be honest with ya."

M must be right. An actual night of no sleep would be like a form of torture. If it were like that, there'd be no kids in the world. It would be the best form of population control.

When big sis had her kids, I was too young to care. When middle sis had her youngest, I was old enough to be in the loop but we weren't living near each other, so I didn't get daily updates. I've never asked her whether sleepless nights are a thing. She's never told me, either. She doesn't look that knackered. Maybe it's all a bit overplayed.

I must get those books from Sophia to learn more about this kids malarkey.

I also must drink some water. This papaya salad is burning my mouth.

"I think I made a bad decision." I gulp the water, submerging my hot lips in the glass.

"There are a lot of chilli flakes in there." M is very observant. "Here, take mine." He pushes his plate of chicken satay towards me.

"No, it's okay. You shouldn't suffer for my poor choice. You've hardly eaten any."

"I've had some. Plus, I want to try yours, anyway."

We swap plates and M starts digging into the flaming hot papaya salad.

"Is it okay?" I ask.

"It's not bad. A bit hot."

"You can take your spice more than me," I say. Then I notice M's bottom lip turning red. Perhaps he can't.

My phone pings. It's big sis, finally.

Oh, that's a shame, lady. Don't worry about it.

Is she serious? *That's a shame?* That's what you say to someone who failed their driving test. Not someone who's lost a baby they thought they had.

M's breaking out in a sweat.

"Are you sure you don't want your chicken back?" I ask.

"It's okay. I don't mind. You finish it off. There are only two skewers left."

"Let's share," I say.

"No it's fine. I'm okay with the salad." Though his flame-tinted mouth tells a different story.

We get back to M's parents after 11pm. The house is quiet. M's sister must be still at her friend's party. M's brother is probably out as it's Saturday night and he's a boy. He doesn't need a special occasion for an excuse. Boys never do.

It's an early night for M's mum and dad, too, as the living room is empty. The TV remotes are parked in front of the flatscreen. The throws are neatly folded into squares. The sofa cushions are back in their place and my trousers are laid out on the sofa, looking shorter, with a freshly sewn seam. Next to it, a freezer bag full of broken basmati rice, which I'd predictably forgotten to get from under the stairs.

12th November, Sophia's library

When Sophia said she had every book ever written on pregnancy, she wasn't kidding. Despite being a mum of one with another on the way, her conception books still take pride of place, dominating an entire shelf on her bookcase.

"This one didn't really work for me, but you might want to have a read, anyway." She points to a thick, hardback yellow book with the words GET PREGNANT in bold white. "This one, however…" She pulls out a paperback with a picture of a chubby baby in a nappy, "It's the best. It tells you everything you should expect before you're expecting. It's practically a blueprint on how to get pregnant, assuming there are no issues, of course."

Her last statement was a bit unnecessary.

"Doesn't all this take the magic away?" I ask.

Sophia looks at me with a deadpan expression. "Trying to conceive is not romantic at all. When you're planning something and it's not working, you have to get military. Once you're pregnant, you can get back to business as usual."

I examine the stack of books she has laid out before me. Pictures of smug, smiley pregnant women. Or smug, smiley women cradling babies. There's one that looks more like a biology textbook I read at school.

"I never knew there was so much to it."

"None of us did, hon," says Sophia. "Nobody tells you this stuff. Asian people struggle to talk about pregnancy, trying to get pregnant and childbirth. Everyone acts like it just happens. I don't know about Bengalis but in Pakistani culture, we don't even like to use the word 'pregnant.'"

"We're the same. People say they're 'not well', when referring to someone who's pregnant. When you're on your period, you're 'ill', too. It can be very confusing. I couldn't figure it out for ages until mum finally explained that ill doesn't necessarily mean cold or flu."

We both laugh.

"I figured that when I was ready to be 'ill'," Sophia does a finger quotation wiggle, "it'd happen. But when you read these books, bloody hell! It's a wonder anybody gets pregnant, ever." She's not filling me with confidence.

I didn't want it to be this way. I didn't want to be reading books. Yet, here I am. Is this the curse of my generation? Overthinking things? Mum once fleetingly mentioned that it took a while for her to have kids. She wouldn't have read any books on the subject. She wouldn't have been able to. They're all in English. She just got on with things. She had to. Life was hard enough for mum, being an immigrant without a network, without friends or a supportive community. She didn't need the additional concern about conceiving.

We, on the other hand, have a manual for everything. If you want to buy some new bedding, you look on Pinterest for inspiration. M needed new TV speakers because the old ones went bust. He scoured millions of reviews online. Everything we do needs an extra level of research. It's the modern day disease.

"How are you feeling anyway, hon?"

I think Sophia is referring to my late period/ false pregnancy.

"I'm okay. A little disappointed but it serves me right for getting my hopes up."

"Don't say that! Don't apologise for getting excited. It's a natural thing to do. And actually, all your positive thinking has done you well recently, hasn't it?"

"I thought so."

"It did as far as I can see. You practically manifested your husband and new life in London. Two things you really wanted."

Sophia makes it sound like I engineered the whole thing in my mind. Also, living in London is a nice bonus, rather than the main perk.

"I hope you're not worrying about it." Sophia looks at me, eyebrows furrowed, like she's doing all the worrying for me.

"I'm not worried at all. Honestly, what is there to worry about? Forget me, anyway. How are you getting on?"

Sophia looks way more pregnant than she actually is. Her bump resembles middle sis' when she was almost due. Maybe it's because she's so short.

"I'm feeling a lot bigger second time round." Sophia pats her belly. "Other than that, it's been a little bumpy. I'm so glad my mother-in-law's got Imran. She's been having him more often since I shared my news. Which is as much a benefit for her as it is for me." Sophia looks to me for agreement. "It keeps her busy. Also, I'm a lot more nauseous than I was. I've completely lost my appetite. I can barely eat this grapefruit. This is only the first trimester. Who knows what I'll be like for the next six months?"

I noticed a peeled, dried looking grapefruit half covered in kitchen tissue. I was hoping she'd offer it to me. I love grapefruit, even if it's parched. I've been sat here for over half an hour and Sophia hasn't offered me even a glass of water. I guess when you're pregnant you can get out of hosting formalities.

There's a slam of the front door, then Adnan pops his head round, looking down through his glasses. "Hello, hello."

"Hiya. Are you alright?" I ask.

"All good. I just picked my car up from the garage. Do you want a brew?"

I smile appreciatively, as I've been gasping since I got here. I love seeing Sophia, I really do but these days we only ever meet at her house. Restaurants and cafes are off the menu. I get it. Having a pre-schooler and being pregnant means she can't be bothered going out. However, I wish she'd specify a slightly more convenient time instead of 2pm, as that's the Bengali lunch hour. I'm starving. I hope the tea comes with biscuits.

"Is hubby picking you up?" asks Adnan.

"Yeah, he should be here any minute now. Then I'm off to the in-laws," I say, with an unintentional sigh.

"Oh yes, the 50-50 rule," says Sophia, smiling at Adnan. "One night at her mum's, one night at the in-laws."

I'm not sure I like Sophia and Adnan smirking at my expense. Only I am allowed to lament the 50-50 rule.

"You should tell him to stop by for a brew," says Adnan.

"He won't be able to. We're heading straight back to London. The traffic is always bad on Sunday."

"I'll let you off, then. But bring him round more often."

"I will. Now Ramadan's over, we'll be able to socialise a bit more."

"Good." Adnan scratches his greying hair, which now just sits round the sides of his head. "I can give him some tips on his dress sense. Cable cord jumpers are a bit preppy."

I can't tell if Adnan is joking or not, but given that he is wearing a forest green chunky knit cardigan, he's not one to talk. He just needs a pipe and slippers and he'd be set.

"Don't forget to take your books." Sophia pushes the pile in my direction. Another smirk at Adnan.

"Sophia was buried under that pile before we had Imran. Hopefully, you won't need to read all of them."

I feel my face heat up. Isn't this breaking girl code, bringing your husband into the conversation?

Mercifully, the doorbell rings. I'm relieved to hear M exchanging pleasantries with Adnan at the door. I'll skip the tea and make a polite exit.

"Here he is! Come in, come in. I was just saying you should visit us more often. We barely see your wife these days."

Don't come in, don't come in, don't come in, I plead silently with M.

"I can bob in for a minute." I hear the sound of shoes being removed.

Damn.

"Nice to see you," says Sophia as M comes into the front room. "I've just armed your better half with some books." She smiles and raises her eyebrows.

M lets out a stifled giggle, as that's all he can really do in this situation.

"This is the bit where we try to put you off kids by telling you how bloody hard they are," says Adnan.

"No, they're not! We're meant to be saying positive things." Sophia pokes him in the ribs.

"That's not what you said this morning, when you were all gassy."

Another jab in the ribs from Sophia, as Adnan puts his arms up in defence.

I'm glad they're back to poking fun at each other, rather than at us.

"And how is it all going?" Adnan asks M, looking down through his glasses.

M looks dumbfounded. Is Adnan asking him about our conception journey?

"Erm... yeah, good."

Adnan looks at M as though he needs some more details.

M still looks dumbfounded.

"We better hit the road," I say. "We'll have tea another time."

"Yes," says M, with a thinly disguised sigh of relief. "Let's do that."

M has never moved so quickly. Within minutes, his shoes are on and he's out of the door, leaving me with an armful of pregnancy books. In his rush to get out, he'd lost all sense of chivalry.

As we hastily reverse out of Sophia's street, we are left with the image of her and Adnan waving, with a mutual raising of eyebrows.

18th December, Canapés

Now this is nicely done. Very nicely done. Julia's engagement couldn't be more different from mine if she tried. She's hired a swanky garden museum in central London. In among the foliage are posh people drinking champagne from skinny glasses. They're in evening gowns, making my green wrap dress look casual. And it's in the evening, which is so different to my daytime gig, which needed to accommodate restaurant workers such as my own brother-in-law. Also, unlike my engagement, there don't seem to be any unwanted relatives, invited out of obligation.

Well, almost.

"Gosh, it's been how many years now?" asks Julia's mum as she greets me with two air kisses.

"It's been ages, auntie. Maybe since school? Or college?"

"Oh lovey, we're all adults now. Call me Gaynor." She smiles but her cheeks remain taut. Has Julia's mum, I mean, Gaynor, had Botox? "I think it might have been even longer than that, come to think of it. Last time I saw most of Julia's friends was probably at school prom. But I don't think you went, did you?"

The waiter comes over with a tray of drinks, helping to deflect from any more othering.

"Do you want a drink of something?" Gaynor asks.

Every glass on that tray looks the colour of piss and is filled with bubbles.

"Mother, you know she doesn't drink!" Julia comes over and puts her arm around me.

"Of course!" Gaynor slaps her unnaturally smooth forehead. "I forgot. How could I remember? You always keep your friends away?"

Julia purses her lips.

"Anyway, where is this husband of yours? Julia tells me great things."

I scan the many ruddy faces to spot M in conversation with Miles. Both boys are dwarfed by an imposing statue of a winged goblin that looks ready to gobble them up. This museum is weird.

A waiter comes round with cucumber canapés. M grabs one. Miles doesn't. Then, a second waiter offers what looks like a mini shortbread. M grabs one of them, too. You can take the boy out of Droylsden. At least he's smartly dressed, in tan chinos and a navy blazer. He's almost coordinated with Miles, who's wearing a blue jacket and cream trousers. Miles looks rather animated, gesturing towards the wisteria wall, which looks more gothic than Instagrammable.

"I hope he's imparting some traditional values to Miles," says Gaynor.

Cue an eye roll from Julia.

"I'm just saying... It took him long enough to propose. They did things in the wrong order." Gaynor elbows me, as if we're colluding. "When they moved in together, I thought they'd have a baby out of wedlock."

"Mother!"

"It's the done thing now, isn't it?" Gaynor sips her champagne. "I was so excited when Julia mentioned that you were getting married. In such a short space of time as well. No messing around. In my day, Julia's father and I courted for five weeks, then he proposed! There's no point practising forever. But yes, I was so pleased and relieved. I thought you might have to have an arranged marriage. You were telling me, weren't you, Julia? How that still happens in the Indian culture."

"Bengali, mother!" Julia's eyes widen, horrified.

"Sorry, of course. That's what I mean. Anyway, must dash before I say something else that puts my foot in it. It's the fizz." Gaynor gives Julia an air kiss and saunters off.

The waiter comes round with more drinks.

"Are these orange juice?" I ask.

"Yes."

Finally. "Great, I'll take one."

"Me too." Julia grabs a flute and takes a swig as though it's something stronger. "Just for that, I'm going to have a bloody long engagement. Two years minimum," she says.

"I thought you didn't want that."

"I do now. I bloody do now." Julia downs some more juice, emptying half the flute.

On the plus side, M and Miles are chatting more than ever. There are only a few pauses when M grabs a canapé, or another glass of Coke. Miles, meanwhile, is showing more restraint, having nursed the same glass since we arrived. Does he not know it's a free bar?

I head over to see what they're talking about.

"What did I miss?" M asks as I join them.

"Nothing much. Mainly Julia's mum, who you'll get to know really well," I tell Miles.

"We already know each other pretty well. She's a hoot!" Miles snorts.

I say nothing. It's a good thing I didn't trash talk her.

"M was just telling me about your engagement. Sounds a bit different to this one."

I nod, as I'm not sure how much M has divulged.

"Julia would love to have a big party with all the frills and as many occasions as possible," adds Miles, taking the smallest sip from his glass.

"I think all us girls are a bit like that," I say.

"I was going to keep this party low key." Miles sighs. "Drinks with friends. Bit of food. Then the parents got wind and invited themselves."

That's funny, I thought this was low key. There's no seating. We're all standing around and chatting with the smallest bites to sustain us. I'm hungry and my feet hurt.

Miles continues: "My mum and Julia's mum started plotting and decided to book out this place. We were thinking of hiring a bar in Shoreditch. Or in the West End. But my dad is a trustee here, so he insisted. Speaking of which, I think I've been summoned." Miles walks off to a thin, tall man with a full head of white hair in a neat side parting. I'm guessing it's his dad.

"How many canapés have you had?" I ask M.

"Dunno. Wasn't counting."

"Well, don't load up. They'll probably be serving food soon."

They didn't serve food. That's practically blasphemous.

M was right to load up on cucumber canapés and little prawns on cocktail sticks. I'm starving.

"Burger and fries?" M asks on the drive home.

"Yeah, go on then."

M navigates towards the nearest drive-thru.

"We should plan our next holiday," he says.

"Where were you thinking?"

"I dunno, really. Somewhere in the Far East. Get in another big trip before kids."

"Good idea, how about Japan?"

"Japan would be good. But their winters are really cold," M informs me.

"Wait. When are you thinking of going?"

"I was thinking this winter, maybe. Or maybe next spring at the latest. I'm sure we can get something pretty decent last minute."

I have a think. "How about Bali?"

"Maybe..." I can tell M already has an idea, though he doesn't want to be so bold as to share it. "Or we could go back to Malaysia. I did like Kuala Lumpur and it's not like we got to see it properly, as it was our honeymoon." M raises his eyebrows and winks.

I have reservations. "I don't think I like the idea of holidaying in the same place twice. There's so much of the world to see."

"True," says M. "Let's think about Bali. Anyway, did you enjoy tonight?"

"I did, but I kept thinking how Julia and Miles' parents aren't that different to mine, after all."

"In what way?"

"The expectations. The pressure to do things in the right order. The knack to embarrass us kids. I think Julia's mortified by her mum for different reasons. I guess it's the universal thing, parents being embarrassing, just in different ways."

"Probably." M nods. "I guess our embarrassing stuff was around money. Or lack of. But, to be honest with ya, everyone was the same. All my mates' dad's worked in factories, too, or restaurants. We were all a bit skint so we knew not to expect much."

I think about that. M's always fit in and been comfortable in his skin. I remember when Julia came round to our flat and M was having a late lunch. He was eating chicken and rice with his hands, in the traditional Bengali way. Julia tried her best not to look at this most novel spectacle. Doubtless, she'd only seen pictures of people eating with their hands. I couldn't tell if her look was that of deference or disgust.

I was mortified. For him and for myself. I felt exposed, so unapologetically Bengali. I would never do that. I learnt my lesson early. Once, middle sis' teenage friend, Kelly, knocked on our door and I was still eating. It didn't occur to me to wash my hands before I answered. I figured Kelly wouldn't even notice. But she did. She leaned towards me, trying to peer round the door, and uttered the dreaded words: "What's that on your hand?"

She was referring to the turmeric-infused oil slick.

"Wash your bloody hand?" middle sis whispered as she shooed me away from the door. She was embarrassed, too. She also went through that phase of struggling to fit in. Of wanting to pretend that we're not that different from everyone around us.

"Look over there." M interrupts my thoughts, pointing towards Tower Bridge, my most favourite London landmark. It's illuminated red and will make for a good photo. I open the window.

As I take a blurry photo (how do people take pictures from moving cars?), I say to M: "The light just hits different here, doesn't it?"

"Huh?"

"Never mind."

My phone rings. It's Bushra. What does she want at this time of night?

"Hey, you okay?" I ask.

"Yeah, yeah. I'm good. What you up to?"

"We're just on our way back from an engagement party. Remember my mate Julia? You met her at my hen do."

"Aww, is she engaged?"

"To Miles. I'm not sure if you saw him at my wedding."

"I can't remember... erm, let me think. Miles... Miles... Oh yeah! The posh lad? I mean, she was well spoken, too. But he was like a posh southerner type."

"That'll be him. Anyway, how's you?"

"I'm alright, yeah. I've been so busy with work and stuff. They've got me doing loads of nights with the marketing events and all that jazz. So... yeah. Nothing new to report."

She's tiptoeing for some reason. Is it rude to ask outright what she wants? M is clearly eavesdropping as he's turned the music down low.

"Yeah, so... I was actually gonna ask you something, if it's not too embarrassing. Is M there, by the way?"

"He is."

"Right, okay. Tell him I said hi."

"Bushra says hi."

"Hello!" M shouts as he leans over towards my phone.

"Hiya," Bushra returns M's greeting with equal enthusiasm. "So, erm... I wasn't gonna ask anything because I don't wanna make a big thing or nothing. Actually I'll just message, if that's okay?"

Bushra is being very strange.

"Is she alright?" M asks as I hang up.

My phone pings. "Let's see, shall we?"

Hey, sorry for being abrupt. I didn't wanna say too much in front of M but I wondered if he's spoken to Kamran? We messaged a bit and he talked about coming up to Manchester one weekend but he's gone quiet. Let me know if you've heard anything x

Oh, crap. My matchmaking mission! I forgot all about it, as I was busy trying to get pregnant. How long ago was their date? One, maybe two months ago? She asked me to put in a good word back then and I never did.

I feel awful. I did what everyone used to do to me when I dared to follow up on someone I'm interested in.

Let's see if I can rectify this.

"Has Kamran mentioned anything to you about Bushra?"

"No. That's old news, isn't it?"

"Is it?"

M shrugs. "I thought it was. Didn't they have a one-time thing ages ago? There's been another girl since, to be honest with ya."

"What? What other girl? Is he seeing someone else?"

"I wouldn't call it seeing her. You know what he's like. He's just one of them blokes that's never serious with anyone. I told you that when you wanted to put them together."

Oh gosh. Is this my fault? Did I set Bushra up for a fall?

"Why didn't you mention this other girl before?"

Another shrug from M. "I didn't think you'd be interested, to be honest with ya."

For a man who thinks I'd care about what biscuits he had at work or when a colleague farts, M is most inconsistent in his behaviour.

I'm going to have to do it. I need to be the bearer of bad news. I can't put it off. If I don't call Bushra tonight, I'll bloody forget tomorrow, as I've become so flaky. Plus, Bushra will be awake. She's a night owl.

It's the hardest news to deliver. Instead of atoning for what I did to Sonali by making a match for Bushra, I'm telling her that Kamran is a total tosser.

"I asked M about Kamran..."

"Yeah..." Bushra can't hide her eagerness.

"Erm... well... the thing is... erm, he's... he's not worth your while."

Silence.

"I'm so sorry. M's found out he's seeing someone else. I don't know how much you guys were chatting or what the deal was but I wouldn't waste your time with him."

A longer silence.

Please, Bushra, say something.

My mouth keeps rolling: "You can do better than him. He's a playboy. M says he's not that serious. I just figured with you both being Pakistani and similar - not similar - but sort of I figured he might want to settle down or at least date. But it seems like he doesn't, even though he's dating some-one else. Erm... are you okay?"

I can hear Bushra's shallow breath through the phone. Is she crying? I didn't realise how much she liked this guy.

"Of course! Yeah, it's fine. I mean, he's a prick because he promised to come up to Manchester and he asked me to go down to London again. We'd been chatting a bit but obviously he didn't take it seriously. Anyway, whatever. It's... whatever. God, why are all men such bastards?"

She laughs half-heartedly. I wish I could speak to her in person but we're a couple of hundred miles apart and this couldn't wait until my next trip. She deserves better.

"Oh well. Back to the hunt, I guess," she says, dryly.

"You will meet someone. Someone good for you. You know that, right?"

"I hope so. But I sometimes wonder."

Bushra sounds so much like I did not long ago. She's in that phase. That abyss between being happily single and hap-pily settled. That bit when you really want to meet some-one but you feel it won't happen. You feel like you're jinxing yourself by daring to even dream. And along the way, fate, men and life keep proving you right.

I've failed as a friend, just like others failed me. It never made sense to atone for Sonali by setting up Bushra. That wouldn't help Sonali. It wouldn't make things good or balance out the universe. In this brutal, competitive world where it's every woman for herself, the good deed for one doesn't cancel out the other.

6th January, How does anyone get pregnant?

Well, my new year has got off to a flying start. One of my retained clients, an airline recruitment firm, has delivered some bad news – they are terminating their contract with four weeks' notice. I say bad news, but they were a massive pain in the arse to work with. Typical recruiters, making everything about metrics and not understanding the nuances of PR, which isn't always easily measurable by revenue. In fact, it rarely is. They don't call it fluff for no reason.

Anyway, while they were a pain, I will miss the monthly retainer. I'm not looking forward to doing my accounts this summer.

Never mind, let's spin this into a positive. The unwritten rule is that I can officially start delivering a sub-par level of work, so the time I would ordinarily dedicate to polishing turds and making them media friendly, I will spend curled up with a book. And top of my to be read list are Sophia's pregnancy manuals.

I start with the one she said was her favourite. It offers up a number of fun facts.

- *Only 3-5% of the semen has sperm cells.* What are the rest for?

- *The journey to find the egg is long and exhausting,*

> *like a hike.* Is this influenced by the endurance of the man? M is more sedentary, if I haven't said it before.

- *Sperm has to compete hard to reach the egg. The chances of success are one in a million.* One in a million? Did I read that right?

- *Getting to the egg is long, exhausting and full of traps for the sperm. Most will die trying. Only the fastest and most resilient sperm will make it.* Right, so survival of the fittest.

How in the hell do people actually get pregnant? It's like an immaculate conception.

I look out of the window of our second bedroom/home office. I can see directly into the high-rise apartment opposite. It's mostly full of working couples or singletons. However, this particular flat has the telltale sign of children. There is a scooter parked against the Juliet balcony and a scribbled rainbow is stuck to the window. That couple managed to have a child. They managed to conceive against these impossible odds. As did so many others. But how? If this manual is anything to go by, we all need a divine intervention.

I flick through the pictures of smiley pregnant women of different races. It's a win for diversity but these pictures look contrived.

The next section talks through the signs of pregnancy:

- Nausea with or without vomiting

- Increased urination
- Fatigue

I had all those symptoms when I thought I was pregnant. Including my period being late. But it wasn't to be.

Then I land on the words... chemical pregnancy.

Apparently, it's a very early pregnancy loss that occurs before or at five weeks. Most people don't even realise they've experienced a chemical pregnancy as they may not have taken a test or missed a period.

Did that happen to me? Oh, how I wish I'd taken a pregnancy test. Then I would've known. It wouldn't have mattered or changed the outcome either way. However, I would have known what happened and understood these feelings. I would've felt justified in my disappointment.

People don't talk about pregnancies until they've had the 12 week scan. It's because it's too early to say and things could change. I never understood that. Surely, if you lose a baby, you'd want people to know why you're feeling and acting the way you are? How can we experience our emotions freely if we have to stuff them down?

I read on. A chemical pregnancy isn't really a pregnancy because it isn't viable.

The book goes on to tell me that some women so desperately want to be pregnant, that their brain tricks them into believing they are. Their body mimics the symptoms of pregnancy. The aching, the tenderness, the sense of something happening. Yet, it's all by the power of imagination. Is that what I did? Did I create an imaginary pregnancy? So it wasn't a pregnancy in the first place? I don't know. I don't know what I should call it or how I should feel. I wish I'd done a test. I wish I had a label, a word for all this.

17th January, 'Twas the night before Eid

'Twas the night before Eid but nothing was magical. It's like a survival test at my mother-in-law's.

M and I drove up after work (well, M did the driving) and after a quick dinner, I'm waiting for the real work to start.

"What do we need to do first?" I ask M's mum, though I'm scared of what the answer will be.

"Nothing yet. Let's rest first."

That's the predictable answer I didn't want to hear. I'd rather get it over with by having a head start, then an early-ish night but that's not how this goes down.

My mother-in-law is savouring her cup of tea while watching the Bangla channel. The only saving grace is it's the second Eid, Eid-al-Adah, so we haven't had 30 days of fasting beforehand. At least I am sustained with food for what's to come. Glass half full.

"I already prepare dough for samosa. You need to get more ready for yellow *bora*," she says to M. "I already ask your little brother to do handesh mix so no need for that."

When is M's big brother coming? I need backup in the form of his sister-in-law. The more hands, the better tonight.

It's gone 10.30pm by the time we start anything. First order of the day is the rolling out. I take my seat next to M's little sister and brother to begin the conveyor belt process. The little sis and I are rolling the dough into neat circles, then using the lid of a pan to cut out perfect rounds. His brother then cuts the circle in half and fills with keema, before folding into a triangle.

One thing I will give this family credit for is their equity during Eid preparations. There is none of this leaving-the-wives-to-get-on-with-it nonsense.

M's little sister has outgrown her teenage phase and likes to help, even if it's slow progress on her part. I can see her struggling. She over-rolls. The dough breaks. She huffs and starts again, piling the dough back into a ball.

"Do you want to swap?" M's little brother asks her.

"Yes, please." She switches seats with her brother.

There is a knock on the door. That will be M's elder brother and family. That's a relief, my mother-in-law is hovering near the cooker, which means the frying is about to start.

M's sister-in-law bounds into the room, red-faced and flustered. "So much traffic! So much traffic you wouldn't believe. The kids didn't even sleep in the car. They need to get into bed soon." She comes closer to give me a hug. "Routine goes all out of the window on these weekends."

She then hugs my mother-in-law and says: "I'll sort the kids first. I'll send them upstairs so I can carry on."

We continue folding and rolling. Folding and rolling. Folding and rolling. It's quite therapeutic. There is also a warmth around the table. We're laughing and joking about who has rolled the most samosas. It reminds me of home.

"Yours looks like Australia!" M's little sis laughs at her brother's effort.

"That's a shame. I was going for a heart shape."

M, who has emerged from the toilet after 20 minutes, rolls up his sleeves, literally, to get started on making the dough. This is by far the most arduous task of all. It needs strong hands. He's getting his elbows in, kneading and pounding at the flour, water and turmeric combination.

"It's too dry. See? It be cracking." My mother-in-law pours water from the freshly boiled kettle.

"Hold on!" M pulls his hand out of the dough mix before being scalded by his mother.

"*Dooro!* I used to do this all time! How come I no burn hand?"

She shows M her bangle laden hands, which are thin, veined but remarkably burn-free. She is hard-core.

"How's your work going? Did you make a course, or something?" M's little brother asks me.

I forgot that I told him about my course. I wish I hadn't, as I haven't had any more sign-ups since that meeting last summer. Since then, I've replicated the formula several times. Host a workshop, offer an intro, launch into the sale of the course. Rinse and repeat. Yet, there have been no more takers. It's not quite the money spinning, retirement plan I had thought. This also creates another dilemma - will I have to go straight back to work after maternity leave? I was hoping I could have a career break or work around a baby. Now, I'm not so sure if I could afford to. Best stuff this thought into the back of my mind.

"It's going good," I say.

Luckily, M's brother isn't one for follow-up questions.

M's sister-in-law comes downstairs, having put the children to bed. Another plus of having kids. She managed to stay holed up there for half an hour before joining the domestic bliss. She was probably napping herself.

"Did you bring any rags with you?" she asks me.

"Rags?"

"Old clothes you don't mind getting dirty."

She gestures towards my kameez, a pink and gold number, which is far too fancy for this work. It is covered in flour. When I come up north, I always bring my best dresses. I feel like I have to, being the visiting daughter-in-law.

M's sister-in-law is wearing a yellow and black check tunic that's bobbly and ripping at the seams. I think she's got the right idea.

"I didn't think of that," I say.

"Next time, bring clothes you don't mind getting dusty and smelly."

Noted.

"*Eh-heh,* look at clock! We need start frying," my mother-in-law announces.

My sister-in-law's face drops. She knows this task is assigned to her.

"I can do the frying," I say, against my better judgement.

"No no! You got work hands. Don't want to burn," says my mother-in-law.

M's big brother isn't part of this merry band of workers. He always gets out of it. Why is that? Where is he? It doesn't seem fair. M's dad doesn't help either, but he's old and I'm brainwashed by rules of patriarchy, so I let him off.

There's more rolling, folding, kneading and frying. Lots of frying. The yellow bora situation is particularly cumbersome. After I roll out some rounds, my mother-in-law pulls out an implement I'd never seen in my premarital life. It's like a pizza slicer with a frilly blade. I'm instructed to cut the edges of the folded dough with it. My triangles aren't very neat, so my sister-in-law takes over and my mother-in-law picks up the frying duty.

It's quite seamless, really. I imagine this is how fast food chains operate.

In amongst all of this graft, I manage to check the time. It's gone 12.30am. If I was in London, in my own home, I'd either be fast asleep, or watching a late night movie with M at the cinema. I definitely wouldn't be doing this. Eid at my mum's is a more low-key affair. She makes spring-roll pastry samosas ahead of time and defrosts them on the day. She'll make a chicken pulao, too. There is none of this 50-item menu malarkey. I look around... there are mountains of food everywhere. It's like meal prep on crack. On the kitchen counter, there's a round wicker tray loaded up with samosas. Next to the cooker, there is a silver dish piled high with handesh. The table where all the rolling is happening, is covered with a dusting of white flour. Both rolling pins are utilised, while there are glass bowls containing various fillings of keema, potatoes, desiccated coconut and curried lentils. There's even a bowl of shredded beef, which my mum never makes.

My father-in-law comes into the kitchen.

"What is all this? Think you've got enough?" he says to his wife and I can't tell if he's joking or not.

"We need to eat!" She looks at him and smiles.

"Did you get your Eid outfit?" M's dad is a man of minimal conversation but he is sure to ask the same question every Eid.

"Yes," I reply.

"And you?" He looks at my big sister-in-law. She smiles and nods.

I find it adorable how he wants to check in and make sure we are clothed for the occasion, even if we stink of onions.

By 1.30am, we call it quits. There is no more space to put anything. No more kitchen tissues left to drain the oil off any fried goodies. No more energy left in anyone, not least my mother-in-law, who has collapsed on the sofa in front of Bangla TV. As I get into bed, M asks if I'm okay. It's his standard welfare check.

I nod, whilst yawning.

"Well done, babe," he says. "It'll be nice to eat it all tomorrow."

I sneak a peek at M's slightly rounded tummy. It's going to expand an inch in 24 hours.

"Tired?" he asks.

Another yawn from me.

"Good thing you weren't in this family back in the day. We cooked until 3 or 4am."

"That's mad! How did you get up in the morning for prayers?"

"Dunno, to be honest with ya. We just did. So count your lucky stars."

Lucky me.

Before I go to sleep, I check Naila's Instagram. She's posting on a daily basis so there's always new material.

I wonder what her Eid is like? There won't be any kneading, rolling and frying going on at her in-laws.

I open her feed to see a picture of her with Darren. Their cheeks are pressed together as she is holding the phone to take a selfie, cradling her stomach. She doesn't look like she's done any cooking. She's not wearing rags, she's wearing green contact lenses. They suit her.

She captions the photo: Pre-Eid dinner with my boy. Feeling blessed. #Alhamdullilah

She is the worst.

18th January, Eid day...

Everyone gets done up nicely for Eid. They dress in their finery and go house-hopping, visiting various relatives and acquaintances and munching on different samosas. This girl, Farheen, who's sitting here in front of me, is wearing false eyelashes. Eyelashes, I tell you! That seems like the ultimate decadence for such an occasion. I can count on one hand the number of times I've worn false eyelashes.

Farheen is married, too, but she doesn't have the appearance of a married woman on Eid. The face that suggests toil. A hint that she's been through the wars. The aroma of fried oil that the morning shower hasn't managed to wash off. She looks splendid. This 22-year-old bride is wearing a blood red maxi dress with a gold jewel-encrusted neckline. Her hijab is the same gold of the stonework. And there's one big hint as to how and why she had so much time to dedicate to herself. She didn't stay at her in-laws the night before. She's been at her mum's all week. Said mum, an auntie that's not quite an auntie but a distant relative of M's, has brought Farheen over, along with her daughter-in-law.

The daughter-in-law is as glamorously dressed as the daughter. She is wearing a green maxi dress with the same gold neckline. They must've bought it together to be all matchy-matchy. She doesn't look like she's been folding hundreds of samosas the night before, either. I wonder if the mother-in-law just gets on with it.

That said, one of the good things about slogging away into the early hours the night before Eid is that there's hardly any tasks today. We've already had two sets of guests and all I had to do was microwave the samosas as they were already fried. My mother and sister-in-law took care of the chicken pulao this morning. They must've got up before seven. I rolled out of bed after nine, as that's all I could muster. Luckily, nobody said a thing.

"Try some samosas," I say to Farheen, who hasn't touched her plate.

"I couldn't. I just can't. Sorry, excuse me." She walks out of the kitchen and into the downstairs bathroom.

What was that about?

"You want to see if she okay?" my mother-in-law asks me.

I guess I'm the closest to her age in this room. M's sister-in-law is assuming kitchen goddess duties, replenishing the depleted salad by cutting cucumbers, tomatoes and onions. As her visits are less frequent than ours, she makes up for it by doing overtime in the kitchen.

"She's not well," the softly spoken auntie tells us.

What could it be? A stomach bug? Norovirus? Good old fashioned shits? Damn, are our meat samosas undercooked? I have yet to try them on account of guests constantly being in my face.

"How long?" my mother-in-law asks.

"Four months," Farheen's mum replies.

Oh, she's talking about *that* illness. The one that lasts for nine months and results in a baby. Gosh, she's only 22. That was the last thing on my mind at that age. Not least because I didn't have a husband.

"She really been struggling. Sickness like never seen," says her mother. "Nargis never have like this."

Her daughter-in-law says "hmm," in agreement. I guess her name is Nargis. "I just had swelling. Like, a lot of water in my ankles. Never any sickness," she says, proudly.

How the hell do you get watery ankles, of all things? Must look that up in Sophia's pregnancy book. For now, I have to deal with the actual pregnant girl.

I knock on the bathroom door and wait outside patiently.

She emerges, face looking drained. Still beautiful, though, with eyelashes intact.

"You okay?" I ask.

"Sorry... It's the smell of curry and spices. I can't handle it."

"That must be a nightmare. Can you eat?"

"I can eat fine. I can have curry and everything."

That's convenient. Selective nausea.

"But I can't stomach when it's being cooked. When my mother-in-law is making dinner, I can't stand it. But it's hard with mother-in-laws. You feel like they're judging if you don't help out. I can't do it. That's why I'm at home. I'm gonna stay as long as I can."

I rub her back. "At least your mum's taking care of you."

"It's brilliant. Don't get me wrong, my mother-in-law is taking over all the cooking and stuff. I don't do anything but you just... sort of feel it. She won't say anything. It'll be just like a look. But that one look is enough."

I understand what she's saying more than she could know.

"How are you feeling, sickness aside?"

"I'm nervous. I'm scared of childbirth but I'm glad I've got my mum here. My in-laws are only down the road, too, so there'll be plenty of people wanting to hold the baby."

I think about how my mum lives 200 miles away. I won't be able to bank on her cooking and keeping me fed whilst pregnant.

"You'll be fine," I say, though I have absolutely no experience to back this up. "Things will fall into place."

I can't breathe for my own bullshit.

She splashes her forehead with some cold water and rejoins the women in the kitchen. It seems, however, that she should've sat this one out as talk has taken a turn.

"She had really bad depression," the mother-in-law says, referring to Nargis, who doesn't seem too perturbed by the revelation. Perhaps it's something that's been widely discussed before.

"I did. I had it bad," she says. "The only way I got through it was because mum took the baby," she nods towards her mother-in-law, who returns a smile. "She kept her every night. My daughter is 10 now and I feel completely fine but when I had it, it got me bad. It couldn't have been easy for mum." She squeezes her mother-in-law's hand.

"No, it be very hard. Especially as I have trouble sleep at night, anyway. But what do to? I had to help."

From the matching outfits and mother-in-law playing night nurse, I'd say this daughter-in-law's got it good. As she looks to her samosa-laded saucer, I see that Nargis is wearing false eyelashes, too.

I'll never be the girl with long lashes. I'll never be immaculately dressed on Eid. It's sad, really. When I was living at home, courtesy of being in a white area, we barely had any visitors or anyone to visit. Auntie Jusna would rear her head when they weren't busy doing other things. Or we'd go to theirs. That would be about it. Here, there is a conveyor belt of guests. Most of whom don't remember my name, and the family connection often gets mixed up in my mind, but still. We are around a community of people. Yet, even now, when I have reason to get dressed, I buy a cheap outfit and don't style my hair after washing it in the morning as there simply isn't time.

My bargain long gown is proving a nuisance. I keep tripping over it as I make the frequent commute from kitchen counter to microwave and back, topping up a plate with samosas each time. How come we always end up hosting? Why don't we go house-hopping? It always baffles me and I never quite got the answer. Every Eid, people come to us. We never go to them.

M's pretend auntie and her party of three finish up with a kiss on both cheeks and a request for us to go to their house. It's the usual empty gesture and I reply with the usual: "Will do, Inshallah," knowing full well we won't.

If you've gathered by now that I'm not fully comfortable with the way things are here, you'd be right on the money. Maybe I never will. Maybe I'm not meant to. Perhaps every married woman has that little niggle about having to go to her in-laws. Maybe every woman has that sense of urgency when it comes to leaving. Perhaps every woman sends a sneaky message to her husband saying: *Where are you?!* when she wants an escape plan.

More guests arrive. M's sister-in-law has gone upstairs and I don't know whether it's for a bathroom break, a bath or a nap. All I know is she's been a while and there are questions regarding her whereabouts.

"She be watching children. She been up very early and finished late last night," my mother-in-law says.

The first bit was a lie. The children are in the front room on the PlayStation.

It's like there's a code. We must never say a daughter-in-law is tired, or can't be arsed with the formalities that Eid brings. They have to be busy doing something, otherwise what possible excuse could they have for being holed upstairs when there are guests downstairs needing to be served? Our mantra is never complain, always explain. Or, more accurately, always come up with a reasonable excuse that doesn't convey our true feelings.

The guests have brought kids of their own, so now the house is bursting with people. The hallway is full of shoes and sandals and there's a distinct smell of socks. The men have gone to the front room, except my father-in-law, who assumes his usual spot on the one-seater sofa in the lounge. He doesn't shift for anyone.

M, wearing a navy blue panjabi, comes in to the kitchen with a saucer containing nothing but a slick of tomato ketchup.

"Need to replenish supplies," he says.

As we are running low, I must be resourceful. I sparingly add the coveted meat samosas, with a more generous mix of the less desirable coconut-filled ones.

I make up another plate of samosas, and place it in front of the aunties. I can't remember if these ladies are real aunties or not. Must ask M later.

One lady is wearing a peacock print saree, which is both bright and ambitious given the weather and her age. The other lady's outfit is hidden under a black burka.

Big sis-in-law comes downstairs offering salaams and naturally slides herself into the conversation. "Let me see your Eid outfit, aunty."

She approaches the lady in the burka, who dutifully lifts her top up, seemingly forgetting that my father-in-law is in the room. Luckily, his eyes are focussed on the television, which is currently showing a documentary about village life in Bangladesh. Her flashing reveals a garish pink paisley print maxi dress. I can see why she kept it covered.

M comes into the room again. He has a tear in the side of his panjabi. When did that happen?

"Shall we go to your mum's in a bit?" he asks me ever so quietly, as if it's a cardinal sin for other people to hear that I may want to see my own mother on Eid.

"Yeah, that would be good."

"Okay then, I'm just gonna see Jam and then we'll go in about half an hour. Is that alright?"

It's not like I can protest publicly but my sixth sense tells me that it won't be half an hour. Nothing is so brief when it comes to Jam.

"Are your parents well?" asks the lady who flashed us all with a hideous outfit just moments ago.

I wouldn't know. I haven't seen them yet, I think.

"Yes, they are," I say.

"What you make today?" my mother-in-law asks.

"We did *bora, shingara, handesh*. You know, same, same." Peacock print lady moves her head from side to side.

Her paisley print wearing companion adds: "My bahu was like, let's make *pita*. I say why make so much!" She laughs, playfully punching the arm of her daughter-in-law, who sits with us, looking very made up with her coiffed hair loosely covered with a red neck scarf. From bits of conversation, I know that this daughter-in-law is from back home and came to the UK after marriage. She lives with her in-laws, so I imagine the domestic demands are much higher. Yet, she doesn't look like she's been cooking all night.

When do these women find time to get ready? She's got kids, too. Her youngest is a toddler. I had a hard enough time waking up at a respectively early hour, washing my hair, and then applying two dabs of blusher. I didn't even have a chance to dry my hair, which is never good. I look like a trapezium. My hair is flat on top and gradually wider towards the end.

"He likes *pita*," the daughter-in-law says.

I'm assuming she's referring to her husband. She wouldn't dare use his name, just as I don't use M's in front of my in-laws. We like to keep things vague.

My mother-in-law smiles, pleased and impressed. "Me and my daughter-in-laws were up till 2am last night, making all these things. Samosa, beef samosa, *bora*... The work doesn't finish."

Oh, I get it. This is a pissing contest, with a spicy kick.

While I'm sitting on the toilet, on a pretend comfort break, I decide to check out what Naila's up to. This might seem like borderline stalking but if she insists on putting her life up for public consumption, I'm going to consume.

There is a picture of her wearing a short, red salwar kameez with a lace trim. Hands on her hips, one leg sticking out. She's standing in front of a house with a sage green front door. It's definitely not uncle Tariq's high-rise flat. Perhaps she posed in front of a random house, like many influencers do. I wouldn't put it past her. The caption reads: Eid Mubarak from me and mine to you and yours. #Alhamdullillah.

Twat.

It's 5pm. The brightly dressed ladies have gone and I'm washing their crumby plates and saucers. When is M going to turn up? I think he needs a new watch, because this isn't half an hour by anyone's timekeeping. He has no sense of expectation management and has this annoying, debilitating inability to say no, especially when it comes to Jam.

"Come here! Come look!" my mother-in-law shouts from the other room.

What is it now? What's happened? What have I done?

As I walk in, she points towards the TV. "Look, this our village in Bangladesh."

On the screen, there is a man talking in mother tongue, wearing a red lungi, against a backdrop of reeds.

I don't see the emergency.

"Every week they show different village in Bangladesh. You should watch this. They show yours one day. Do you have the Bangla channel in London?"

"I think so?"

"You think? You never watch it?"

"We don't have time."

"Make time! This be important. Watch these programmes and learn about your 'desh. Otherwise, how else you know? You never go back there. You young people all same. I tell him to go Bangladesh, see his village. He no interested."

I don't blame M for not being interested. My few trips back home hardly left me wanting to revisit.

I last visited Bangladesh nearly a decade ago, when my grandma passed away. I remember the big house that we shared with my dad's brothers. It was like an ivory tower. Literally, in that it was painted ivory, like most mansions in hot and humid Bangladesh. And figuratively, in that there was no escape.

I would spend days roaming around in that house. I can picture it now. Black and brown speckled tile flooring. A big, long, formal front room with uncomfortable wooden settees and red cushions lining opposite walls. A gigantic picture on the wall of a very official-looking man in black glasses with neat, grey hair. A former president, maybe? I never asked who it was. I never cared, really.

Another room, less grand, with seating along one wall and a small TV on the opposite end. This room led to a double door, opening to a net lined wall to keep the mosquitoes out. On the other side is where they kept the cow that would be sacrificed for Eid. There were some chickens that would peck around the back of the house on a makeshift farm, if you will. Fresh fruit and vegetables grew abundantly.

Now I think back, the place was so huge there were parts I hadn't seen. I guess they were the servant quarters, kept out of sight. The one worker I did see was the kitchen lady, Mona and a teenage girl, Shefa.

I spent most of my time holed up indoors. Apart from the occasional walk along the front yard, when it wasn't too hot, I sat inside under the spinning ceiling fan. I'd watch the hours go by. Despite this being the motherland, it did not feel like home. Visitors would come every so often, second cousins and the like. We would occasionally go to someone's house but this was a brief punctuation in weeks of nothingness. There was nobody to take us anywhere and mum was nervous about me venturing outdoors unchaperoned.

"It's not safe. They'll know you from UK," she'd say when I'd ask to go to the shop.

It was in stark contrast to my life in the UK, where I was free to come and go and I had my own money. In Bangladesh, I couldn't even walk down the road to buy a packet of crisps. One time I asked Shefa to grab me some. She promised she would but never did. I guess I wasn't important enough to have my request fulfilled. I never bothered asking again.

One time, I napped during the day, out of sheer boredom. I woke to find that my family had left to go into town. They were likely headed to the local plaza, where you could get sarees, bangles or anything you like.

I don't know why mum didn't take me. She should've woken me up. She knew I was bored shitless. It didn't help that the domestic staff decided it would be fun to taunt me about this. "Oh, they didn't wake you? I told them they should wake you. Now you're all on your own," said Mona as she watched TV with her feet up on the stool, with nobody there to reprimand.

I wanted to cry. I was so fed up and frustrated in this place that was so alien to me, but I couldn't cry. That's what they wanted. A reaction. I couldn't do it. I wouldn't do it. I wouldn't give it to them. I remember being so angry at mum.

"So what if you no go? It just be shopping. You no miss anything."

She said this is as she unloaded the bags of saree blouses, shawls and cotton maxi dresses bought for herself and my sisters.

I didn't go, so I didn't get to choose anything. It seems like it was always easier to exclude me from these things because mum knew I would never make a fuss. I was the good one. The sensible one. I remember, right there and then, thinking I do not want to go back to this place.

I don't care if it's the motherland, I have no connection there, and my family had made zero effort to instil any love for Bangladesh.

I wonder if I'd visit with M. I wonder if it will be more fun with a husband, who'll take me out and I'd get to see places. If we don't, there's no chance in hell that our kids would go back. That part of our history would be wiped away, just as the mother tongue gets diluted as we immerse ourselves in the western world. It's sad to think that part of my heritage will be lost and I'll be a stranger to the place that runs through my blood. But it is what it is. So despite my mother-in-law's enthusiastic discussions about Bangladesh, I can't drum up the same interest. I'd love to be proven wrong one day.

M finally comes in. "Are you ready to go, then?"

He asks me as though I've been the one holding him up. I nod in agreement.

"Cool, I'm just gonna go to the poop station and then we'll get going."

That'll add on another 20 minutes, then.

As M disappears into the bathroom, there's another knock on the door. God, who is it now? I'm hoping it's M's older brother, returning from the shops with snacks of some sort.

It's not. It's another cohort of ladies whose faces I vaguely recognise because I've probably seen them once, or twice, in the duration of my marriage.

M's sister-in-law goes over to hug one of them.

"It's been years. I can't believe it!" she says, as she grasps the hand of the lady.

This woman is incredibly tall for Bengali standards. She must be about 5ft 8in. She's wearing a grey, billowing maxi dress, and has apparently shed some weight.

"You're like half the person you were! I don't believe it!" M's sister-in-law gasps and looks over to me. "Can you believe it? She's changed so much!"

I look at this lady, with her hair in a bun, adding extra inches to her height, and a grey scarf loosely draped over the top. She has thick, winged eyeliner and some silver, shimmery blush highlighting her already high cheekbones. Nope, don't recognise her. I, therefore, couldn't verify if she has lost half her body weight.

One thing I can be sure of is that with the arrival of new guests, it's going to be difficult to escape to my mum's.

There's another old lady, who is dwarfed by the newly slimline, tall lady. She comes closer and rubs her nose against mine. The spiky hairs on her mole tickle me. Unfortunate.

As nobody's making introductions, it's a game of Guess Who. I'll stick to informal pleasantries without daring to call anyone auntie or sister. It's the safest way.

M comes out of the poop station looking like he wished he'd stayed there.

"Salamalaykum. You okay, affa?" he asks the unusually tall lady.

Right, that's a big sister, then. Possibly many times removed. At least I have some context.

M doesn't know what to do. We can't very well leave now, can we? He should've come home ages ago.

He looks at me and mumbles. "What do you want to do?"

Cheeky git! Pinning it on me! I can't declare that I'm desperate to get out of this house in front of his family and some new guests. I shrug my shoulders and retreat into the kitchen to microwave some more samosas. I reckon a plate of six should be suitable, unless someone tells me otherwise. I'm not sure if there are any other male guests in the front room. They always head straight in there, lest we should see each other and cause a calamity.

M follows me. "Do you wanna get going?"

"I wanted to get going ages ago."

"What was that?"

Of all the bloody times to go deaf, he chooses now, when I'm trying to be secretive.

"I said I wanted to get going ages ago. I've been waiting on you." I say this through clenched teeth to hopefully muffle my sound and convey the resentment I'm feeling at the situation.

M looks wide-eyed and chastised. "Sure, that's fine."

I go into the living room and lay the samosas with a side of ketchup on the small table in front of the tall lady.

"Do you need to microwave more? Are there any guests in the front?" my mother-in-law asks.

How the hell should I know? I don't know why she's asking me.

"It be just my son," the old lady says. "Don't make anything. We ate when we came. Why you do all this? I just come to see you."

It's a sweet suggestion but we all know if we didn't serve samosas, our name would be mud.

"Uh... we'll get going," M mutters to my mother-in-law.

She looks up. "Go? Oh, yes, yes. Of course. You must see your family on Eid." She looks to the ladies. "Her father getting older. Not so well. She must see him."

Since when has my dad been unwell? And he's not that old.

"Yes, yes," says the old lady. "Always see your parents! You never know how long they be around for."

That's a bit morbid. But I'll take it and bolt out of the door before any more guests come.

After a few minutes of silence, initiated by me, M asks the inevitable: "Have I done something wrong?"

I sigh. "No, I just wanted to get going."

"I know. As soon as I saw Ruqya affa, I was like *'oh man'*."

"What about before then? You said you'd only be at Jam's for half an hour."

"I didn't mean to take so long. I got to Jam's and he wanted to show me his new jacket. He's going to one of those Muslim dating events and wanted to look sharp. Then he started banging on about how hard it is to meet someone. You know how he gets. He makes it hard to leave."

Usual story.

I have to choose my words wisely. "Eid is rubbish at your house. No dawats. No dressing up nice to go out. We just cook loads and stay at home while everyone else comes to us. Why don't we ever go to them?"

"Dunno, to be honest with ya. We've always been like that. When it comes to Eid, mum wants to stay at home. Bit rubbish for you."

Think positive thoughts. Think positive thoughts. He's a good husband. There's no point rocking the boat.

I arrive at mum's to find middle sis, big sis and little sis congregated in the dining room. M goes straight to the front room where the men are. I catch a glimpse of dad, sat on the Ottoman stool against the radiator.

It's his usual spot when guests are around. He's wearing a light grey kurta with a dark grey flowery border. He looks well, despite the ladies of Droylsden tempting fate. I'll catch him for small talk later. First, food.

There are a few leftover samosas in a colander. I'll happily have them.

"You alright, little lady?" asks big sis.

"Yeah, I'm fine. A little tired, that's all."

"Lots of cooking?"

"Yeah, the usual. We finished up around 2am last night."

"Blimey! I can smell the oil on you now!"

"Really?" I sniff a strand of hair. She's right, even the morning shower hasn't managed to wash off the deeply enriched cooking oil. That's intense.

Big sis still hasn't said anything about my non-pregnancy text message. It's weird, as it's not like we haven't been in touch. She messaged me a couple of weeks back asking if I want to attend a mehendi party in London. Someone from my brother-in-law's side. Obviously, I said yes, because an invite is an invite. Yet, no word on the possible miscarriage/late period front.

She could at least offer an extra tight squeeze instead of the standard, soulless hug. Maybe she's forgotten? Maybe she thinks it's no big thing? Should I bring it up? It was a big deal to me. No, it's not worth making a fuss in front of everyone. She might be thinking the same. Save it for a time when there aren't multiple family members milling around.

"Never mind, girly," says middle sis, smelling my hair, then frowning. "I had to do some frying this morning. And make a Tandoori chicken before I left my in-laws. It's never a party for us ladies."

"Speak for yourself!" says big sis.

"Well, except for the ladies who get married in the 'desh," middle sis adds with a sneer.

Having got married in Bangladesh, there aren't any cooking responsibilities for big sis beyond her own family, and it shows. She's wearing a navy saree with gold thread work. She has her hair up in a bun and her eyeshadow matches her outfit.

Middle sis, however, is less put together. Her hair is scraped back into her usual ponytail. She's without a speck of makeup, bar a swish of blush.

I always thought big sis drew the short straw having a husband from back home with a poor command of English. Having to be in charge of everything. Sorting the bills, mortgage and doing all the frontline household admin. However, there is a silver lining on Eid. Those days are all about her getting ready, looking nice and spending time with her family. As opposed to me, splitting the day in two, with a bigger proportion devoted to my in-laws.

Mum squeezes my shoulders whilst inhaling my hair. I'm getting paranoid now. "It be only once a year you have to do these big things. Best do what you can. And when you have time just escape little bit."

Eid comes around twice a year, actually. That aside, mum has some stellar advice. I must be better at escaping. My big sister-in-law did the lion's share of frying. However, she managed to excuse herself for prayer, toileting (both herself and her children) and bedtimes.

Damn, I need a baby.

26th January, Yellow is my nemesis...

It will be my five-year wedding anniversary this year. M is my soulmate and has made me feel more comfortable in my skin than ever before.

He is a testament that I am worthy of a happy ever after. That I am worthy of love. Though he rarely says it these days, I know he thinks I'm perfect. Scratch that, he fancies the absolute pants of me. He wouldn't have me any other way. He likes me just as I am.

Despite this, and despite 31 years of living in this skin, I am still not fully accustomed to it. Yes, I'm more comfortable, but not as comfortable as I should be. Not as comfortable as my sisters are.

As I stand in front of the full-length mirror of my built-in wardrobe, I get that familiar pang. It's less frequent nowadays, but right now, I can feel it with full force. It's niggling at me, nagging away. It's telling me this lemony shade of yellow is not my colour.

Yellow is my nemesis.

Fucking yellow.

I hate it when Bengali people have colour schemes for weddings and all the associated parties. You have to abide by it. Even if it's a shade that you really don't feel is you.

Yes, I wore yellow for my mehendi but I also wore a shit-ton of makeup. I was painted so golden that I could have draped a luminous pink saree and still looked great.

Today, I don't have a shit-ton of makeup applied by an artist. I'm applying it myself and that is rarely a good thing. My smudged eyes are more down to consequence than design. One eyeliner wing is slightly fatter than the other. The foundation that usually brightens me up is making me look chalky. Why is that? Why is it that the same makeup I wore to Julia's engagement and looked rather fabulous (if I say so myself), is looking so crap now?

Come to think of it, how come I can pull off yellow in a shirt, or even a dress, yet when it's a saree it looks bloody awful? What's that about? Granted, when I ordered the saree online, I thought the shade was more buttery than citrus but the issue is deeper than that. I'm comfortable in any shade of western clothes but the exact same colour in an Asian outfit gives me a bout of self-hating colourism. Suddenly, yellow is darkening, red is darkening, blue is darkening.

It's a painful reminder that despite all my preaching about fair isn't beautiful and colourism is outdated, these views have been etched into my deepest layer.

"Can I come in, lady?" big sis asks, although she's already entered the room.

Oh yeah, the mehendi is for one of my brother-in-law's cousins and I'm now having second thoughts about going. M is unable to attend as he's gone up north to see his mum. She's been unwell with flu, which resulted in a scary trip to A&E with chest pains, though she was out within 12 hours. M was still understandably worried, therefore broke the one visit per month mandate and is visiting just a week after we were last there.

I do sometimes wonder what the future will hold. I worry that we will have to go back up north. Don't get me wrong, I miss my family and we always say eventually we will make the move. But I worry about what that means. What it entails. What the expectations will be. I can just about do the one weekend per month. I can just about manage being on my feet for a couple of hours, chopping, descaling, washing, rinsing, more chopping, stirring and doing any other menial job that goes with being a sous chef to my mother-in-law. I can cope with the stench of fried onions that seeped into my skin, my hair and every orifice because my mother-in-law doesn't open the window or use an extractor fan. It's okay to do this once a month. If we moved back, it wouldn't be once a month. These are conversations M and I tiptoe around. He always assures me we would never be expected to move in with my in-laws but how can he be so sure? What if it comes to a point when it's necessary? His younger brother will get married. His sister will get married. What if my in-laws are left on their own? Will we have to pick up the baton? M is reliant and reliable, as I am with my family. We both carry a burden of responsibility and the worry that comes with it.

Then, I think of my parents, with no sons to live at home with them. What will happen to them? What's the default these days for Bengali people in old age? What's the expectation? If M is indeed right, and I wouldn't have to live with my in-laws, then great, woo hoo! Happy dance! But what would that mean for us in the future? Will care homes become more commonplace in Bengali communities? We're increasingly hearing about older people who don't live with their grown and married children. The last woman to join middle sis' husband's family has now left the house. That's the youngest brother's wife. It was expected he would stay at home but he didn't. The parents now fend for themselves. As far as I know, they're fit enough and up to the task. However, what happens if they need round-the-clock care? What will become of them? What would become of any of us, when we get old and we need help?

"Did they not have any other shades in the shop?" Big sis interrupts my train of thought.

"Shades of what?" I needn't ask. Her face speaks a thousand words. "I bought it online. I didn't know it'd be this... acidic."

"Well, it looks okay, I guess. What about your mehendi saree?" Big sis puts her hands together as if she's got an idea that's going to save my face, literally.

"You mean I should wear my mehendi saree to someone else's mehendi, who I barely know?" When I say it out loud, it makes me wonder why I'm even going.

"It's just... I'm sorry to say it, lady. I know it's really annoying when you've got your heart set on something. It's just not very flattering. But whatever. Whatever you feel comfortable in. Just saying, that's all."

She is more than just saying. She's planting the seed of a fucking oak tree in my mind. Why does she do this? Why is she doing this when we're about to leave? The taxi is coming in a few minutes. We have to make our own way there as her husband and kids have gone ahead early to help out. I don't understand what he's helping with. Surely they've got their own catering?

My phone rings. It's Reena.

Big sis carries on admiring herself in the mirror, oblivious to any social etiquette of leaving the room while I take the call. She is so annoying. She still hasn't mentioned anything about my almost pregnant situation. I thought she might at least share some words of comfort now we're alone. I can't bring it up to her. That would involve talking about feelings. We don't do that.

"Hey, you okay?" I ask.

"Look who finally answered!" shouts Reena. "Where you been? Too good for ya mates now you've got a bonking buddy?"

I let out a howl. That was unexpectedly funny.

"No, I've just been busy with stuff. Sorry." I don't even have an excuse. I can't remember what I've been doing.

"Yeah, yeah. You've changed, mate. I knew you would. Anyway, I'm changing, too. Got my own bonking buddy now, innit?"

"Wait. What?" I really wish big sis wasn't in the room so I could have an unfiltered conversation. I can't use the word bonking around her. I think humping and boning will be off the table, too.

"I've met someone and I'm getting married!"

"What? When did that happen? Last time we spoke, you were single."

"The last time we spoke was five months ago. You don't keep in touch no more."

"Am I really that bad?"

"You are but I'll let you off. I still love ya. Anyway, I can't remember if I was seeing him when we last spoke but I kind of didn't wanna tell anyone straight away. You know how it is."

"We're like soul sisters," I say.

I shared my news with Reena at the last minute, too. If my mum had her way, I wouldn't have told any of my friends until the wedding day itself, as she was so worried I'd jinx myself by daring to share my happiness.

"When's the wedding?" I ask.

"This summer."

"That's quick!"

"You can talk! You hardly gave me time to get an outfit for your wedding."

"To be fair, I barely gave myself enough time to get an outfit for my wedding!" I laugh.

Reena sighs. "When it was your wedding, I was thinking about when I'd meet someone. It had been ages since I'd dated. Everything was taking time. So I figured I'd have to -"

"Reena, I'm so sorry. I know it's absolutely rubbish but we're literally on our way to a mehendi party, and the taxi's just pinged my phone to say it's a few minutes away."

"Yeah, no, don't worry. You get going. I'll catch you properly later. And I'll send you details of my hen do. It'll probably be in springtime."

"That's great. It'll be like the old days," I say.

I'm aware how abrupt I was on the phone but I have a nosey listener hovering nearby.

Big sis flattens her saree over her front and it stubbornly crumples back up again. I'm really not sure about the half-silk aesthetic. It's meant to be luxurious, but the saree she's wearing is so stiff she might as well be wrapped in tissue paper. It's like the cotton sarees mum buys from Bangladesh that have been hardened up with starch. It's weird.

"Can you check if any of my back is showing?" Big sis turns around.

"One of your fat rolls is visible." I pull the stiff achal up to meet the bottom of her blouse.

"There's no need to be like that, lady. Is it because of what I said about your saree? You're not that bothered, are you?"

And there it is. The rhetorical question to cover all shitiness. Those two words, *are you,* followed by a question mark, means you can't object. That would make you a bad sport. We have to suck it up and take it on the chin. Bloody hell, sometimes it's like we're the royal family with our stiff upper lips.

"Actually, I am bothered. You do this all the time."

"Do what?" big sis laughs as she asks. She's doing it again. Minimising her micro aggressions.

"This! You always do it! The lot of you. But you're the worst."

"What do you mean, lady?"

That's it. Decades of hurt flood out of me in the form of one searing memory I thought I'd long forgotten.

"It's like that time in Bangladesh when we were all out playing guess who's holding the sweet in the front yard and me and middle sis were the last ones standing." I know it sounds stupid out loud. I don't even remember the point of the game but this is so important to me I have to carry on.

"And then the little cow Mina gave everyone a clue by saying *'darky, darky, darky'*! And then the other cow, Shahida, said to me: *'It's you holding the sweet, because you're the darky and she's white.'* And you laughed! You're my big sister and you laughed!"

My hands are trembling. I can't believe I'm sharing this. I can't believe it's been there. All these years. It's not even something I think about. But now, the memory and feeling of my 14-year-old self is as clear as crystal.

Big sis is smirking. She wants to laugh. Why does she do that? It's the worst thing. She's doing it again. Minimising. "I don't remember any of this."

"You wouldn't! Why would you? It didn't matter to you but it really hurt me. And that's just one example. I felt that all my life around you."

"Blimey, lady. Of all the times to bring this up."

"There's never a good time! You never give me a chance to speak about the real stuff. You never bother getting back to me about most things. It's only when you're in London and you need somewhere to stay, or you want someone to come with you to the saree shops. That's when I hear from you. When you need something."

"That's not true! You've forgotten all the things I've done for you. And instead you remember all this random stuff from years ago that I can't even remember so I can't defend myself! That's your problem. You hold onto things and you take everything to heart."

"And your problem is you're a cold bitch and you don't care!"

"Well… that's a bit out of order." Big sis is scrambling for words. "And it's not like you haven't had jokes at my expense. You used to say I had a fanny like a rugby ball right after I had my boy."

I try not to laugh at her use of the word fanny. Plus, I'd forgotten about that. "You found it funny! We all did!"

"I had to, didn't I?" says big sis. "Everyone was laughing. I'm a good sport like that. Anyway, if I'm so bad, why are you even bothering coming with me today?"

"I won't. I've changed my mind."

"Don't be silly, lady! You're all ready now. What would your brother-in-law say?"

"He'll probably say nothing. Like he always says nothing. Like he's been trained to say nothing. Like you expected him to say nothing when you collected him from Bangladesh."

Big sis' face drops.

In a flash, the taxi rings to say it's arrived and big sis heads out of the door alone. As the fire door slams shut, I can't recall answering the phone to the cabbie. I can't remember whether I told her the taxi arrived or she just went. All I remember is she didn't say a word. Perhaps I didn't, either. It was obvious at that point that I truly wasn't going to the mehendi to assault people's eyes with my acidic yellow saree.

14th February, Happy Valentine's Day to me

The thing with falling out with someone that you rarely speak to and only see once every few months is that you don't get proper closure. You can't resolve things, so you carry on with your business as usual every day, not realising that you had a fall out.

Not that we ever really had closure.

In another lifetime, big sis and I lived under the same roof. As there was a gaping age gap between us, our fights were few and far between, and they didn't last long. They couldn't. We shared a dinner table and, at one point, a room. There was no space for grudges.

The real squabbling was between her and middle sis. Their fights were epic. Shouting, arguing. I never knew what started it but it always seemed fairly trivial. A snide remark, a stolen lipstick. They would never hash it out. It would end when one of them started speaking to the other. The white flag would usually be in the form of a cup of tea, or a reminder that their favourite programme is on. Like I say, we don't really talk about feelings.

Big sis and I could ride things out in the same fashion. I'm sure she's forgotten about our little moment. It's probably for the best if she has forgotten. I know I went below the belt but I hold firm that she hit me first.

Anyway, tonight's not about fighting, it's about love. It is Valentine's Day after all. All my single life, I hated the 14th February. Friends would get cards and chocolates. I wouldn't even get flowers from my mum and I certainly wouldn't buy myself flowers. Who does that? I'm pretty certain it is a day designed to make singletons feel awful about themselves. It's a load of commercial rubbish and arguably the most pointless hallmark of the calendar year. That said, after years in the single wilderness, I'm conforming.

Following much deliberation of where we should eat, tabling options such as fancy tasting menus in central London or afternoon tea, we reach a decision after a long day of work.

"Brick Lane?" asks M.

"Why not?" I say.

We make our regular walk through Altab Ali Park, then cross the road at Whitechapel High Street to get to Brick Lane.

The beginning of the Lane starts off as Bengali as back home. There is a convenience store with its name written in both Bangla and English. A group of old men in a mishmash of styles - panjabis, prayer hats and suit trousers - walk past us.

"Let's go get *paan*," I hear one man say in Bengali.

There is a chorus of: *"Oy, oy!"* in agreement as the men head towards their after dinner equivalent of a beer.

"I never understood the thing with *paan*," I tell M. "I tried it once. It was like chewing on a leaf and wood chips. At least that's what it felt like."

"I tried it once, too. It's not for me, either. My mum and dad don't even have it that much. It only comes out when guests are around. It must be a social thing."

Despite these men being in their 60s or 70s, they're charging ahead of us at an impressive speed.

"It's not bad, having a bit of a crew at their age. Those old timers probably have more of a social life than we do." M laughs, though we both know it's true.

"You've got Jam."

"Yeah, some of the time."

As we move further into Brick Lane, we find more trendy pop-ups housing kitsch coffee places or dessert parlours. The clientele has changed, too. There's not an old group of Bangladeshi men in sight. Instead, there are young couples walking with interlaced fingers. A group of friends, clad in all black and chunky steel-toe boots, tights and fluffy coats, stomp past us. Across the road are a bunch of girls dressed like they're on their way to a hen do, with pink sashes over their white outfits. A guy walks past in a grey suit, headphones in, looking straight ahead. He likely lives in a trendy end of town, like us, where all the new build apartments bridge the East and West. He might be a neighbour, though we would never know.

We are closer to Shoreditch than Aldgate now. As we reach the last block of Brick Lane, we realise that we have eaten at every restaurant worth eating at.

To our left is an outdoor dining/drinking area, playing host to more friends than couples. They're so young, so free. They don't have anywhere urgent to get to. Laughing and joking and clinking glasses, they will party into the night.

Hold on, what is wrong with me? They're not living the dream I always wanted. On closer inspection, I don't think they're even that much younger than me. There's a guy among them that looks over 40. If I was to make a broad guess, I'd say they won't be having a nice meal. They'll be drinking and chatting and then making their own way home to their respective flat shares. Okay, that's super judgemental but I feel like I'm not a million miles away in my observation. Especially given the prices of accommodation in London. Nobody, but nobody, is living in a flat by themselves. Not in these parts, anyway.

I never wanted that. I always wanted to be coupled up. I'd be envious of other relationships. So why do I envy these guys now? Why do I always think the grass is greener?

"Shall we try that Thai place?" I ask, before we get into the part of town that is more bars than restaurants.

"Sounds like a plan, Batman," says M.

Three prawn crackers in, M has a confession. "I bought you a card..."

I have a confession, too. "You didn't need to. I haven't got you anything."

"It's alright. I haven't written in it yet. I didn't get a chance. I was walking home through Blackfriars and the card shop options are absolute pants. So I went into that rip off card shop and then, by the time I came out, I was getting late to meet you. And then obviously when we got home, we pretty much came straight out." M takes a deep breath. "Anyway, your card's at home. Just in case you think I haven't got you anything."

I wasn't expecting to be whisked off to Paris every year on Valentine's Day. However, I hadn't quite anticipated such a steep decline in chivalry since those early benchmark years. I can't even say anything, as I haven't got him a present. We're just as bad as each other.

"Oh, and the other thing is…" M does a lip grimace not dissimilar to my mum's. Why is everybody looking like her these days? "Jam messaged me earlier to say he's in London. Obviously Valentine's Day means nothing to him, so I doubt he realises what day it is. He wanted to join us." M's grimace turns into a look of sheepishness. "What should I say?"

"Does he want to come round later? Or join our dinner?"

Oh God.

"I don't know." M shrugs. "Either, I guess."

Oh God. God. God. The bar really has fallen to the ground.

I reluctantly reply: "Yeah, why not? If he can make it in time, he can join us for dinner."

No sooner had I said that, M's fingers are tapping on his phone, summoning his best friend over. Jam must've been waiting round the corner for the go-ahead, as he arrives around the same time as our mains.

"Do you want anything?" asks M.

"No, no." Jam shakes his floppy fringe. "I had a late lunch. I'll just have a bit of what you guys are having." He raises his hand to the waiter. "Could we get another small plate?"

Oh dear.

"Is that Tom Yum soup?" He nods towards what was supposed to be my main. "I haven't had that for ages."

"Do you want to try some?" It seems like the only polite thing to say, doesn't it?

"Nah, you carry on. If you can't finish it, I'll have the bit at the end." Jam takes the last prawn cracker and loads his small plate with more rice than it can hold. M's rice, I should add. "I see the rose sellers are out in full force today. I hope you treated your lady."

M laughs. "We've moved on a bit from the plastic roses. That was far too fancy."

"Now I get a card that's not been written in," I say.

Jam raises his bushy eyebrows as if he's stumbled upon a domestic. Truth is, I don't actually mind that much. M's half arsed nature gives me plenty of material, should I turn my makeup blog into something about relationships. My last post was about what lipstick to wear on Valentine's Day. Perhaps my next one can be about how to kill your husband when he doesn't get you an appropriate gift?

"At least that means you can recycle the card next year," says Jam with a laugh. "It's still better than anything I've been getting this year. Or giving."

"No girls on the go?" asks M.

"Unfortunately not. There aren't any meet-ups outside of London. There was a girl I was speaking to a few weeks back but you could tell she was way too high maintenance. She expected me to pay for everything. Once, I suggested we get a Chicken Cottage after the cinema. She wasn't impressed with that. It's like she wanted a three course meal at 11 o'clock at night. Nothing was open!"

"She's after the high life," says M.

"It's not even that. I don't mind paying for the first date, or whatever. I just don't think it should be expected all the time. We met up a few times and every time I got the coffee or the food but then she took the piss. She wanted me to drive around looking for something that would be open. It's not London! There won't be any hip 24-hour places in that neck of the woods."

"I take it you're not seeing her again?" I ask.

Now it's Jam's turn to look sheepish. "Maybe just once. She asked if we can meet up when I'm back. Obviously she's over the Chicken Cottage. And she is pretty nice. I'm not going to lie."

Ah, the pretty face. It makes up for a multitude of sins.

"Anyway, what are you guys doing afterwards? There's this programme I want to tell you about. It's a murder case. Basically, it's about a guy in America who killed his wife and whole family. We should watch it."

I guess there's no baby making on the agenda this Valentine's Day.

I send a sneaky message to Julia:

I hope you're having a better Valentine's night than me. Just be glad there's only two of you. Three's a crowd over here.

28th February, Designated letter reader

It's the half term holidays. I am at mum's. This also means that at any moment big sis might be joining us. You'd think we'd know with a reasonable amount of notice which sisters, if any, would be coming this weekend.

Nope.

Despite being over 100 miles away, big sis still doesn't know until the very last minute if she'll be making the journey to come and see her parents. It's a story as old as time. Mum would be nervously anticipating whether to make one curry, or six, just in case she turns up.

Mum would also be wondering whether big sis will be getting a lift from her hubby, or slumming it on the train. If the husband comes, mum would need to make a fish curry. A proper fish curry that involves descaling. None of this crack open a tin of sardines or defrost some prawns nonsense. Big sis' husband hasn't changed his Bangladeshi palate in all the years he's been here. He likes fish curry and not much else.

Middle sis is also terribly last minute in letting us know whether she'll be gracing us with her presence. Again, it's down to whether her hubby can bring her or not.

These kept women. I hope I'll never be that way. I hope I remain independent. Always.

"Your big sis no coming." Mum reads my mind. "But other lady be here soon."

"You mean middle sis. Your other daughter?" I ask mum.

"Yes, yes. Who else?"

Having only just settled in myself, as I stepped off the train at Stockport half an hour ago, I'm eager for lunch.

"Rice not ready yet. Let it bubble properly."

"Since when have you reverted to boiling rice in a pot?" I ask. "I thought you were all about the rice cooker these days."

"I heard on Bangla channel rice no good when use rice cooker. Water be full of starch that stay in your body and make cholesterol. You should stop using rice cooker, too. I see your husband. His body getting all big and heavy."

I'm going to ignore the well-meaning fat-shaming of my husband. "Who said this? One of the unverified doctors on those talk shows?"

"Yes. One of my doctors. Just because they no English doesn't mean they no qualify. Always think you better. Anyhow, before you eat, I got *lit-ool* job. While house be quiet and before children come. You know how crazy it get when they all come, especially now with small one."

"What's the job?" I'm bracing myself.

"Just to look at *lit-ool* letter?"

"What letter?"

"I *do-noh*. That's why I ask you check! I think it from NHS so best you look for me. Don't want to miss important appointment."

"Mum, you know there's another English-reading girl in the house?"

"Yes but she have no time. She be studying and working."

"I'm working, mum!"

"No, but she be proper working. In office, for people. She got boss. Real boss, not like you."

I begrudgingly read the letter that's laid out for me on the dining table.

"What is it? Is it bad news?" Mum does a fake gasp. She is so extra.

"It's a breast screening. That's a pretty standard thing you're meant to do every few years. They have a translator available, if you request it."

"What day is it for?"

"Let me check... it's this Tuesday! Mum, this letter is dated last month. You need to check your mail as soon as it arrives. Or get your other daughter to check it. You can't leave these things. They're important."

"Hmm. That be true." Mum nods. "Can you come?"

"Come where?"

"*Dooro!* To appointment! Where else?"

"It's in the middle of the week!"

"But you flexible with work, no? Isn't this best thing with you being boss? If you come, it would help. I can pay train ticket. Or give you half money. Train fare be expensive these days."

"No, mum! I can't come to your appointment next week. You can't expect me to do these things anymore. Not when there are other people who are more than able to help you. You don't actually need anyone to go with you. There is a translator, as I said. I can call them and arrange that for you. I'll have to do it on Monday, as the line isn't open now."

"Why line not open? It's a weekday! What kind of NHS is this?"

"They have limited hours, mum. I'll take the letter back to London with me."

Mum looks down. "How I go on my own? They have to look at boobs and things. It be embarrassing."

"It's not embarrassing. It's totally normal. And you should have been prepared for these things."

"What things?" mum asks.

"Needing to be able to speak English and do your own stuff. It's annoying that my life's work is being your receptionist. Every time I come home, every single time, there's always something. There's always some bloody letter or call to make and these things aren't easy. The lines are never open on the weekend. I have to do it from London and sometimes the person wants you to verify that I'm actually your daughter and you give me permission to discuss your personal details, when of course you bloody do! Who else is going to do it? You won't be able to do it yourself."

A knock on the door interrupts my rant. Just as well, as I might have said some potentially mean things, like my mum is a burden. I know I'll regret it later. But, oh my life, she makes my blood boil sometimes. It seems like you either have to have a job, a proper job where the boss isn't me, or have kids. Otherwise you're lumbered with everything. Or maybe that's just my lot. Maybe it's my default to be the dead cert. The one who gets everything done. After all, I always have. I pride myself on being reliable. The best girl. The good girl. Look where it's got me. A lifetime of letter-reading, translating and ferrying around.

"Look who it is! Alright girly." Middle sis greets me with a hug and this is followed by a line of hugs from her three children. But not her husband, obviously. If I've not said it before, I'll say it now. We do not hug our brother-in-laws. Not ever.

"Where's your fella?" middle sis asks.

"He'll come over on the weekend. I thought I'd come early for a couple of days."

"Oh nice, lady of leisure now, isn't it? Can come and go as you please."

"As you've been all your life. Anyway, I'm not really a lady of leisure. I'll make up for the time I'm taking off in the evenings. Clients still expect my work to be done."

"Yeah, yeah. You're not fooling no one," says middle sis, elbowing her hubby.

"That's not bad. I wouldn't mind giving up teaching to run my own business," says my brother-in-law.

"You've got the car business. Buying and selling?" I sometimes hear the odd anecdote about him acquiring a knackered BMW, souping it up in some garage and selling for a profit.

"Nah, it's small change. Not quite ready to quit the day job yet." He smiles.

"An unpredictable monthly income and demanding clients who want more for their money isn't all it's cracked up to be," I say.

"*Heh,* who got no income?" Dad comes in from the front room, newspaper in hand, at the sound of financial trouble. Not that he can bail anyone out. He's been retired for years.

"Salamalaykum," says my brother-in-law, straightening up and standing tall(ish, he's only about 5ft 7in) in the company of his father-in-law.

I find this hilarious as my dad, who looks even more diminutive in his blue collar shirt and baggy suit trousers, is hardly someone who commands attention. At least not in my eyes. He's dad.

"*Eh he, Bala nee*? I didn't hear you come." Dad assumes the usual Bengali formality.

"Why you all stand here in hallway? Let *damand* come in," says mum, ushering us all to make way for the man that's been a groom, as she puts it, in our family for over a decade.

"I wish I'd get this kind of greeting when I go to my in-laws," I tell mum once we're in the kitchen.

Mum scoffs. "You know it be different for ladies."

"It shouldn't be."

"Of course it should not be! Nothing in this world is fair for women. We always have to *com-per-mise*. But you no complain. You have it very easy, Mashallah. No live with in-laws. Only have to show best face for one weekend in month. Anyhow, no time to talk about this. You take through these samosas."

I dutifully take the saucer of samosas with the accompaniment of ketchup squeezed into a small bowl. Mum is right, I should be grateful. And I am. I know I've got it good. As she says, I only have to show my face once in a while. My life in London is great and beyond anything I could've expected, especially given the views on life post-marriage drummed into me from an early age. Yet, when I'm over at my in-laws, elbow deep in flour or crying from cutting onions, it's hard to practice patience, or count my blessings.

Since I've been downstairs, I've had four missed calls from Bushra. Better see what this is about.

"Mate, you are not gonna believe this," she begins.

"What is it?" I ask.

"Right, if I tell you, you can't tell anyone."

I'm assuming I can tell my husband if her news is funny, relevant or too juicy to keep to myself. After all, he's not anyone. Plus, four years into marriage, we need all the talking material we can get.

"Okay, I won't say anything. What's up?"

"So I just... God, I can't believe I'm saying this. I can't believe this happened!"

"Oh no! Is it Kamran? He's not been back in touch, has he?"

"No, not that prick."

Phew, that eases my guilt. "What is it, then?"

"You won't believe it." Bushra sounds like she's short of breath. "I'm going to tell you this thing, yeah..."

This better be worth all the preamble.

"You know how I said I'm kind of open to being introduced by my family. Like, even more now, after what happened with that dickhead, Kamran. He was such a knob."

"Yeah, total knob."

"Exactly. So I had my first blind date today. I said to my mum, I don't wanna see a photo. I don't wanna see a CV. I just wanna meet them. I didn't even want their name…"

"How did you know who you were meeting, then?"

"That bit was easy. I said I'd meet in the whitest part of town possible, in a cafe that was maybe a right-wing meeting ground. That way, we would be the only Asians there. There'd be no danger of me getting off with a skinhead."

That's actually a rather cunning plan. I'm impressed with Bushra's ingenuity.

"Anyway, guess who it was?" she asks.

"Why would you assume I'd even know? Just because I went through the arranged marriage process, it doesn't mean we all have one big WhatsApp group."

"You wouldn't know him through the arranged marriage process, you donkey. You know him from work. Or at least where you used to work."

"Work? We didn't have any other Asian people at work. Except for… Wait… Do you mean you went on a date with -"

"Don't you dare!" Bushra shouts down the line. "Don't you dare laugh."

I am indeed trying not to laugh. "Ahmed? Is that who we're talking about? Ahmed from work? You went out with him?"

"Yes! Bloody Ahmed! Like you said, there aren't any other Asian men at work. So yeah, I went out with Ahmed from work. Ahmed with the Harry Potter glasses. Big Ahmed." The last aside is laced with guilt. "Turns out he's blooming Mirpur like me. From the same village in Pakistan."

"That's nice. Though I assumed he would be from the same part of Pakistan as you."

"What?"

"Not in an ignorant way but just like many British Bengalis come from Sylhet, I figured that most Pakistanis are from Mirpur. At least that's what I learnt from my Pakistani mates at uni. Anyway, I think we're missing the point. You went out with Ahmed! I bet you were mortified when you first saw him!"

Bushra hesitates. "Erm… yeah, at first. Obviously. Then I thought: well, I'm here. He's seen me, I've seen him. I couldn't exactly walk out. So I sat down. Obviously, it was awkward at first. Neither of us knew what to say and then we kind of just started… talking. It was crap like work and stuff and then he told me how his dating situation, or lack of, has been going. I'm not gonna lie, he had more chat about him than I expected. I figured he'd be one of those… I don't know… he's a clown, isn't he? We all laughed at him at work. But when I was chatting to him outside the office, he was actually alright."

Bushra pauses. I don't have words to fill the space.

"Are you laughing?" she asks.

"No! I'm just taking it all in. Why would I laugh?"

"Come on. Why would you not laugh? He's Ahmed. The one we've always took the piss out of."

"So what's the deal? Was it just a nice chat? Or do you mean you kind of like him?"

"As if! I don't fancy him, obviously. 'Cause, you know…"

"I don't think I do."

"You know what I mean. He's a bit of a big fella, isn't he? Emma would have a field day if she found out."

"You told me before Emma?" I suddenly feel very included. Bushra and Emma are thick as thieves. Partying together. Working together. I didn't expect to be privy to anything first.

"Of course. You know how it is. You know the extra baggage that we have to deal with. It's easier to talk to you about this stuff. And for now, I want to keep it between you and me."

"It doesn't really matter if Emma finds out, does it? It's not like you're going to be... or.. unless you're going to see him again?"

I gasp. She likes him. Bushra likes Ahmed. Bloody hell, I did not see that coming.

"Don't!" says Bushra.

"Don't what?"

"Just don't!"

"Are you going to see him again?"

"I don't know. This is what's so annoying. When I got to speak to him outside of work, in a different context, he was actually okay. Maybe even normal. He was weird and creepy in the office. A bit of a try hard. When we met up, he was nice. He paid for everything. We ended up having croissants and pastries and hot chocolate."

"You were there for a while, then."

"Too long, mate. Too long. That's why I'm all confused now. How did I end up spending an afternoon with someone I'm so grossed out by and not hate it?"

This is my cue to impart some sensible advice. "Maybe you're not grossed out by him anymore. Maybe back in the day, when we worked together, we were a bit shallow."

"Shallow? No way! I've dated ugly blokes before."

"Come on, we were all a bit shallow. Also, Ahmed was an easy target. Do you remember the work do when Amy was bitching about him and we all felt bad but nobody wanted to say anything because it was easier to listen to her? Maybe there is something to be said about the guy who isn't the fittest in the room. Maybe those guys are the best. After all, I married a bald guy, which I never thought I would. Now I can't imagine myself with anybody else. I mean, maybe someone with better timekeeping who finds it easier to say no would be nice. That aside, I wouldn't change him."

Oops. I didn't mean to make that more about me than her.

"You're right," Bushra declares. "Kamran was proper fit and he turned out to be a bastard. Why are all the bastards fit?"

"Oh, Bushra. I think womankind has been trying to solve that mystery forever. Anyway, do you want to see Ahmed again?"

"I don't know. Can you imagine what Emma would say and everyone else?"

"Who cares! Look, Emma and everyone else isn't going to live your life for you. Nobody else is going to find you a man. If you find someone decent, even if it is Ahmed, give them a chance. You never know. Worst case, if he's super chivalrous and buying everything, then you get a free lunch, dinner or coffee or whatever."

"True. I guess it's also a good thing we're no longer work colleagues. He left about a year ago, so I don't have to worry about bumping into him in the office. We've exchanged numbers and we'll see what happens. Who'd have thought it? Ahmed's normal."

"Who indeed," I say.

"Thanks though, yeah."

"For what?"

"For being you. You're a good mate."

"I'm not really." I feel myself blushing.

"You are. You really are."

2nd March, Patience

Have sabr. Have sabr. Have patience. Be patient.

Patience, patience, patience.

I figure if I say it in both languages, it's more likely to stick.

You see, patience, gratitude and all of that is a worthy thing but it seems the hardest to practice when I need it the most.

"Do you want a hand?" says M, coming into the kitchen as I'm cutting the fat, veins and other gross bits off a raw chicken.

"No, you're alright. No point in both of us getting salmonella."

I'm struggling to separate the thigh from the drumstick. They did a half-baked job at the butchers, as it should be ready cut. It looks like I'll have to cut every single piece of chicken into even smaller pieces. My mother-in-law doesn't like big chunks of meat in her curry. She says it stops the flavour getting into the chicken. I say it's a stingy attempt to make the meal go further.

"Here, hand it over." M takes the knife out of my hand and presses down on the handle, cutting clean through the chicken bone. "Right, what else needs doing?"

"I need to stir the onions to make sure they don't burn."

M walks over to the tall, deep pot. "Who shall I talk about while I'm stirring?"

Would it be bad to say his mum? Probably.

My mother-in-law walks in, having returned from reading her prayers.

"Do you want to read namaz?" she asks me as she puts her socks back on.

"No, I'm not well."

M looks at me, concerned. "You okay?"

"I'm not well as in on the blob."

He doesn't say anything, no doubt processing that I've had another false alarm. Then he simply says: "Ah, okay."

What else can he say? What else should he say? There's not really much point in saying or doing anything. It is what it is.

But... this time, I was so sure. I was so bloody sure. I felt it. I felt it in my core. It wasn't just the aches, the heaviness, the tenderness. My body was working to produce *something*. I've heard about some people bleeding during pregnancy, so I did something I didn't do the last time. I took a pregnancy test. I didn't tell M about this. He had no idea I was carrying the small plastic wand in my bag, all the way from London to Droylsden. He didn't need to know.

I sat astride my in-laws' garish green toilet, looking at my pregnancy test. I was willing it: *please be pregnant, please be pregnant, please be pregnant.* Then came the sign. The small line that told me it wasn't to be.

I'm not upset. I'm not emotional. I'm... disappointed. I'd rather not be pregnant and have regular periods that come on time so I know where I stand. Instead of this nonsense. My own body is teasing me.

I can tell M is disappointed. Even M, with his unrelenting positivity, is finding this testing.

I'll message Julia when I get a minute. A Chancery Lane meet up where we put the world to rights always helps feed my soul.

"Shall we make some prawns? What do you think?" my mother-in-law asks me.

Before I can answer, M says: "What do you want to do prawn for? We've got enough food? Don't do anything else."

My mother-in-law's eyes change as she nods: "Yes, yes. Of course. Okay. Of course, there's no need. We won't make anything else. Got plenty."

Bless my M. He has his moments but, fundamentally, he is a good boy.

It's a rarity when we're all sitting down to eat in the living room. Even M's younger brother and sister are there.

"So I'm thinking of having a balayage next. What do you think?" M's little sister asks me.

"Is that kind of like blonde streaks?" I know nothing of hair dye. I briefly dabbled when I was 20 and obsessed with having hair that was anything but black. I coloured my hair as much as my strong pigments would take and ended up with something of a red hue.

"I can't imagine you with red hair," says M's little sis when I share this story.

"I was cool back in the day. I even considered going slightly purple."

"Purple?" M's brother looks up from his plate.

"Yeah, not in a dramatic way. I wanted a deep purple-ish black. It sounds a lot better than it is. I wouldn't have looked like an aubergine."

"I'd dye my hair, if I had any," M's brother laughs at his own joke.

My mother and father-in-law watch us with smiles. I don't think they get the gist of what we're saying, but their look suggests they are happy that we're all getting on nicely.

M has the same expression. I know every time we go up north, he has an air of trepidation as much as I do. He's worried about a mood swing, a tantrum, a domestic chore that's a step too far. I do my best to not whine and just get on. For the most part, that works like a charm. Until it doesn't.

"There's some leftover pizza, if you want it, from last night," says his brother.

"I'm alright, thanks," I say. "I had enough of it last night. I think the spiciness didn't agree with me. Putting green chilies on a pizza is a bit much."

"That's the best one," says M. "Then again, I'll play it safe, since we've got a four-hour drive back."

"Yeah, you don't want any emergency stops on the motorway!" M's little sis giggles.

M's dad presses his palms onto the coffee table to help hoist himself up.

"What do you need, baba?" I ask. "I can get it."

"I need some water. Not too hot, cold water with a bit from kettle." He says this every time as though it's a new order.

As I get up, he settles back into his chair. He is the opposite of my mother-in-law, the culinary machine.

I wonder if the relentless cooking is something she always loved. Or was it something she started after having children, a habit born out of the desire to feed them Bengali food? I'm caught between resenting the job of helping, while also being grateful when eating.

Back in London, curries are a weekly effort. Even then, it's a poor effort. There's always something amiss and M and I struggle to put a finger on it. Either there aren't enough onions, or they're not melted enough, or not browned properly. Or a spice ratio is off. I never get that golden red tint that my mum or mother-in-law's chicken curry exudes. Mine is always a bit soupy, a bit watery. So, yes, while I would rather be spending my weekends with my feet curled up and watching the telly, I also want to eat home-cooked food and I'm beginning to realise that as a grown woman, I'm not going to be fed and watered and waited on hand and foot. I have to do it myself or at least help in the kitchen.

There's a routine in Droylsden. We travel up on Friday night and there's no cooking to be done. Everything is laid out for us, too. Sometimes three curries are ready and waiting.

Saturday is the hard slog. We have a slow breakfast and a lazy start. At midday, the cooking commences. This can go on for hours. Then we get to eat the spoils. My mother-in-law is painfully slow at prepping. She's a contrarian. On one hand, she is a force of nature when getting things done. Yet, at the same time, it's a leisurely pace. *Good food takes long time*, is her mantra.

Saturday evening is a break for all concerned. No cooking, just takeaway. Come Sunday, it's time to go. Though as today shows, it doesn't stop my mother-in-law trying her luck and introducing a couple more dishes to the menu, even though we have food from the day before. Usually, M puts a stop to it, if he gets back in time from seeing Jam or whatever else can distract him from having to stay at home. And then he gets an earful from me.

I wonder whether this tradition of Bengali feasting will be lost in years to come. I wonder whether it's fading already. We modern girls have to balance careers with cooking. With so many conveniences on our doorstep, such as takeaways, sandwich shops and sushi at the end of a workday, it's all the easier not to cook. I guess when I have kids of my own, they will be brought up on an eclectic diet of pasta, chips, curry and whatever else is languishing in the back of the cupboard. There'll be an end to this. Gone will be the days of two or three different curries per meal. I feel both glad and sad about that.

M's little sis washes up while I wipe the dishes.

"I don't know how you manage it all," she says.

"What do you mean?"

"Working and then coming here and cooking. Mum always says to me: '*What you gonna do when you get married?* She thinks I'm lazy."

I used to think she was lazy, too. Best keep that thought to myself.

"You've got a few years before you have to worry about that," I say.

"I don't know. I'm finishing uni soon. I wish I'd gone away, then I would've been a bit more house-trained as I'd have to pull my weight." She gives a wry smile. "I couldn't go because mum was worried what people would say."

What would people say indeed? The reason many of us girls are held back. I feel a pang of guilt, as I feel some of her mum's reasoning was due to the ground rice based fallout we had years back. I remember being so exasperated from having to constantly cook while she came and went as she pleased, that I planted a seed in M's mind that she might be up to no good. I wish I hadn't said anything.

M stands at the doorway, as if he's not sure whether to enter. He's got his plotting face.

"Is it okay if we leave in about an hour?"

Gladly, I think. "Yeah sure."

He's still hovering at the door. I wish he'd spit out whatever he wants to say so we can all crack on with our day.

"So... Jam called. I might pop over and see him. Just for like an hour. It's been a few weeks since we met. Is that okay?"

"Yeah, go."

M bolts out with his figurative permission slip before I can change my mind. "See you in a bit."

Famous last words.

It's been an hour and a half, not that I'm keeping tabs or anything. I'm on edge as I'm sat with a cup of tea and my mother-in-law. My father-in-law has gone for a nap. M's little sis is upstairs. His brother has gone out. I can feel it coming.

"I know," M's mum declares, putting down her mug. "Shall we do kebab? What say you?"

"I don't know, mum. Do you have mince ready?"

"I got half KG in fridge." M's mum smiles. "I thought I best keep fresh, since you all here. Might be nice."

Of course she has a stash ready for such an occasion.

The food processor is turning into my worst enemy. I'm not grinding rice, I'm blending onions. I've never blended onions for a kebab. I usually chop them as finely as I can (which is still pretty coarse). This is new.

Blending aside, I'm miffed. Where the hell is M? Why does he always do this? Why does he always go out at the last minute? If it's not a quick game of golf, or a cheeky burger, it's Jam. It's almost always Jam. Despite seeing him less in London, they catch up just as frequently up north. That's the thing, now he's not in London, in our faces all the time, I feel I can't moan so much when he sees him here.

So annoying.

My face is getting warmer. Have patience. Have patience. Have patience. But we have pots of curry! We've just eaten! Why are we making kebabs? There's no space in the tummy for kebabs! I bloody want a doggy bag to take home with me, though.

My mother-in-law is adding the exact spice proportions to the keema. "If you done onion, now you can mix it."

No thanks, I'd rather not, goes my inner monologue. I reluctantly bring over the jug of blended onions. Just then, as if like a movie, when the hero appears at the very last minute as the heroine's life is at stake, M strolls in.

"What's going on now?" he asks, looking around the kitchen for clues.

I say nothing. Instead, I shoot daggers with my eyes. Sharp, lethal daggers.

"I thought we do kebab before you go. You can take with you," says my mother-in-law.

"Leave that. There's no time now. We need to get going."

If only M was here to say that an hour ago. There is no consideration for the fact that I've got work tomorrow. By the time we get to London, it'll be after 11 o'clock. It's too late for a proper shower. Courtesy of having thick, strong Bangladeshi hair, there is definitely no time to wash and dry it in the morning. It's like my mother-in-law doesn't think about that. It doesn't occur to her that I might not want to get smelly and sweaty on a Sunday evening. Then again, why would it? She's never worked in the corporate world. She doesn't need to think about these things. It's not malicious. She just really likes to cook.

M's mum looks deflated. "No worries. I just fry them quick for you. Then you can have it for snack when you get in."

I feel like I'm breaking some daughter-in-law code but I go upstairs to get changed into a more appropriate public facing outfit of a fresh-smelling salwar kameez with discreet pink beading. It's slightly more suitable for a service station burger and chips run.

Annoyingly, the kebab is really nice. Just how does she get that spice mix right? I never get to see. When you're a sous chef, you watch bits of things happening and have a small part to play, but you never get the full picture. It's like seeing the trailer of a movie.

The kebabs aren't the only thing we've brought with us. My mother-in-law insisted we take the rest of the chicken curry but I felt bad as she'd done the hard bits. I just bashed some ginger and garlic in support.

"It get old. Who else eat it?" she said.

"What would you have later?" I asked, secretly happy about the prospect of not cooking the next day.

"You know I no eat at night! I just have toast. Your father-in-law have fish. And the younger two usually don't eat same curry twice. No point wasting."

Despite her insistence, it felt like more of a symbolic sacrifice. A way of making amends for dropping a last minute kebab job on me, even though she did most of the work in the end. So there you have it, I'm loaded with containers of curry, kebabs and guilt.

However, what's weighing me down most is annoyance towards my husband. He always does this to me. He always leaves me in a tricky situation. He knows there's likely to be a last minute job if we linger too long. As the space between lunch and dinner widens, he knows damn well we'll end up cooking some random dish that is totally unnecessary. Why does he do that? Why does he leave me in the lurch? Is he testing me? Is it subconscious?

"Are you alright?" is his standard question as we leave Droylsden to join the motorway.

I don't respond and carry on eating my kebab.

"Save one of those for me!" he says.

He doesn't deserve one.

While I'm hating my husband, I recite my mantra. Have patience. Have patience. I can hear my mum's voice in my ear. *Don't make small matter big.*

"What were you doing with Jam?" I ask.

"I went to his house. He's getting some work done to his mum's place. So just chatting, really."

"You said you'd be an hour and you were gone nearly two hours."

"Yeah, I was about to leave and then he started talking about some girl he's met online. He went round in circles procrastinating about it. Basically, he likes her but she said she's not willing to relocate. She wants to stay near home. And guess where she lives?"

"No idea." I look out of the window.

"Devon. Of all bloody places. She wants him to relocate to Devon! So he's not sure what to do."

"I take it he doesn't want to live by the coast?"

"No. Who would?"

"Well, that's that then, isn't it? If he's not going to relocate and she doesn't want to move, it's a non-starter. What's to procrastinate about?" I don't get why these situations, which are obvious for all to see, are so complicated for these boys. "Did you realise you were gone for ages?"

M stutters. "I- I didn't straight away, to be honest with ya. Then, I checked the time and realised I better get a move on."

"Good, I just want to check that you knew. I'm not always sure if you're aware how long you keep me waiting. If it's nothing life-threateningly important, I don't see why you can't cut the conversation short."

There's silence for a moment. Then M says: "I tried."

"Next time, try harder."

M doesn't say anything, neither do I.

Have patience. Have sabr. Have patience.

13th March, A joyless day

"Come and look at this," I say to M, showing him my phone.

He puts down his bowl of muesli to take a closer look. "Who is that and what am I looking at? I can't see beyond the surgical gloves. Wait, is someone have an operation and they've put it on Facebook?"

"Well, it's on Instagram, and it's Naila. Looks like she's at the dentist getting an implant fitted. Of all the things to share on social media."

"Why would she put that on there? Surely she wouldn't want to advertise that she's getting a fake tooth. Wouldn't that imply she was toothless to start with?"

"You used the right word there, advertise," I tell M. "It's a paid partnership. She's advertising this private dental clinic and they're giving her a tooth in return. I bet she wishes monetisation was a thing when she had four teeth removed to fit her braces."

"So first she had too many teeth and now she's not got enough!" M laughs.

As far as guys go, I've picked a good one when it comes to bitching. He loves it.

"How much do you think she makes from those posts?" asks M. "It's got to be worth it to share your false teeth."

"I don't know. It'll be more than me, that's for sure. The best I've ever got is some free lip balms."

"That's not true. Remember, you got those chocolates? I benefited from that as well." M strokes his belly.

"Oh yeah, I forgot about that. Maybe I'll get more free stuff as I write more blog posts. Though I think I'll draw the line at posting when I get a filling, or my teeth cleaned."

"That's where you're going wrong." M shakes his head. "You should be sharing all the personal stuff, like how I'm trying to knock you up and it's not working."

He laughs. I don't.

"A bit soon?"

"Just a tad," I say, sipping my lukewarm tea.

"I'm just joking! I hope you're not worrying about anything."

"You know me. I do like to have something to worry about at all times."

"Don't add this to the list. It'll be fine. You'll be preggo in no time and moaning about your swollen vag."

I nearly spit out my tea. "Vag?"

"Isn't that what happens? Swollen something, isn't it?"

"I think you mean swollen ankles?"

M shrugs. "I don't know you women and your weird bodies." He takes another spoonful of muesli before reaching for his backpack.

"I might have to lend you Sophia's pregnancy books to get you familiar with the way things work. Anyway, on that note..."

"You're pregnant?"

"No, but I'm considering getting ovulation sticks."

"What sticks?"

"The ones I mentioned, where you pee on them and it shows when you're fertile, or something or other. It might help things move along."

Another shrug from M with a slight huff. "It's up to you... if you want to."

"Why? You don't agree?"

"I just don't think you need to worry about it." M picks up his laptop from the floor and puts it in his backpack.

He heads towards the door and I follow closely behind, intent on getting to the office early. There's a bum fight these days for seats. I guess that's the downside of hot desking.

As M holds open the pine effect fire door. I tell him: "Like I say, I like to have something to worry about at all times."

How dare people question my worth?

Joy has called an emergency meeting to discuss 'ways of working'. What is to discuss? The whole point of flogging an online course is that there's only one way of working – she does the course and doesn't bother me about it.

There's not meant to be any after-care or client liaison. Otherwise, I might as well keep her on retainer and bill her every month, rather than a one-off fee.

The only good thing is that Joy is coming to my office, as she works from home. It saves me a journey, while also giving me the opportunity to show off my workspace.

Joy speaks in such a slow, careful, deliberate way that I'm hanging on her every word, thinking it's the last. She does my head in.

"You see... the thing is..." Joy takes one of the free mints from the bowl in the centre of the large table. That bowl has housed the same green, stripey mints since I started here. I'm not sure how often it gets replenished. "I feel like there's a bit of a disconnect between what I expected the course to deliver, and what it actually did."

"In what way?" I ask.

"It's just... well... for what isn't a small sum of money for me... after all, I'm only a humble slimming coach, I expected more bang for my buck."

"Okay. Is there anything specific you feel was lacking in the course?"

"Nothing specific but the reality of implementing the learnings is a lot more than I expected. I just... I think... I don't want to be negative and certainly don't want to devalue your work but I'm not in the right frame of mind to focus on PR right now."

I take that to mean she hasn't bothered finishing the course. "Have you implemented any of the learnings? As in, have you approached any journalists or tried to get any stories together? Or written a press release?"

Joy does that face again, where she's trying to locate the source of the imaginary fart. "I've not gone anywhere near doing that. I don't feel that I have the confidence."

"That's the point of the course. If you did all the modules, and I know there's quite a few but if you went through them, you would see that it covers everything to give you the confidence to approach journalists."

"No, I get all of that and, honestly, this is not about you. I think you're great and the couple of modules I did looked fantastic. It's just that I'm not in a place right now to make it work. When you pitched it... and, again, this isn't a criticism of you, perhaps it's more the way I view things... but, when you pitched, I genuinely thought it would be something I could do around my work. That it wouldn't be too time-consuming."

My heart sinks a little. Have I misled her with my marketing spiel?

Joy goes on. "Had I known I'd need to spend hours online, watching these videos and then on top of that," she scoffs, "actually implementing everything. I haven't got time for it right now."

"I did clearly set out a whole list of modules. I mentioned that there's 30 videos and that each video was no longer than half an hour but no shorter than five minutes." I don't want to sound defensive but I have to fight my corner. "I thought that was clear enough for you to gauge that it's going to take you a few hours to get through. It is one of those things, what you put in, you do get out and -"

"Yes, yes, of course," Joy raises her hand as if to stop me. "And like I say, I don't want this to sound like a criticism of your course. Or you, for that matter. I think you're fab. I'm just not in that place right now. Perhaps when I have a PA, or increase my team, I'll have more time. Then, I can perhaps think about doing your course. Or maybe even outsourcing PR, if I have the budget. Having said that, for now, it's not for me." Joy unwraps the mint. The sound of her untwisting the plastic wrapper goes through me. "And I know that I've gone well past my 30 days..."

"It's been quite a few months," I say.

"I'm aware. I'm fully aware of that." Joy shakes her head, letting her brown bowl-head hair swish animatedly. Why anyone has that haircut, I'll never understand. "But, if at all possible... and I ask this as one businesswoman to another." She reaches across the table as if to hold my hand. Weird. "You know how stretched we all are right now. Clients are tightening their belts. Everything's getting more expensive, all of that. So... if at all possible, I wonder whether there could be some grace and you could issue a refund?"

I am well within my rights to say no. I clearly stated there is a 30-day money-back guarantee. It was as simple as can be. Now, she's trying to go back on that as if we did business on a handshake. Businesswoman to businesswoman. The cost of living is affecting us all, not just Joy, who is sunburnt, having returned from a trip to the Algarve.

Then, my PR politeness kicks in: "That should be fine, Joy."

Benedict keeps giving me furtive glances from the corner of his eye, as I'm silently seething at my desk.

I've been avoiding him of late after his awkward expectation of a freebie course from me. It was the epitome of entitlement. However, the curse of being a part timer means I have to take whatever seat is available. Today there is a full house, except for the one place next to Benedict.

"I'm going to grab a coffee. Do you want anything?" he asks.

"No, I'm alright," I say, continuing to punch away at my laptop.

"Are you sure? Someone's brought in some biscuit samples."

"No, I'm good."

I have never refused a biscuit. It's just not in my DNA. However, I've lost my appetite. Joy hit me where it hurt the most. She questioned my credibility and challenged my work in the most backhanded of ways. Every echo of 'you're great', 'you're fab', was a patronising slap in the face.

All my life, I've been able to bank on my career. I wasn't the prettiest or the most popular but I was a workhorse. I was a grafter. I was proud of my achievements. I *am* proud of my achievements. When I embarked on this solo PR journey a few years back, it was daunting. I wasn't hiding behind the banner of a big company. I was representing me. People were paying for me.

This course was supposed to be the next big thing in my business. It was supposed to be the game changer. The one where I productise my business and make a scalable income. Yet Joy's rejection has got me questioning it. So far, I've had three sign-ups. I've had plenty of people feigning interest but reluctant to put their money where their mouth is.

There's another reason I'm beat up about this.

Doing an online course that doesn't require me being so hands on was my ticket to becoming a successful working mum. I know that I won't be able to do this PR game with a baby. I can hardly take media calls in the middle of the day when I've got a screaming newborn. And yes, I do think about these things. I think about the five-year plan.

I wonder what it would look like for me. I know I can already write off my mum and mother-in-law as help as they are hundreds of miles away and, truth be told, if I lived up north, they wouldn't be able to be of much help, either.

I don't resent that. It's just a fact.

The other option, of course, is paid childcare. Nannies, private nurseries and the like. I just never thought I would do that. I always thought the baby would be with me, just as I was with mum my whole life. Mum never worked. She never had the chance or the choice.

In some ways, it made things simpler for her. There wasn't a dilemma. It wasn't even a consideration that she'd go to work with small children, or ever. But for me, with one foot in this modern world, as a forward thinking career woman, and another foot deeply entrenched in Bengali culture, I'm torn right down the middle. I figured I'd make a sustainable income from this course, whilst being a mum. But it's not panning out like that. It's not selling itself and I'm not making money in my sleep.

The story you're constantly fed about this hustle culture, this 'you can have it all and make your dreams come true', it's all bullshit, isn't it? It's a load of rubbish to trick you into thinking you can do it. To make you chase Nirvana. Chase that rainbow, yet each time you get closer, it gets further away before you have a chance to touch it.

Anyway, those are my thoughts right now and I'm not exactly sure how much sense I'm making, even to myself.

It's bloody hormones, you see. That bloody time of the month, taunting me when I'd most like to be rid of it, for nine months at least.

I need to distract myself. I'll check my personal emails. Maybe I'll get a message from a PR company trying to send me free lipsticks to review on the blog. That'll cheer me up no end. No lipsticks, but an email from a Varsha Patel. Who is that?

I open the email, and then remember it's Reena's sister, who I've met only a handful of times in my life.

It reads:

Hi, as we prepare for our little sister's wedding, we have been busy arranging something more important... a big fat, gu-jji send off!!!

You are cordially invited to Reena's hen do.

Venue: Stomping Ground, Islington.

Date: 10th of April.

Time: 8pm till late.

Theme: Easter bunnies.

If you want to gift Reena something, just hand it to me or Veena on the night. Don't feel obliged, obvs.

We're looking forward to a night of boogying, Gujarati style.

Love from the chicks, Veena and Varsha.

That sounds like fun.

It's also way more effort than any of my sisters made when I was getting married. They didn't organise a hen do.

I had to sort out a family dinner myself, and even then they couldn't be bothered turning up on time.

Stop, stop it now! No need for negativity. I'm happily married. Everything turned out fine. Glass half full. Glass half full.

"Excuse me," says a voice from behind.

I see Jasdeep. He's not said a word to me since that weird meeting where he spent the whole time bragging about himself. What does he want? I bet he's remembered that he messaged me online. That's why he's probably been avoiding me. This is my chance to confront him. It's the best time to do it, as I'm pissed off already.

"Can I nab that empty mug?"

"Sorry?"

Jasdeep gestures towards my desk. There is an empty, coffee stained mug. "I've got biscuits at my desk. Can't have them without tea and there's no more mugs in the kitchen," he says, as he reaches for the mug and walks away before I have a chance to say anything.

He'll keep.

Despite my better judgement, I go on Instagram to check the latest status of Naila. I don't know why I do it. I'm a masochist.

Unsurprisingly, she has a new post, with a photo of her holding a strand of her hair, which has taken on a dirty blonde shade. She's piercing the camera with her eyes, sporting hazel contact lenses. Her pout is full and she has a fistful of rings. The caption reads: *I'm a boss bitch, yeah, what you get is what you see. All those basic bitches got nothing on me.*

Oh, she's a poet and she didn't know it.

10th April, Typos

I feel like an idiot, sat on the Tube wearing bunny ears. I'm getting side eye from the girl next to me. Now I think of it, my novelty headband is slightly at odds with the rest of my sensible outfit. Grey jumper dress, leggings and ankle boots are more dress down Friday than raucous hen do. Anyway, she's one to judge. Green tights with matching ballet pumps? I didn't realise it was panto season, Tinkerbell.

I rarely make Tube trips on my own in the evening. Or at all. I walk to work, or get the bus if I'm feeling lazy. When I have to hotfoot to a networking event across town, I'll keep my Tube stops to a minimum, sometimes getting off earlier and walking extra. I'm sure I've got some low-level anxiety about the underground, which I should get checked out at some point.

I'll message Julia. I'm sure she'll find all this hilarious.

Hey, guess who's sat on the Tube wearing bunny ears? Also, when shall we meet up? I miss your face.x

When was the last time I saw Julia? Surely it wasn't as long ago as her engagement? We can be flaky with keeping in touch, but this is on another level.

Let's see when we last messaged each other. That's weird. The last two messages were from me and she never replied. Rude. I get that she's engaged but surely she could hold off on the 'Misters before sisters' mantra until she's married.

I wonder who will be at the hen do. I wonder if there'll be anybody else not drinking. As I've realised throughout my entire life, it's never fun being sober, not least when everybody's pissed.

As I get off the Tube, I'm thankful that the restaurant isn't too far from Highbury and Islington. However, as I approach, I'm not sure if I've got the right place. From the outside, it doesn't even look like a restaurant. It's more like a dingy club, painted black with small, steamed-up windows.

The inside doesn't fill me with confidence, either. I don't want to sound like an old woman, but the music is a couple of decibels too high for my liking. They're pumping out some good R&B, which reminds me of my uni days. Then I realise it's not really a restaurant. Well, there are tables dotted here and there, but the lighting is dim and there looks to be a stage for live performances. There's even something of a makeshift dancefloor. Perhaps that's for later.

"You made it! I thought you wouldn't come," says Reena, pulling me in for a tight squeeze. She's already tipsy. I can smell it on her.

"Am I late?"

"Yeah, but you always are, so never mind. Come and sit down."

Reena parks me on an empty chair and heads to the other end of the table, flicking her nylon veil over her shoulder while she walks. As she stumbles on a chair blocking her way, I notice she's gone for the full bunny look, complete with a pom-pom on her bum.

Reena has a lot of friends. They've taken up the long table and overspilled into nearby booths. I never had a big group of friends. I gathered pockets of friends from different aspects of my life. Julia from school, Reena from university, Bushra from work.

Before I was made redundant from my last job, Bryony and I had become fast friends. We were adamant we'd keep in touch. There was a concerted effort at the beginning with various text message exchanges. Then, life inevitably got in the way. There was no longer that commonality of a shared office, which made it so much easier to keep in touch.

I don't recognise a single face here. I thought there'd be a couple of girls that I knew from uni. Perhaps Rekha? Or Shradda? No such luck.

The girls on either side of me are locked in conversation with those seated next to them. With their backs to me, I can only see swathes of black, shiny hair. This is awkward.

The girl sat opposite, perhaps noticing my loneliness, pushes a bottle of red wine towards me.

"Oh, no. Not for me. I don't drink."

"What?"

"I said I don't drink."

The girl gives me a thumbs up. "That's really good. I should stop. You know every January I think I'm going to go dry. And then -" she swirls a glass around in her hand.

She speaks some more but her voice is muffled under the thumping music. I have to smile along, hoping she doesn't ask any open questions that I won't be able to hear.

I could do with some moral support. I check my phone. Maybe Julia has replied. Nope, nothing. She is terrible these days.

The girl next to me passes a basket of prawn crackers. "Most of the food is cold now but these are still good."

I grab a cracker before saying thanks, as I'm ravenous. I haven't eaten anything since lunch. Having swallowed a crunchy mouthful, I turn to see who my generous feeder is. Bloody hell, it's Sonali!

"Oh, my days! I haven't seen you in time! How you doing?" she says, a smile as wide as I remember.

"I'm – I'm good. It's been... what? 10 years? You haven't changed."

"I have! Two dress sizes bigger these days." She tugs at her ribbed black vest. "It's you that's not changed. You're literally the same girl that used to eat shit loads and never put on any weight. I always hated you for it."

"I didn't realise you and Reena knew each other."

Sonali grabs a cracker. "You don't remember? You introduced us. At your 21st. Well, small world that it is, I ended up working with her sister when she moved to London."

Reena's sister is in London? It now makes sense why the hen do was here. They're probably all staying over with her.

"Actually, I've been meaning to get in touch with you. I saw your Facebook status had changed to London. I'm guessing that's where your guy's from?"

"That's right," I say.

"We should link up while we can. I'm still in Barnet for now but then I'll be moving to Leicester when I get married."

I gasp. "Oh, that's amazing! You're getting married! I had no idea!"

Sonali looks at me funny. I don't blame her. Why would I have any idea that she's getting married? We haven't spoken in a decade.

"You know how it is." She runs her fingers through her long, straight hair. I catch a glimpse of a ruby and diamond rock. "I didn't want to go all out on social media until we're married. Never know who might jinx you."

"I thought it was just us Bengalis who believed that sort of thing."

"Nah, we're extra about it. My mum was convinced I wouldn't get married, so we went to India, did some prayers and now we're all good." She laughs.

"Tell me about your guy, then?"

Sonali looks wistfully. "Well, he works in IT, which I know is very boring and typical for an Asian boy. He's a software engineer. We've been dating for a year. Oh, give me your number. I'll send you an invite for the big day. It's been too long." Sonali pulls her phone from her back pocket. "It's a shame, we were tight in uni, I didn't want to lose touch how we did. In between you've got married and everything!"

Sonali and I have lots to catch up on. It turns out she works in project management, a career I'll never fully understand. She went back home after uni, just like me. It's interesting to see the parallels between us. She has the usual family pressure and went on a bunch of non-starter dates before meeting her man.

"How did you and your fella meet?" Sonali asks.

"The usual. Through friends, kind of a blind date." I've become better at covering my secret over the years. "You?"

"Same."

A girl from across the table slides a tray of shots in front of me. She looks up and mouths: "Oops, sorry." Word must have got out that there's a Muslim among them. She nudges it towards Sonali.

"You don't mind if I drink, do you?" Sonali grabs the small glass and downs it in one big gulp. "Eww... that was nasty. I'm not having anymore."

"Don't be a lightweight!" I hear someone shout.

"I'm taking it easy. I haven't eaten much but I'll have some prawn crackers to line my stomach."

"Oh, shut up!" says Reena who's audible even from the far end of the table. "It's my hen do. You're gonna drink."

"I might just have one more." Sonali downs another.

I look around me. Shots everywhere. Empty glass bottles. Empty glasses. Girls throwing their heads back, guzzling booze.

There is more alcohol than food around here. I haven't spotted a single menu. No more food is shuffled in my direction, though I have been offered various drinks.

What is everyone eating tonight? I spot one half-empty basket of bread and a demolished plate of nachos on the other end of the table. On one overspill table there's an empty saucer that doesn't look like it had much on it to begin with. I spy a bowl of untouched olives with cocktail sticks. I'd happily have one of them right now but they're too far away for me to reach.

It looks like I'm the only sober one here. I don't really know what to do with myself. It's not like I can be loud and lairy with them. When you're not emboldened by drink, you just look silly. While everyone around me is losing their inhibitions, mine are very much intact. Plus, like many a work social I've been on, when everyone's drunk, everything else seems magnified. The chatting sounds like arguing. Someone looks like they're about to cry, while another girl strokes her hair.

Four more shots later, Sonali is in a confessional mood. "I actually met my man online."

"Really? I thought you said you met through friends?"

"That's the official story. I didn't want to say at first. I wasn't sure what you'd think of me. It's a bit sad, isn't it?"

"It's not sad at all." I wonder whether I should be equally forthcoming about how M and I met. I consider it for a second. No, too many people have the story of how we met through friends. It's not worth muddying the water now.

Reena shoves in next to me, almost pushing me off my seat.

"You guys know each other, don't you?"

"Yeah. Apparently, I'm the one that introduced you both," I say.

Reena looks puzzled. "Oh yeah, I forgot about that. You felt left out because we bonded over Sambuca shots while you were drinking Coke."

Hmm. Is that how it was?

"I remember that." Sonali laughs. "You said something at the time about not mixing friends because you end up being left out when we're all drinking."

I must have selective memory. Was I jealous of their budding friendship? More to the point, was I so honest about my jealousy?

Sensing she may have touched a nerve, Reena says: "Ignore me. I'm a bit hammered."

Another girl, who looks like she headed straight out after work as she's in a sleeveless ivory shirt and black trousers, grabs Reena by the arm. "Come on, you owe me a dance."

"Hold on. Only if these two come with me."

The makeshift dancefloor looks full but I reluctantly follow Reena as I don't want to be the bad sport. However, I'll excuse myself from any bumping and grinding. I'm a respectable, married Bengali lady, after all.

As we head on to the dance floor, there's barely space to breathe, let alone bust any moves. Then I hear a voice speaking in the direction of Sonali: "Excuse me, fatty, can I get past?"

It was barely audible, disguised in the muffle of the music, which is now blaring but I heard it. Sonali casually looks from side to side, as though it's part of her dance routine. I think she heard it, too.

"It's a bit hot here, isn't it?" she asks me.

"Yes," I reply. "Do you want to sit down?"

"Yeah, let's do that. I'm not in the mood for dancing."

I follow Sonali back to the table but I can't get that throwaway comment, from some idiot, out of my mind. And given the sudden lack of small talk, I don't think Sonali can, either.

That's what I hate about bars/clubs/makeshift dance floors in restaurants. They give people free rein to be twats. In any other scenario, nobody would be so rude to another person. You wouldn't squeeze past someone in a restaurant and say: *"Excuse me, fatty, can I get past?"* You wouldn't say that in a supermarket? Or at work? Definitely not at work. HR would have your head and rightly so.

It seems that such unfiltered nastiness is the reserve of drunk knobheads in noisy environments. It seems okay and justifiable to say it because they've had a bit to drink and the room is too noisy, too stuffy, too uncensored for people to care. It's like all etiquette, human decency and basic manners are left at the door. And the food looks shit. Who wants shrivelled olives? I should've known. I should've expected the worst from a place called Stomping Ground.

I've decided I hate hen dos. I'm going to text M. He said he'd give me a lift home but was expecting to do so around 1am. It's barely eleven but I'm ready to call it a night.

"How are you feeling about moving to Leicester?" I ask.

"Not great. We've had many arguments about it but there's no way he'd move to London. He's a typical good Gujji boy. Wants to be near his mum and dad. I guess I should be grateful I don't have to live with them. There was another guy I was introduced to before him and he was in an extended family. Three generations. That's a lot of people packed into one big house. I couldn't do it. That'd drive me mad. What about you? Did you live with your in-laws?"

"No. Never did."

"Seriously? Didn't they expect you to, even for the first year?"

"M works in London, so it was a no brainer that I was going to transfer over to be with him. As his parents are up north, it was never really a conversation."

"That's great. I've heard too many horror stories about people living with their in-laws. It's much better if you can have your own space. So, what else is new with you?"

"Well..." I wasn't going to say anything, but given that Sonali is fairly tipsy, she likely won't remember. "M and I are trying for a baby."

Oh damn. Damn. Damn. I said it. I wish I could take it back. It feels so presumptuous to throw that out into the universe, when I haven't got any pregnancy news to share.

"Good for you guys," says Sonali. "I don't think I'll be far behind you. As in, we'll be trying after the honeymoon. That's the downside of getting married late. You've not got too much time to mess about."

"Getting married at 31 is hardly considered late these days," I say.

"It is according to the nosey auntie's at the community centre. I'm always hearing about ticking clocks and what not. I'm really happy for you though, mate." She throws her arm around my shoulder. "I'm guessing, given that you're here, your husband is pretty chilled with you going out."

"He is but, to be fair, this isn't my average night out. We're usually going to the cinema on a Friday night, or dinner. It's all very civilised and grown-up."

Sonali laughs. "I remember at uni, when we'd talk about getting married, you said your family are a bit more traditional. You expected to have an arranged marriage like your big sister who got married in Bangladesh. Though she seems really happy."

"You met my big sister?"

"Yeah. I spoke to her when she and her hubby picked you up at the end of the final year. I remember your poor brother-in-law had to lug your suitcases down two flights of stairs."

The memory makes me uncomfortable and regretful of the things I said. My big sis and her hubby took me to and from university every year. Nobody else could. My brother-in-law was the only one who had a car back then.

I forgot all about that. I also forgot about my very real fears of what to expect from marriage. Thinking back, I had low expectations and *this* isn't a life I expected to live. That explains a lot. I think it explains why I'm so thankful for my lot, which perhaps makes me overlook certain indiscretions, like my husband's terminal lateness or being Cinderella on Eid.

"I guess us Bengalis aren't as backward as I led you to believe. Speaking of uni, do you remember that lad, Ritesh?"

"Erm... I don't think so. Remind me, was he on your course, or something?"

"Yeah, the marketing communications module. I think he fancied you."

"Did he? I don't even remember what he looks like. Anyway, what was his surname again?"

"Erm... Solanki, I think."

Sonali looks down at her ring. "Then it wouldn't have worked, anyway. Wrong caste. My dad would hit the roof. He's still funny about that sort of stuff, even in this day and age. Also, Sonali Solanki... bit of a tongue twister."

"What the fuck? What the actual fuck?" Reena shouts as she stumbles towards me, knocking into a chair en route. She's like a raging bull.

"Huh? What happened?" I ask, feeling that this might be some kind of weird drunken rampage.

"What was that message about? I hate Hindus?" She's leaning over me, finger pointing in my face.

"What message?"

"You just text me, saying: I hate Hindus." Reena pushes the phone into my face.

Oh, my life. There in front of me is the message sent from myself, saying I hate Hindus. It was meant to say I hate *hen dos*. It was meant for M, not Reena. Bloody typos and bloody smart phones. It's so easy to send something to the wrong person.

"Why did you come here if you hate us?"

A few of Reena's friends, undoubtedly Hindu, look up to see what the commotion is about.

This is very awkward and I can't help but laugh. It is ridiculous. Of all the things to get wrong and of all the places to do it and of all the people to be around. It's hilarious.

"I'm sorry. Let me explain." I'm still laughing. "It was meant for M."

"So you say shit like that behind my back?"

One of Reena's friends, who is dressed like an Easter bunny, grabs Reena's shoulders as if to hold her back. I need to explain myself properly before this turns into a very one-sided religious war.

"It was meant to say, I hate hen dos. It was a bloody typo! Obviously, I don't hate Hindus, otherwise I wouldn't be here. Come on! I've been to your mum's house and had her chapattis. You taught me how to make chickpea curry. Why would I hate you?"

Reena's clenched teeth soften to a smile. "Awww, mate. You're a funny bugger. And I love you, too, my Bengali babe." She then whispers: "So you really don't hate Hindus? It's okay if you hate these other girls. Half of them are here to make up numbers."

"I really don't hate Hindus. If I did, it's not something that I'd say in a text message. Far too incriminating."

Reena hugs me, squeezing tight. "Sorry, I jumped the gun. I'm a bit smashed."

"I know."

Still in half an embrace, she pushes me into the chair for a deep and meaningful conversation. She is now holding my hand, interlacing our fingers, as though she's about to say something very important. "I just miss you, you know. We were so tight. I know it's not just you, it's me, too. But we hardly message. So I thought maybe over time you'd developed a bit of a hatred for Hindus. I don't know. I couldn't think of any other reason why you would say something so weird. I did think it was strange that you'd send that to me. Of all people. A Hindu."

"Yeah, that wouldn't be wise."

"But why do you hate hen dos? Are you not having fun?" Reena strokes my bunny ears.

"It's not that. It's fine. I don't want to be a boring cow. It's just that I'm the only one sober and it feels a bit awkward. And I don't want you to have to accommodate me."

"I get it. It's like when I go to Burger King and I'm the only one not eating beef so I can't have the quarter pounder."

It's nothing like that, but I nod along.

"I think your hen do was better, anyway," says Reena.

"Are you joking? I thought it wouldn't be raucous enough for you."

"It was nice having proper conversations with your mates. Some of them were geeks but it was nice." Reena lets out a small burp. "Let's try not to be strangers and make time for each other. Who knows where we'll be in a few years? Sharing our major life changes over text is shit. We need to get together more. Let's make it a thing."

"We will," I say, checking the time on my phone. "Listen, I've been pretty hard-core and stayed up till 12. Would you mind if I called it a night?"

"No!" shouts Reena. "Don't go. It's my hen do! I won't drink anymore. We can have Cokes and just chat."

I appreciate the gesture, even if it's empty. "Don't be silly. This is your night. Anyway, I told M to get me about now."

Reena gasps. "Shit! Is he making you leave early? Is he coercing you? Or being a controlling bully?" She leans in closer and I can smell her vodka breath. "Is he a narcissist? If he is, I'll have him. Just give me the word, I'll smash him up."

"He's none of those things. I suggested leaving at midnight. He said I should stay out longer, probably because he wants extra PlayStation time with his mate, Jam."

"He's gonna collect you?" Reena leans back in her chair. "Oh, in that case, I take it back. My fella wouldn't do that. He'd tell me to make my own way home."

"I can't wait to meet your man," I say. "Let's arrange something after the wedding."

"Okay but when we do meet, don't tell him about anything I said."

"Sure, but you haven't said anything bad about him."

"Haven't I? Oh, that's good. I can't remember." Reena leans in again. "Between you and me, I am a bit buzzing."

"I know. You said."

M can't stop laughing. "You messaged your Hindu friend, saying *I hate Hindus*, at a hen do where everyone is Hindu?"

"Pretty much."

"That's brilliant!" M almost squeals. "It's probably the funniest thing you've ever done."

"Does it even top -"

"Even that." M doesn't need to elaborate. My funniest funny will remain a secret. "It even tops that."

Once M has managed to compose himself, he asks: "That aside, did you have fun?"

"It was okay." I look out of the window at the revellers still enjoying their night. "Actually, it was a bit crap being the only sober one when everyone else was drinking."

"Yeah, I know what you mean. How come she doesn't have any other Muslim mates? Are you a special project?"

Now it's my turn to laugh. "I don't know. In other news, I bumped into an old uni friend that lives in London."

"You've got an old uni mate in London?" M asks.

"Yeah. We lost touch."

"Did she come to our wedding?"

"No, but she's getting married and we might score an invite to hers."

"Good stuff. We could do with another wedding. It's been a bit of a drought recently. Better keep in touch with her to make sure you do get invited. In all seriousness, keep in touch with your mates."

"I know, I know. You're so much better with your friends. I think, for me, it's an out of sight, out of mind thing. When you're at uni, you're in a bubble. You're on the same course, you live together. You're sharing a bathroom and sometimes toothpaste. You think you'll be besties forever. It's like that with work friends, isn't it?"

M leans back in the driver's seat. "That's happened to me at work a lot. I've got loads of people's numbers in my phone and I never call them. Anyway, you should stay in contact with this girl. It's nice for you to have other people as well. I know you've got Julia but..." M stops himself. "Yeah... it's good for you to keep in touch."

He doesn't need to say it but we both know it. M is Jam's ride or die, and vice versa. I don't have that with any of my friends. Much of it is my own doing and I feel like I use every excuse under the sun about it. I'm busy being a wife, even though my husband doesn't expect anything of me. I'm busy being a career woman, so wouldn't send too many sneaky messages at work. I'm busy doing home stuff, so there wasn't time for extended lunch dates. I don't like too much screen time, which is problematic in this day and age when the phone is a primary mode of contact.

It makes me think about big sis. I should reach out. Our argument wasn't about her disliking my yellow outfit. It's about a ton of stuff that she doesn't even remember. Yet, in amongst all the deep- seated resentment, I forget all the good she's done for me.

16th April, Biting the bullet

I've only gone and bloody done it. I've only gone and bought myself ovulation sticks.

It's come to my attention that being half arsed and trying, but not trying, isn't really working for M and I. This whole, I'm-not-really-bothered-it-will-happen-when-it-does-but-I'm-bothered-when-it-doesn't-happen, is getting tiresome. I've accepted that perhaps M and I are one of those couples that won't get pregnant at the drop of a hat. I need to be strategic. So, along with charting my period, I've decided to get those pesky ovulation sticks to know when I'm fertile.

However, getting hold of those bad boys was no mean feat.

I didn't know which section of the store to look in. Would it be with period towels, feminine hygiene, or the baby section? After scouring the entire store, I managed to find pregnancy tests. I didn't need one of those just yet. I was afraid the search was going to be futile, therefore decided to do something cringeworthy. I asked for assistance.

I grabbed some muesli and a granola bar to disguise my true intention and went to the till. It didn't help that there was a man in a pinstripe suit behind me.

"Have you got ovulation sticks?" I said in the quietest voice imaginable.

"Sorry, what's that?" was the inevitable query from the cashier.

"Ovulation sticks. For f-fertility?" I said, louder this time, enough for the entire store to hear.

The lady smiled and lead me to the aisle next to the pregnancy testers. It was there, in plain sight, but I didn't know what I was looking for.

Anyway, now I'm faced with a new dilemma. When do I start these things? It requires 30 days of tracking and we're going on holiday in two weeks.

If we wait until we're back from Bali, that's a whole 34 days wasted. A whole 34 days in which we could've been trying. Moreover, perhaps an exotic destination is the best place, as we both would be free of work and the stress of day-to-day life.

If I start them now, I'll have to stop before we go to Bali. That wouldn't make sense. You can't monitor your fertility for half the month. It doesn't work like that.

"How does it work?" M asks, examining the box as we sit in front of the telly.

"I've got to pee on one every day. Then it shows which days I'm producing eggs. Or something like that."

"That's a lot of wee."

"Hopefully, I won't pee on my hand like I normally do when I have to provide a urine sample."

"Nice. It's a good thing we don't hold hands anymore." M laughs. "Then what happens? What if that doesn't work? Where does it end?"

"Well, if that doesn't work, we'll have to see what the issue is."

"There won't be any issues," M says, with his usual unwavering enthusiasm.

"Let's hope not."

M shuffles closer and puts an arm around me, ovulation box still in hand. "Remember, I said about how you're a worrier? Well, don't worry. There isn't an issue. It's not even like we've been trying properly."

"Maybe that's the thing. That's why I've got the sticks. We can start trying properly."

"Sounds a bit clinical." M moves the box around in his hands, like it's a new pair of trainers.

"Also, and I might be fretting over nothing, but I haven't heard from Julia in a while. She hasn't replied to my last messages."

"That's odd," says M. "Does she normally do that?"

"She's always busy and we can go for months without seeing each other but she usually replies to my messages."

"Have you called her?"

"Not yet."

M tuts.

"Don't you tut at me!" I snatch the ovulation sticks back and pretend to whack him with the box.

M covers his face in mock defence. "You women don't half complicate things. If she hasn't replied, give her a call! If she doesn't answer or ring you back, then you can worry. At the moment, it might be nothing. She might not have even seen your messages."

I lower the box down. "Sometimes you do talk sense."

I dial Julia's number. It rings twice before the line cuts dead.

M, who is waiting as eagerly as I am, raises his eyebrows. "Maybe there is something to worry about."

"Right, thanks for that. It's really helpful."

Just before bed, I get a message. It's from Julia. Thank goodness. My mind was doing a number on me. I was trying to recall our previous conversations to see if there's anything I said that would've offended her. I could only assume that this radio silence meant she was upset with me. To hear a ping, with her name attached to it, is a welcome relief.

Hi, sorry I haven't been in touch for a while. I needed a bit of time to myself. I don't want to go into it, but between you and me, I found out I was pregnant just before my engagement party but then I lost the baby soon afterwards. We didn't make it to the first scan.

Oh no.

I reply straight away.

I am so, so sorry. I can't imagine how you're feeling.

Shall I tell her about my situation? Would it help ease the pain? Perhaps it will.

I wasn't going to mention this, but I thought I was pregnant, too. Twice. It turned out I wasn't as my period came later. I don't know if they call it a chemical pregnancy. It's horrible and confusing, so I get it. Sending hugs and here to talk whenever you want x

Should I have said that? Am I making her bad news about me? Damn, why do my fingers type before my brain has a chance to process things?

My phone pings. Phew, Julia is still in discord. That's good. She replies:

I'm really sorry to hear that. But being late for your period is NOT a miscarriage.

8th May, On top of the world

We should do a trek up Mount Batur, he said. It's a volcano, he said. It will be amazing, he said. Imagine the views, he said.

The thing he didn't say is that this excursion involves waking up at 2am. *2am.* That's the time I just about drop-off on some nights, especially when staying away from home in an unfamiliar bed. This bed, and the entire hotel, is particularly unnerving. It's grand, gaudy and creepy. The lobby is filled with every kind of stone monument imaginable. There are giant, life-size dragons, marble monks, an imposing Gothic bat, and many bronze statues. It's like they robbed a museum.

Another thing that's not exactly helping me nod off is the huge concrete lizard on the wall opposite our bed. It's like a creepy cornice. How was that a good idea? Who sanctioned that? Its head is raised, watching me as I sleep. It makes the real lizards that occasionally scurry up the wall appear miniscule. The scary decor only adds to the island vibe, with the constant hum of insects outside and the buzz of the ceiling fan above our heads.

I have this annoying habit. When I have to get up extra early, I cannot sleep the night before. I'm not sure whether it's excitement, anticipation, nerves, or a bit of everything. Last night was no different but I had some added thoughts. Julia and big sis were revolving around my head. Thoughts about whether I said something wrong, or where it all went wrong. The most uncomfortable feelings are the most confrontational. They just don't stand down.

Then there's the other thing. I have been diligently peeing on a stick. Every evening, I cross my fingers that it will be time. That tonight will be the night. So far, I've seen nothing. No rise in hormones to suggest I'm fertile. I haven't told M any of this. It's a worry I'm carrying alone, as it dawns on me that all may not be okay. No wonder I can't sleep.

My eyelids were finally getting heavy when the alarm rang. M snoozed it four times before realising we were in danger of missing the trek. I wouldn't mind missing it, had it not been for the fact that we'd paid upfront.

"Do you think there's a breakfast box?" I ask.

"There should be. That's what the concierge told us last night. Though I don't think I can eat much at this time in the morning," says M, rubbing his eyes. "What a disgusting time to be awake."

Well, it was your idea to climb the volcano, I think. Ever since M floated the idea on the second day we arrived in Bali, I've been Googling obsessively, trying to verify the safety of a live volcano. Apparently, it hasn't erupted in years. Perhaps it's due? I scoured the travel websites to gauge the internet's thoughts on the matter. Annoyingly, quite a few people said it was an enlightening, moving experience. I bet they're glass half full, permanently positive people like M.

I haven't told mum about the trek. She's already a nervous wreck about me travelling so far that I'm closer to Australia than the UK. The entire island is full of Antipodean tourists. From the roads congested with motorbikes, to the restaurants, cafés, and beach club, you can't move for back-packers from down under.

This is the furthest I've been away from home. The journey was exhausting. I couldn't sleep while M snoozed away. The turbulence made my stomach churn. My heart skipped a beat when we'd fly over open water. I spent the entire time watching movies back to back while praying under my breath that we land safely. I wasn't the happiest of flyers.

"I was thinking, if we can't handle climbing the volcano, we can catch a truck," I say.

M looks at me with raised eyebrows.

"I've checked it out. You can sit on the back of the truck and it will take you to the top. Same views, less endurance."

M laughs. "Seriously? No truck will go that high? It won't be possible. The terrain's too rugged for that."

That's not helping my anxiety.

"Are you sure? I read about the truck on a travel blog. The girl who wrote it got a free trip to Bali."

M throws his head back in disbelief. "Then why are you reviewing lipsticks? We need free holidays!"

"I wish. But seriously, if I struggle, don't leave me."

"Leave you? That's exactly what I was going to do. I was planning to abandon you at the bottom of the mountain, to be eaten by wolves."

"There are wolves?"

"I'm joking, man," says M in his appropriated Geordie accent. "Don't worry about it. You can do this. Otherwise, you'll end up an old woman that sits at home all the time."

Damn. Am I that bad?

"It'll be fine," M continues. "We'll have fun. Think about it, if it was that dangerous, do you think they'd be letting people do it?"

"That's true. If anything does happen, like the volcano erupts, my mum will have your head."

"If the volcano erupts, we'll escape the wrath of your mum, as we'll be dead, anyway."

My face drops.

"I'm joking, man!" Another butchered attempt at a Geordie accent.

As we head down to the garish lobby, I am delighted to find that there are indeed two boxes waiting for us.

"For your breakfast, madam and sir," says the kind concierge.

"Let's take one," says M. "It might be too much carrying two up a mountain. We can share one between us."

Is this my husband? This goes against his very nature, not making the most of a culinary freebie, even if it is a dry bread roll with a miniature tub of butter. I ignore his suggestion and grab both boxes.

"Do you really think we'll eat it all?" M looks at me in judgment, takes his box and puts it back on the counter.

"I sure will try." I turn to the concierge. "Where do we get picked up for the excursion?"

"You have to go to the entrance of the hotel, madam."

Is he serious? The entrance is a solid mile away from the actual lobby. It's not a straight road, either. There's a treacherous forest, with buzzing fireflies, mosquitos and many a temple in between. It's as though you have to go through an entire village just to get to the hotel.

"Would you like a golf cart to take you?" asks the concierge.

"Yes please," M and I say together.

So much of Bali reminds me of Bangladesh. Every time I've been back home, I'd spend a couple of nights in the village where mum grew up. We couldn't stay any longer. It wasn't comfortable. We would miss the air-con, the TV and lack of insects. Don't get me wrong, the ivory tower in town had its share of bugs but the village was on another level. I'd seen spiders as big as my hand. The geckos are so brazen that they didn't stay on the ceiling or the walls. They'd stalk the floors, making me want to wear socks, even in the unimaginable heat.

However, one thing that was beautiful about village life in Bangladesh was the fresh air. The town was stifling and not just because I was stuck indoors 90% of the time. The humidity, the pollution from the many cars that competed for space with rickshaws, all of it contributed to making Sylhet town a big smog. In the village, there was open air and freedom, too. My cousins and I would walk to a nearby shop and buy a bottle of Sprite. There wasn't the same fear of – I'm not sure what - kidnapping? Ransom? Human trafficking? Mum had this deep, deep worry that if I ventured out of our town house, I would never return. In the village, I was free. For that, I loved it.

Ubud is much like the village in Bangladesh. I am even more free here, so much so that I'm trekking up a live volcano with my daredevil husband. If only mum knew.

As our golf cart bumps along the windy path, we pass a group of men and young boys sat in congregation at a temple veranda, singing at the top of their lungs. They're beating drums, clicking castanets and making a glorious racket. What a life! What an amazing, simple life. They seem to be cut off from the modernity of smart phones, one-upmanship, comparison-itis. I bet they're not checking their Instagram constantly to see what their cousins are up to. I bet they're not in a constant battle with themselves, not knowing what they want from life, always looking over to the other side, where the grass is greener. They seem content. Doing the same thing, over and over, but not minding at all.

Further along, there are a couple of stalls, and a kiosk. As hotel guests, we get ferried straight to the lobby, therefore can never stop to check out their wares. They sell Coke in glass bottles, though it looks like they're never bought, never drunk.

As we finally pull up to our entrance, we are dropped rather unceremoniously outside on the main road, in the pitch black. I'm not scared. I'm safe. I've got M, my safety net. Even if he nearly did me out of a breakfast, he's my safety net.

"What if they forget to pick us up?" asks M.

Okay, the safety net just slid from under me.

"They wouldn't, would they?"

"No, it should be fine," says M.

We are both staring into the abyss. There is not a tuk tuk, car, motorbike, or human in sight. All I can hear is the buzz of bugs hovering around us. I get the lightest of whacks against my arm, my shoulder, and my cheek. Occasionally, something settles on my skin, likely a mosquito smelling foreign blood.

I can hear mum's voice in my head: *You shouldn't have done this. Why you agree to such madness? Anyone could attack you now and there'd be nobody to help. What your husband do? He be one who put you in danger! Trek up a volcano... Hmmph!*

Just as I'm wallowing in worry, a van pulls up in front of us. Phew, we haven't been left for dead. That's always nice to know.

In the van are a bunch of tourists. One girl, Natalie, has travelled alone from America.

"You're so brave," I can't help but say. Yes, I'm echoing my mother again.

"It's something I've always wanted to do," says Natalie. "I recently broke up with my boyfriend, who was going to come on this trip with me, so I thought, fuck it, I'll go by myself. I don't need a man."

Natalie, with her friendly smile, low maintenance blonde, plaited hair, double layered vest and wrists covered in beads, really does look like she doesn't need a man. She chooses independence, adventure. She finds people to talk to wherever she goes. She is staying in a hostel with other back-packers, which takes care of any loneliness.

Then there is me, with my trainers, tracksuit bottoms and sports top, reluctantly going on this trek. I barely get the Tube without M. I couldn't imagine going abroad alone. Na-talie is probably the same age as me, yet so different. The only thing we've got in common is our plaited hair. It's the default style to both stay in place and look chic.

Also in the van is a family, all speaking Italian. Then there are a few Aussie guys. They are rowdy, so my unconscious bias tells me not to elicit conversation. Judgemental, I know.

We stop at a roadside cafe. Natalie gets a bottle of Coke, while I open up my breakfast box. In it, there is a bap with a scrambled egg filling. There is also a cube of cheese, and a foil covered container, which I pull back to reveal the jewel in the crown – nasi goreng.

"It's alright, isn't it?" M says gleefully, inching closer.

"Hands off! You had your chance and chose to leave your box because you're too cool."

"Can I have a spoon of it?" asks M.

"I'm joking. Of course you can." I pass the container to him. "Let this be a lesson. You do not throw away free food."

"How long have you guys been married?" asks Natalie.

"It'll be five years this September," says M.

"That's great. Congratulations. And how did you guys meet?"

As we are thousands of miles from home, it feels safe to tell Natalie the true story. We share how we met online, having been through numerous routes to meeting a partner. Natalie then shares a story about her Indian friend at University, who had an arranged marriage. Everyone knows a brown person.

"Anyway, we figured we'd get these big adventures out of our way before we decide to be grown-ups and have kids," I say.

"That's the way to do it," Natalie says. "If you haven't stayed in a hostel, and got bitten by bedbugs, have you even really lived?"

I wouldn't take it that far. I still prefer my hotels and creature comforts.

Natalie shares stories of getting a fish pedicure in Vietnam and being frightened of losing a toe. I share the story of our trip to Hong Kong, where M was held back by security personnel at the airport, most likely for having a Muslim name. We were the only brown faces on the plane. Halfway through the anecdote, I can see from Natalie's face that our tale doesn't have quite the same nostalgic charm.

M and I polish off the egg sandwich, which smells rather rotten. We are then summoned onto yet another vehicle, this time a much bigger bus with more tourists. Good, I think. Safety in numbers. Some people are chatting, while others are trying to sleep, having had precious shuteye stolen from them. Annoyingly, I'm far too awake to sleep now.

Natalie sits in front of us, having become unofficial friends. Unlucky for her, the person next to her is snoring loudly, head pressed against the window, mouth open.

When we disembark the bus, we are greeted by a small, thin man called Ricky.

"I will be your guide," he says, emptying a bag of flashlights on the floor. "Who needs torch?"

I'm guessing we all will. Unless some among us have night vision. There is a scramble as everyone tries to grab a torch. It looks like there won't be enough to go around.

"We can share," says M, as Natalie grabs a torch and looks guilty, having taken the penultimate one.

"How is that going to work? With one of us having a torch?" I ask.

"No, no, I get more," says Ricky, before shouting something in Balinese to his colleague.

"Don't worry, we'll be okay," says M.

"You guys sure?" asks Natalie.

"We'll be fine. We only need one between us." M looks at me, expecting me to agree. I don't. He's being bloody chivalrous with the wrong person.

Luckily, Ricky comes back with a flashlight in hand and shines it on my face. "Got one!"

"Thank you, I see that." I grab the torch from him, before someone else needs it and M decides to forfeit my safety out of politeness.

As we walk away from the distant lights of the bus, I realise just how important the flashlight is. I can't see a thing. There isn't a light source beyond our little torches with their narrow range of field. Here, at the base of a volcano, I am as far away from the bright lights of London as can be. I'm already having second thoughts.

"Okay guys, let's go," says Ricky, with a bit too much enthusiasm for my liking.

The first few steps are easy enough but M warns me it will get steeper as we go along.

"Good job I've got my own flashlight," I say.

Some people are pacing ahead and within minutes, our group gets divided by the fastest, the intermediates, and slow coaches. I am in the slow coach side and despite M making big strides up the rugged mountain, he is staying in the slow group with me. Natalie has gone ahead. I think she's intermediate.

I get chatting to another girl, Isla, who is from the UK. She says she's come with her boyfriend.

"I wanted to get this trip in before I knuckle down and do a postgraduate course."

"What will you do?" I ask.

"No idea! I've been travelling for the past three years, so something that pays well!" She laughs. "Possibly law?"

Travelling for the past three years? That seems like such a freeing, alien concept to me. A gap year would've been out of the question, as I was never able to go travelling with friends, let alone by myself. It's not the done thing. For me, rather than go find myself on the other side of the world, I went headlong into my career.

Isla, meanwhile, has been planting trees in Brazil, farming in Australia, backpacking through South America, and teaching English in India. As my eyes get used to the dark, I can just about make out her face and see that she's much younger than me, yet has seen so much more.

Oh, stop it. Glass half full, glass half full, glass half full. I'm getting to see the world now and staying in nice hotels while I'm at it. I've hardly got room to complain.

About half an hour in, we stop for a water break. That's when I realise the back of my t-shirt is wet through. M, too, is sporting some rather fetching damp patches under his arms. Isla, in her trendy racer back vest and cropped leggings, has no such tell-tale patches.

We continue on the journey to notice a newlywed Asian couple in front of us. The occasional flashlight in their direction reveals that the lady is wearing red bangles, synonymous with Hindu brides. Her husband is taking utmost care to help her navigate the more tricky parts of the journey. I am making full use of Ricky, as he holds out his arm for me to grab while stepping onto the bigger rocks. Good job M is not the jealous type. He's far too busy making small talk with Isla's boyfriend.

There's a throbbing pain in my knees. I've gone from stepping to lunging as the mountain gets steeper.

"Are you okay?" M asks, looking back.

"Yeah, but it's getting harder now, isn't it?"

M moves to the side. "Go in front, then I can help you," he says, giving way.

Isla's boyfriend, who had gone ahead, bounces his way back to us.

"Can I go with the fast group? Would you mind?" he asks Isla.

"Go for it," she replies.

M wins on the chivalry front and has made up for his torch light faux pas.

The rocks are getting bigger. I'm not sure if we will make it to the top. I'm getting out of puff, and given the general silence around me, everyone else is, too. All I can hear is the occasional deep breaths, as our stamina is pushed to the limit.

"Not long now, babe," says M.

It's so dark, I can't even tell how far up we are. All I can see are rocks and many overgrown bushes, trees, and hedges immediately around us.

I hear a shuffle of gravel. Someone cries out. It's a woman. More specifically, it's the Indian newlywed lady. I shine my flashlight upwards and see her, sat on her bum, clutching her knee.

"Keep going. Keep going. She's okay," says Ricky to the rest of the group. "I'm staying behind."

Now I'm really nervous.

I don't know if I can make this journey without Ricky to guide the way and warn me when there are tricky, loose rocks to negotiate. In this rare scenario, M is not my safety blanket. He's as much out of his depth as I am.

We keep going, three down, with the newlywed lady, her husband and Ricky left behind in the middle of the mountain. The intermediate group is so far ahead of us we can only see the last group member take a step up before disappearing from view. This is some scary shit.

"We must be near the top now, surely?" I ask anyone and no one.

"Nearly there," says M.

"I hope this doesn't affect my fertility."

"Why would it do that?" asks M.

"I don't know. This seems like an unnatural level of exertion."

M laughs, breathlessly. "I don't think anyone's become infertile from climbing a volcano, have they?"

"There's a first time for everything."

It's getting brighter. I can now make out more of the route. Isla's vest is navy blue, not black, like I originally assumed. The leaves on the branches nestled around the rocks are deep green. There is hope. I can make it to the top. We are so nearly there.

Why are we not there yet? It seems like even thousands of miles away from home, M is just as bad with expectation management as ever. We are still slogging away, with no sign of the summit in sight.

I've now got my hands involved, scrambling up the rocks, grabbing any points to help wrench my body up the steep incline. I have nearly fallen more than once. When I look back to M, I see the mountain behind him and all those rocks we left behind. It looks deathly. One misplaced foot and we're screwed. Why is this kind of excursion even allowed? We should all be wearing helmets, not fighting over torches. I can hear my heart pounding. I should drown that noise out.

"You know those sticks I brought with me?" Hopefully I don't have to say the word ovulation. "I can't tell if they're working."

"What do you mean?" asks M.

"It's meant to show you a line when you're fertile, and I've not seen the line."

"But how long are you supposed to take it? Isn't it over 30 days or something?"

"I started taking it before we came here. I've only got a few left. I should have had a line by now, surely? Either they're not working, or I'm not."

"Shit!"

"I know, right? I thought there might be something wrong -"

"No!" says M. "I just whacked my shin against a rock. I didn't even see it jutting out."

"Weren't you shining your torch?"

"It's too awkward, holding a torch and then trying to climb the rocks. Anyway, it's not so dark now so I thought it'd be okay." M rubs his leg. "What were you saying?"

"Nothing."

It's getting brighter still. We're at that strange part of the morning where night and day meet. Everything is still a little dark and cold but you can feel the day is beginning. You know it's dawn, not dusk.

"Why do people do this?"

"What was that?" asks M.

"Why do people do this? It's madness."

"I can't hear you. Hold on." M grapples to reach the rock next to me.

"I was saying I don't get why people would want to do this. It's like torture."

M rubs my sticky back. I would expect him to recoil, but he doesn't.

"You're doing great. Just think, you've got this far. We're nearly there. Imagine what else you can do."

"I bet you didn't expect this from the girl you met for coffee all those years ago." I try to laugh but the altitude is making even breathing hard work.

"I didn't, to be honest with ya. I doubt any of the other girls I met would be up for this."

"Were there many other girls?"

Now it's daylight, I can see him grinning. "I could tell you some stories."

"Please do. But not right now. I might throw you off the volcano. No one would ever guess it was me. We're the last ones in the group. Even the newlyweds have gone ahead."

"I'll save it for safer territory, then."

"By the way, would you have left me, the way Isla's boyfriend left her, to go with the faster group?"

"I was tempted," says M before tickling me, which isn't the wisest thing to do as we climb a volcano without any helmets, wires or safety equipment. "I'm joking, man! As if I'd leave you."

And just like that, the top of the volcano is within our reach. I'm now practically crawling up on all fours. My plait is frayed. My face is flushed. My body is wobbly. But I made it.

I'm not sure what I was expecting, perhaps a deep pit with molten lava? The summit, however, is just like the base. Rugged and dusty with some plant life. There are no such deep holes that we have to avoid. We can walk freely.

What a view.

It's sunrise and we all bask in the orange light. The coolness at the top is a welcome relief. As my heartbeat regulates, I take in the panoramic view of the lush greenery. There are monkeys! Tiny, adorable little monkeys live on top of the mountain. I read about this on the reviews but I didn't expect them to look like this. I thought I might be intimidated by them but instead, we're intimidating to them. I go near a mother and her baby. The baby monkey hides her face in her mother's chest, just like a human would. She then takes her mum's nipple for comfort.

There is another, even smaller monkey, perhaps the size of my foot, hiding amongst the bushes. As I walk closer, I whisper: "Don't be scared, don't be scared, don't be scared." I keep a respectful distance and, for a moment, we observe each other. She nuzzles the leaves. I try to capture the moment on camera, knowing that no video will ever do justice to this real life experience.

Some people are lifting the monkeys, cradling them, carrying them on their shoulders and taking selfies. I won't do that. This is their territory and they're likely wondering what the hell we are doing here. They're probably sick of this imposition of uninvited guests brought here by Ricky.

M and I sit down on a craggy rock, heads together, exhausted and relieved. We're so far from home, so cut off from our normal life, sharing an experience we will never do again. It would be the right time to take a photo. Just for the 'gram. Imagine how envious Naila would be? She won't be travelling anywhere now she's due imminently. She has to stick to selfies and affirmations in random cafes.

We take a couple of photos, then I decide it's not worth posting. I'll keep this for us as it's more important than social media. It's real life. It's us. It's our moment. Plus, my face looks red and bloated.

"When we get back to London, I think I'll make an appointment with the doctor," I say.

"What for? Is everything okay?"

"Everything is fine. At least I think so. I just want to talk about us trying to have a baby. I don't want to be presumptuous. If there's anything I can do or we should do, it's better to know in advance, right?"

I'm expecting a sermon about not worrying about it. Instead, I get: "Sounds like a plan. To be honest with ya, I think we're fine but there's no harm in speaking to someone."

Another group has clamoured onto the summit of the volcano. They must be the next cohort of tourists as we were the last in our group.

I'm not sure if my eyes are deceiving me (I wouldn't be surprised given the lack of sleep) but there is a man with a baby in a sling. The baby can't be more than nine months old. This guy made the trek the entire way up, carrying a baby? What if he fell? I can't decide if it's brave, reckless, or crazy.

"Can you imagine doing that with a baby?" I ask M.

"No chance. I've got my hands full with you." M nudges me playfully. "Is everything else okay with you? You're very quiet."

"I'm okay. It's just, nothing really."

"Go on. Is there something I should know?"

Well, since he's asked. "Sometimes, it's no biggie, but I think…" I'm trying to figure out how to get this across without sounding like a ball buster. "It's just that sometimes I think I let a lot slide, because I think it's no big deal, and it isn't, but I think sometimes you take advantage?"

M looks confused.

"What I mean is, like when Jam comes over last minute and kiboshes our plans. Or, you say you're going to be home in half an hour and you're two hours late. It's not such a massive deal and that's why I don't say anything at the time but sometimes it would be nice if you manage my expectations. Don't get me wrong, Jam's like a brother. It's not about him. I think I've been conditioned to put up with so much that I don't complain, when a lot of other wives would." I feel like I'm not explaining myself properly. I would've been better off bringing this up as and when the issues occur rather than when we are on top of a volcano.

M puts a sweaty arm around my moist shoulder. Gross.

"Sorry. I can take the piss sometimes. But when Jam messages, he sort of invites himself, and I feel like I can't say no -" M stops himself. "Yeah, I get it. I have issues saying no."

"I'm the same. I'm a people pleaser but I think you're even more so than me. You've got to give yourself some slack. If not for you, then do it for me."

"You're right. I will work on it."

"But this isn't about Jam."

"I get it. I'm also aware of how much you do for my family. I do appreciate it, maybe I don't say it enough. My mum appreciates you, too. She tells me I found someone good."

"I never knew that."

"You know what she's like. She won't want to give you a big head."

"Of course. Can't have that."

It looks like everyone has reached the summit. People are taking selfies and the man with a baby in the carrier has taken him out to be breastfed by his mum. Imagine that, feeding your baby on top of a mountain. Surely that's a bucket list moment?

The mist has dissipated to make way for a burnt orange sunshine.

M rests his head against my shoulder. "What do you think now?" he asks, with an *I told you so* face. "Was it worth it?"

I look around. It's like we're sitting above the clouds. We can see the tops of the tall trees around us. M and I have been to many places and seen many things. The pyramids of Giza, Angkor Wat, the Eiffel Tower, the Burj Khalifa... but this is the only time that I have, quite literally, felt on top of the world. I smile at M. "Maybe."

There are a lot of bleary eyes on the coach trip back. The usual polite chatter among us tourists has died down to make way for peaceful slumber. Whilst on top of Mount Batur, all feelings of sleep deprivation had faded. Now, in the relative comfort of the coach, with its patchy air-con, sleep is overtaking us all. M is already out for the count, as per usual. How I envy his ability to fall asleep within seconds. I'm trying to nod off but I'm oversensitive. I get jolted awake by the occasional beeping from the coach driver. I'm also inherently nosey and see this as my time to look around at the tourists that I hadn't fully been able to appraise on the way here, as it was too dark.

Natalie has freckles that run across her nose. She and her companion, a tall, blonde guy, are the few people that seem to be awake. He looks like a seasoned traveller, just like her, with his deep tan, faded T-shirt, and cargo pants. They're locked in conversation. I wonder if that's a budding romance in the works?

I don't know what time it is in the UK. I'm slightly vague on the date, too. Holidays tend to blur things together. However, I need to text Julia. We need to talk. Luckily, my phone has reception and the bus has Wi-Fi, with the connection popping in and out along the journey. I quickly send a message before it ends up in roaming purgatory. Luckily, I only need two words.

I'm sorry.

Right, must get some shuteye. M's snoring. I'm wondering if I should close his mouth as he looks rather uncouth.

My phone pings. It's Julia.

She replies: *Me too.*

7th June, Tennis

"What brings you here today?"

What indeed.

Dr Wong isn't my regular doctor. That said, I don't really have a regular doctor. Since moving to London, I've only seen the GP a handful of times and there's been a different doctor sat opposite me, asking me that same question. I must say, there is some comfort in the anonymity of seeing a new face each time. There's something freeing about being able to tell this doctor anything, knowing that I likely won't see her again. *Somewhat* freeing, I must stress. I am Bengali. I won't let it all hang out.

"Well..." I begin, "it's probably nothing and I'm conscious of wasting your time." I pause for effect, which is wasting more time.

"But what it is *is*... my husband and I were looking for... thinking of... erm... having a baby. As in getting pregnant. And we sort of have been trying but nothing is really happening. I got these ovulation sticks and I tested them out while we were on holiday and I'm not sure if it's because they're quite far travelled... we went to Bali, so I don't know if on the plane they got ruined or something. But... erm... anyway, they didn't work or it wasn't showing that I was ovulating. So, I'm not sure if that means I'm not ovulating, or that the ovulation sticks got damaged in travel. I don't know.

But yeah, I just thought I should see you and decide if that's an issue, or if there's going to be a problem with me getting pregnant. So that's why I'm here. To cover all bases, really. And... yeah."

I take a breath.

Dr Wong looks at me with the end of her pen raised to her lip, trying to decipher the jumbled rambling I spat at her.

She inhales sharply and says: "Okay. How long have you been trying?"

"I'm not sure. I would probably say about a year. But, like I say, we've not really been trying properly, if that makes sense."

"How often are you having intercourse?"

Blimey! I wasn't expecting to be asked that. Perhaps I should have, given the nature of the discussion.

"I would say probably about twice. A week, obviously."

"Good... good. And how old are you?" She looks up at my screen before I have a chance to answer. "Nearly 32, I see?"

"Yes."

Dr Wong taps into her keyboard.

"Good. Good, good, good." She now turns to face me, palms on her lap. "Right, from the sounds of things, it's not like you've been actively trying. And as for the ovulation sticks, I couldn't tell you whether they were damaged in travel. Regardless, I wouldn't worry about that. You're young, you're healthy, you're fit. No pre-existing health conditions. So what I would say is, if you're having intercourse about three times a week, see how you go for the next year. If nothing happens, then get in touch. Otherwise, if you're two weeks late for your period, do a pregnancy test. It's as simple as that."

"I don't need to do anything else? I was wondering if I should get an ovulation monitor."

"These things have their place but I would suggest you don't overthink it and see what happens over the next year. Nothing that you've told me gives cause for concern. It's all normal. You can look at monitors and the like later on if need be. For now, I would recommend carrying on as you are and perhaps upping the activity."

Dr Wong sounds like she's describing a brisk walk around the park. I'm grateful for that. I'm also grateful to hear that there is nothing to worry about. At least not at this stage.

As I leave the doctor's surgery, I pass two teenage girls with tennis rackets hanging from their shoulders. They're probably part of a club or something. That's nice.

Julia and I played tennis many moons ago. We were never part of a club but we played to our hearts' content. Many a summer was spent at our local tennis courts. I absolutely loved it. It felt so liberating, smashing a ball across the court, letting off steam. It was an outlet for all those emotions, all that baggage that came with being a Bengali teenager in a white town. I thrived on it. I needed it. We stopped around the age of 14. For Julia, rackets were swapped for bottles of cider. Balls were swapped for boyfriends. Had it been my choice, I would've happily carried on.

"Should we find a new meeting spot?" I ask. "The amount of bird shit on these benches is insane."

"I know." Julia frowns. "It's just so hard getting out of work. I appreciate it's a mission for you to come to Chancery Lane but my boss is a real arse if I'm taking more than half an hour out of the office. I'm sure that's a HR issue but I don't want to make a big thing as I need to clock a couple more years at this place before I can get a cushy in-house job with more reasonable hours."

"It's a good thing you've got a flexible, self-employed friend like me, who has a very reasonable boss. Also, I didn't know you wanted to go in-house."

Julia sips her coffee. "I've come to learn that it's probably the end game if I do want to... have kids." She looks down at her half empty cup.

I shuffle along the bench, even though that means sitting on a whitish-green pigeon dropping. "I am really sorry about that. I'm sorry about what I said, too. I didn't mean to compare your situation with mine."

"And I'm sorry for minimising what happened to you. It was a shitty thing to say and I regretted it as soon as I sent that text. That's the problem with phones, hey? Fingers type faster than brains think. And honestly, I didn't even expect to be that upset. When I first realised I was pregnant, I was shocked. I've always said I wanted to get married before having kids. I knew mum would be disappointed. Dad would be the same. So I decided not to tell them. Anyway, I figured we'd bring the date forward and have a shotgun wedding, or whatever it's called. That would appease mum. Then, when I realised I could have the wedding and then have the baby, I got quite excited. Then I got excited about the baby. I got used to the idea. Miles and I were talking about how we would make it work, figuring out the logistics, like maternity leave and going back to work part time. Then I'd go in-house and not have to work like a dog. We started to formulate a plan. A workable plan. That's probably my comeuppance. I don't know if you've heard the saying, *we plan, then God laughs?*" Julia laughs, though it doesn't seem in jest.

I squeeze her hand, and notice she's without her usual manicure. Her fingernails look pale and brittle. "You've always been a planner and you shouldn't change that. Just like I'm always glass half empty and I'm really trying my best to be positive. Maybe we can't shake off who we are."

Julia looks into the distance, where a stream of workers rush past us. "Perhaps we should try. Anyway, whatever, it's done. I got myself all worked up and stressed out. And that's one of the things with all this. The best thing we can do for ourselves and our bodies is relax and let nature take its course. There's a lot to be said for stress being the cause of so much shit."

"Will you try again any time soon?" I ask.

"No. Not actively, anyway. Now that I've had time to take in the news, I've decided to carry on as normal, keep the wedding date for two years in the future. If something happens in between, then great. If it doesn't, we can worry about those things later. Meanwhile, I need to learn to relax."

I sip my fruit cooler. "Shall we start playing tennis again?"

Julia looks at me, dumbfounded. "What made you think of tennis?"

"I don't know. It's something we used to do when we were young. We're still kind of young. It'd be nice to get back into it."

Julia smiles. "Sure, why not? After all, doing some physical activity might help us thrash out our angst and highly-strung ways."

19th June, Hormones

"Hon, when are you going to meet your new nephew?" asks Sophia, holding up her newborn to the screen.

"I'm seeing him now, and I can verify that he is extremely cute," I reply.

"That's not good enough! I need you here, in the flesh. How do you not want to see this adorable face?"

She brings her phone so close to the baby that I can only see a chubby chin, and Cupid's bow lips.

"I am sorry I haven't been to see you yet. It's just difficult when I come up north. I'm at my mother-in-law's, and then my mum's. I feel like I'm fighting for time when I'm here."

"Surely, your mother-in-law won't mind you cutting your stay short to see your girlfriend, would she? It's not like she doesn't get her pound of flesh when you're there."

"I should warn you I'm currently at my mother-in-law's house, sat in the spare room upstairs." I pan the camera around the room to show non-descript magnolia walls, an oak affect wardrobe, and a dusty bookshelf. To be fair, I could be anywhere, with such indistinguishable surroundings.

Sophia gasps. "Gosh, I'm sorry hon. Give my salaam. Anyway, try to come over, please. We'd love to see you."

"Me too. Trust me, you're on my list of baby mamas to visit."

"What do you mean?" Sophia looks like a jealous girlfriend.

"Nothing, it's just my cousin has also had a baby around the same time as you."

"Oh. You've not visited her either? Are you avoiding babies because you've not got your own?" She cackles. A full on, mean girl cackle.

My face drops.

"Sorry hon, I didn't mean it to sound like that. It's hormones. Don't pay attention to anything I say."

Sophia's not wrong. Despite auntie Rukhsana calling to tell me the good news, I've found myself too busy to visit. It's strange that for a girl who documents every aspect of her life, Naila hasn't posted anything on social media since the baby's been born. I spotted a glamorous selfie in a taxi, with the caption: *This is it!* Her husband posed next to the gifted car seat in another photo. Even in the labour ward, she shared a video of her and Darren getting high on gas and air. After that, it's been a social media blackout.

"Don't worry," I say. "I best let you go as my mother-in-law has started a cooking marathon downstairs. It would be rude not to help."

"She doesn't know how lucky she's got it, having a chef to hand. My mother-in-law, to this day, hasn't asked me to help with cooking."

I look at Sophia.

"Sorry," she says again. "Hormones."

I never realised that frying onions to the point of burning could create such a tasty, caramelised effect. It's just one of the things I've learnt from my mother-in-law while assisting her in the kitchen. Today's recipe is chicken pulao. And what's the special occasion? There isn't one.

"Do you want to cook the chicken?" she asks rhetorically.

I wash and drain the chicken, trying my best not to spread salmonella everywhere, and lay out the pieces on the chopping board. Even though they are ready cut from the butchers, I slice the chicken even more, until each piece is barely 1inch squared. Cleaning the chicken is yucky. I hate de-veining, I hate cutting the fat but it's got to be done.

I bring the chopping board, loaded with chicken, over to my mother-in-law, who is softening some more onions in a pan.

"Don't add them yet," she says. "It's too soon. Let the onions dry out a little. Otherwise, chicken end up watery and ruin food."

Another golden nugget.

"You won't have time for all this in London as you be working. But on weekend, try frying some chicken, with haldi, salt and curry powder. Then you can have it with roti. Bit like tandoori chicken."

"I always wanted to know how to make tandoori chicken. Do you know how to make it?" I ask.

My mother-in-law laughs. "Do I know? You no worry, I show you everything."

"You know so much," I say.

"My time be different. Ladies no work. Our job was house. Feeding husband and children. Different for your generation but I can show you few things, so you have these recipes when I'm gone."

When I'm not bemoaning having to cook at M's mum's house, I hoover up these pearls of wisdom. Looking at my mother-in-law, slightly more hunched, frail, and slower paced, I can see she won't be doing these dishes for long.

It's interesting how her cooking, and my mum's, is slightly different. My mum's chicken curry is rich, with a thick gravy. M's mum makes her broth soupy, adding more water and not melting the onions so much. The subtle variation results in a huge change in taste. I still prefer my mum's and M prefers his. I guess that's just how it is.

"Do you want a hand with anything?" M asks.

"I think we've got it under control," I say.

M is loitering. He hovers near the door, neither coming in nor leaving. Obviously, he wants to ask me something. I can guess what it is.

"So Jam called and he wanted to meet up..."

Of course he did.

"I said no." M looks as if he wants a shiny gold sticker.

"Why did you say that?"

"Because it's Jam. We'll plan to meet for an hour. He'll go off on a tangent about something. Then, before you know it, I've sat there for ages without an escape plan."

"Yeah, that sounds like Jam." I add the chicken to the condensed onions. "Food will be another hour, so if you can exercise some amazing willpower, you could meet him quickly and get back in time for lunch."

"No, it's alright. I don't wanna get late."

"What you talk about?" asks M's mum. "You want to go out?"

"No, I'll stay at home."

M's dad walks into the kitchen. "If you're home, do you want to drop me off at mosque?"

"Yeah, can do. Is it a different one?" M asks, confused as his dad normally walks the five minutes to the local mosque.

"No, usual Medina mosque. Just walking be harder. I not been able to go this week, because of pain in leg."

"What pain? Have you hurt yourself?"

M's dad chuckles. "No, no. Old age pain. One day, you know. Then you be telling your kids to drive you to mosque."

"Not that you ever go mosque!" says M's mum, seeing an opportunity to chastise her son. "Why you no go mosque? One day you must answer for everything. I tell you, life be better when you pray. You need make effort to do that. No point praying in your old age to be healthy and well. Don't pray when you desperate, don't wait till the need."

"Will do." M looks at me and smiles. It's something he's heard many times before. "I guess that's me told."

"By the way, if you want to meet Jam, I won't hold it against you. I don't want you to be resenting me for stopping you from seeing your friends."

"It's alright. We'll both be seeing him soon, anyway. He's invited us round for dinner when we get back to London."

"Did I hear that right? Jam's inviting us round?"

"I know, things are changing," says M.

20th June, Mending bridges

It feels like an age since I've seen big sis. The last time she came to mum's, I didn't bother. I was still in the angry phase and wanting to avoid her. I was annoyed at her refusal to acknowledge the way she was, the way she's always been and the way she is now.

I can't avoid the inevitable. On a rare weekend, middle sis is here and big sis is coming later for a whistle-stop visit en route to Oldham to see family on her husband's side. Any and every Bengali person has some relatives, however distant, in Oldham.

"There's this mum that I've made friends with at school," begins middle sis, "and once I offered to do the school run as she was rushing to get back from the dentist. Now, she blimmin' asks me to do the school run every other week. It's one of those awkward ones, where she gives a good reason and it's hard to say no. A few times she's even asked me to keep the kids for a couple of hours before she picks them up."

"Is she working?" I ask, not that it excuses things.

Middle sis scoffs. "No. Well, not really. Not like an office 9-to-5 job. She bakes cakes from home to sell on a stall. That's her business! She might get the occasional birthday or wedding cake order but it's not as if she's rushed off her feet. I don't get it. Her fella's got flexible work, too, as he's a taxi driver. I didn't mind so much at first but when she leaves the kids... they can *eat*." Middle sis' eyes widen. "My goodie cupboard will be emptied by them. Then they start looking in the fridge. They're so different from our kids. Mine will never ask for anything from anyone else, even if they're hungry."

"That's annoying," I say. "You need to teach your kids to be greedy in other people's houses. They don't hold back here."

"Grandma's house, innit? Anyway, I've come up with a name for her. Farida the freeloader."

We both laugh. I wonder how long middle sis spent thinking that one up.

"Why are our kids like that? Wimpy outdoors but giving loads of attitude at home?" I ask.

"We all were, weren't we?" says middle sis. "You were the same. Remember that little cow, Rebecca, who used to bully you in primary school?"

Rebecca? Oh yeah, I'd mentally blocked that out and assumed that my school experience started with Julia. "There was hair pulling and everything. She even said my jumper was horrible."

"It would've carried on as well if we hadn't had a word outside school."

It all comes back to me. Those long forgotten, suppressed memories. "That must have been in infant's school. I wonder if it was racism? Then again, it can't be. She's alright now, I'm on her Facebook and she's a proper lefty. Loves the refugees and everything."

"You were probably a soft target."

"Probably. I remember telling the teachers and they'd be like: '*Oh, just ignore her.*'"

"That's what they do. They don't like to get involved. That's how bullying happens. Honestly, if anyone started on my kids, I'd sort them out good and proper. A few threats work wonders. But yeah, I think we're all a bit like that, aren't we? Little mice outdoors. Probably comes from feeling different all the time."

"Different?" I wouldn't expect middle sis to have those feelings.

"That's how we always were. Never quite fitting in. It's so deeply ingrained that we will never fit in anywhere. I mean, look at the way we dress. Look at how I'm dressed! What is this? It's neither Asian nor English."

Middle sis throws her arms in the air, flabbergasted by her own outfit. To be fair, her black kurta top and cream pinstripe trousers aren't really working for her.

"Do you still feel left out?" I ask. "Even in Bradford?"

Middle sis sighs. "Even in Bradford. I'm constantly displaced."

I thought that was a hang up only I had.

"Then again," says middle sis, "there are benefits to being misfits."

"Are there?"

"We didn't have stirrers living on our street. We were allowed to do our own thing, in a way. I got to go to uni, you got to live away. I remember auntie Jusna trying her best to stir about that but it didn't matter because it was only her. One person in dad's ear wasn't enough. If there was a whole gang of Bengalis on our doorstep, mum and dad would have paid more attention. It's probably about the only plus side, among the many downsides. The biggest one being for mum."

"What do you mean?" I ask.

Middle sis sighs. "She got the raw end of the stick, didn't she? At least we could speak English and try to fit in with people around us. She never stood a chance. Her life was us. Cooking for us. Cleaning and bathing us. There was never time for anything else, like learning English, taking a course, or making friends. She relied on big sis for everything. Filling out the forms, being a translator. Now big sis has moved away and is busy with her kids, mum relies on you. Once you have kids and don't have time for her, she'll be relying on the little one."

That hurt more than expected. "I'll always have time for mum."

"You say that now. Wait 'til you have children. Everything changes. It's not even that you want it to, and that you want to not have time for mum, it's just how it goes. It's a circle of life, isn't it? Mum was probably like that with her mum once she had big sis. Then, she moved to the UK, so she never saw nani at all. You're now miles away. It's not like after having kids you'll be able to hop on a train, like you do now. Everything is harder. And your priorities change. As they should."

"I still think I'll make time for mum."

"We all did before we had kids. But you'll know when you have your own."

There's a knock on the door, which is a welcome relief, as I didn't want to get any further into this. It's too painful.

We go downstairs to see big sis standing in the hallway, in a fashion forward, royal blue maxi dress. Since when did she wear dresses? I rarely see her out of ethnic attire.

"There's no need to stare, lady," says big sis. "It's too hot for salwar kameez."

She's managed to both read my mind and break the ice in one inelegant swoop.

"The trains are getting ridiculously expensive these days," says big sis. "I might have to get the family railcard again."

"Them were the days," says middle sis. "That family railcard took us on so many journeys. Remember those trips to London?" She points at me. "We used to make you wear your hair in bunches so you'd pass for under 14. It's lucky that you've always looked younger than you are."

"Not so much now," I say. "The other day, I went to Tesco to buy a gift for a client. I got this set that had chocolate and a small bottle of wine. Then, I got to the till, fully expecting to be ID'd. The guy approved the purchase without a second glance! I had my driving licence at the ready! He didn't even ask to see it!"

"That's the 30s for you. It's all downhill from there." Big sis looks down at her dress, flattening out the creases over her stomach. "Remember that time we went to London and we had to get advanced train tickets and the cheapest would involve staying for five days? Uncle Tariq's face dropped when he realised how long we would be with them. We more than outstayed our welcome on that visit."

"It be hard for them in small flat. There is barely enough space for own family. When we all came, makes it more difficult."

"You didn't say that when you were pestering me to book the £6 return tickets!" Big sis laughs. "Imagine being able to go anywhere for £6 these days. It's funny, back then it didn't feel so bad sleeping three-in-a-bed sideways. Now, after a couple of days here, I'm ready to go."

"And how long you staying for?" asks mum with a lip grimace.

Big sis looks sheepish. "You see, there weren't many options. It was £48 for a fixed ticket or £137 for a flexible return."

"I see." Mum braces herself. "When you return?"

"Next Thursday."

Mum's face is the mirror image of uncle Tariq's when we also delivered the news of a five-day stay.

We all, including mum, burst out laughing. We've become caricatures of each other.

"In other news, how is uncle Tariq? Have you seen them all recently?" asks big sis.

"Not for a while," I say. "Naila's staying over now that she's had her baby."

"You've not been to see her yet?" asks middle sis, surprised.

"You should go soon!" Mum nods. "And when you do, remember to buy baby clothes. I give you some money and you can give gift from me. Who knows when I be able to go visit them all the way in London. Okay, now everyone eat! Chicken getting cold."

It's the most unusual spread as the chicken is laid out on a baking tray next to a bed of rice. Usually we help ourselves from the kitchen, loading everything up on our plates. The only time we have this much ceremony is when one of our husbands is eating with us.

"How come you've not visited her yet?" Middle sis is ever so concerned about my relationship with a cousin she hasn't seen in years.

I don't want to share the real reason. I don't want to say that I'm not looking forward to the questions, the hints in my direction. All the blatant, unfiltered suggestions that it's my turn to have a baby. I can't cope with all that.

"I just find her a bit annoying," I say. "She's always flaunting her perfect life on social media. It looks like she has all the time in the world to put makeup on and pose. I don't even need to see her, as she posts everything, down to the last fart."

"*Dooro*!"

"Ooh! Do you follow her?" asks big sis. "I wouldn't mind having a nosey at some pictures. I haven't seen her fella, as we never got invited to the wedding. Assuming she had a proper wedding, what with him being an English guy and all."

"She posts plenty of photos of him. Look..." I tap in the passcode on my phone, which is nestled between my plate and glass of water.

"*Acha* enough! No phones when having dinner. Everybody got a phone now, it's like disease. People obsessed. Your little sister always, always on phone. It heating up her hand and face and ear. So many illness come from this," says mum.

The young lady in question rolls her eyes in response. "You can't talk, mum. You're addicted to YouTube. I can always hear the muffled tone of some preacher, followed by a lecture from you."

"*Dooro*! These are important things. Like how to be healthy. Or my Islamic programme."

"Is this the same programme that tells you eating fish is good for you, and other such facts that we learnt 30 years ago?" Middle sis laughs.

"Okay, you all so educated now? Backward mum know nothing? When you have hand problem from always using phone, then you see. So you look at photo and be jealous of cousin later. It dinner time now!"

My smirk fades. I'm not jealous.

"What is this?" asks little sis, prodding the chicken with a fork.

"It's Peri Peri chicken and rice," says middle sis.

"Is chicken cooked," is mum's usual question when it comes to poultry.

"More than." Middle sis grabs a fork. "The recipe said four to five minutes on each side. So obviously I cooked it for 45 minutes on each side!"

Mum cuts open the meat and squeezes it to check there aren't any juices running freely. "Good. You never be too sure with chicken. You need to speak to your little sister about these recipes. Can't cook or even clean! She is so messy, how she live with in-laws when she get married."

"Fucking hell," little sis mutters under her breath.

"What is this fockin' bockin? Real nice language, you learn at uni-barsity?"

Mum is unintentionally delivering comedy gold. We all laugh, including little sis. It's good that she finds it funny. She's got years of henpecking to go.

"Can someone call your dad? He needs to eat. These days, it's hard to get him eating at all," says mum.

"You can't tell from looking at him," says big sis. "He still has a pot belly."

"That belly not going nowhere but doctor told him to stop eating *supari*, now he has sweets. Can you believe? All his life, never touch sweet food. Now he love biscuits, cake, even chocolate! The other day I caught him eating Ferrero Rocher."

"Dad is so classy," I say.

"Yes, very, very classy. Will you call him?"

Before I have a chance to shout for dad, he steps into the dining room and examines my plate.

"*Eh heh*, anything else for dinner?"

"Try it!" says mum. "It be just like chicken roast and rice. You may like it."

"Nah, not me. Not this. Do we have sardine?"

Mum sighs. "I make some."

"I go watch the news then?" says dad. "Then call me when done?"

Mum looks at dad and doesn't need to say a word.

"Okay, I cut onion for sardine first," says dad, going into the kitchen.

"At least he does some of the housework, mum. Unlike mine," says big sis.

"This be nothing! Now I have to push him to go to grocery shop. He want to stay home more and more. Other day

I walk to supermarket, come home, cook dinner, clean up. No rest. Anyway, what do you complain about? You expect your husband to work all night at the restaurant and then make dinner at home?"

"No, I'm not saying that at all."

"Good!" Mum huffs. "You should be grateful for husband. Sometimes you hear of men taking other wives because first wife not good enough."

"Do you personally know anyone who's done that, mum?" asks middle sis.

"No but I saw programme about it on YouTube. Man got second wife because first could have no children. Then, another cheeky man got other wife because he thought first wife be ugly. Shameless man! Anyhow, no matter if I know personally. These things happen. They show on internet so it be true. Be glad for good men that no want extra ladies."

"God, the barometer is set at completely different places for men and women, isn't it?" I say, causing everyone to look up from their chicken. "For men, it's the bare minimum that they're kind and nice and preferably monogamous. Whereas for ladies... can they cook? Do they help out with the in-laws? Can they socialise and interact with extended family? It's like with M, you guys are all saying how amazing he is, how lucky I am and how I should be grateful. And I am grateful, however, I'm pretty good, too! I'm really good to him. I am the one that takes the lead when it comes to dinner most nights of the week even though we both work. We both earn the same money! It's not like he's the breadwinner and I'm the 1950's housewife. Yet, I'm the one that will be stuck in the kitchen for at least a couple of hours whenever we visit his mum. He comes to ours and we get the best plates out and he's waited on hand and foot like a prince."

"Oh, here you go, complain again!" says mum.

"I'm not complaining, I'm just saying it's stupid. All of it's stupid. And you all know it!" I look around at my sisters. Little sis is none the wiser, while big sis is tearing up her stringy chicken by hand, no doubt lamenting this fake-away nonsense.

Middle sis chimes in. "It's like my mother-in-law, when she bangs on about her son working so hard. Being a teacher is so blooming hard. Being the one going to work is so hard. I say to her she's obviously forgotten that being a mum 24-hours a day is bloody hard. Not having a break from small people needing food, wiping bums, entertaining or cuddling is hard. No one sees it like that because it's not a job you can attach a salary to. The biggest problem of all? It's us women who perpetuate this. My father-in-law doesn't say anything. He just has his cup of tea and goes to his room to read namaz. It's the women. It's the mums who've been through it and should know better."

I think about my in-laws' dynamic. It is my mother-in-law who instigated the roster of curries for lunch and dinner. I think the default, the long ingrained expectation is that the women in the house get on with it. Much as I have got on with it in our very modern life in London. Like many of us women get on with it.

Julia gets on with it, because Miles can't cook or clean. Reena will have to get on with it, even though she's dreading living with the in-laws and being chief roti roller when she gets back from work every evening. My mum, my sisters, all women I know, fall into a role that is as old as time. We haven't really moved on that much since the cavemen era, when men would hunt for food, while women stayed at home and lit the fire.

Never mind, when I have kids, whether they're boys or girls, I'll raise them as feminists.

Middle sis washes up, mum and dad go to read evening prayers and little sis hides upstairs. I'm alone with big sis, indulging her in my favourite new hobby, stalking Naila's social media feed. Lucky for me, after a brief silence, she's posted some new material.

"She looks ever so glamorous there," says big sis, examining a photo of her wearing a dramatic, sweeping, red gown, cradling a newborn baby, against a deep blue studio background. "It must be a mum and baby photo shoot. I remember doing those. Except it wasn't me in the photos, just my babies posing as sailors or bunnies."

"It's different these days. Now, the shoot is as much about the mum as the baby."

We scroll through more photos. Shots of Naila in hospital, with the baby clutched to her chest while she's still wearing false eyelashes and a hint of blush. It has the caption: *heart in my hands.*

There's another photo of Naila, dressed in a fluffy white robe, which looks brand new. She has a flawless messy up do, her full lips peachy. Her caption says something about how this is her reality... tired and with eye bags for days. She looks nothing like her description.

More photos include Darren holding the baby with Naila looking on, arms wrapped around his lean shoulders. The caption includes the hashtag #prproduct. Whether it's the baby's clothes or theirs, something was free.

"Her fella is not bad looking, is he? A bit lanky, but not bad," says big sis. "I mean, if you're going to marry out, you might as well make it worth it with a handsome guy."

I look at Darren, with his green-brown eyes and dirty blonde man bun. We've never met in person in all the years I've been in London. I've never really paid attention to his photos before, usually because I'm so fixated on Naila. But, objectively speaking, Darren is fit.

"How old do you think the baby is now?"

"I don't know. A couple of months?" I say.

"Hmm," is big sis' reply.

I know what she's thinking.

"Sometimes months go by without me going round. I don't want to keep bothering auntie Rukhsana for free curry, you see. They'll be busy enough with the baby, so I thought I'd go a bit later, when I've got a free weekend. When she's not doing a photo shoot and modelling one of the free products she's received." I laugh.

"Yes, it does seem like she has a lot of time to do these things. And who do you think takes her photos?"

"I don't know. Maybe Darren?"

"What do you think he does for a living? He must have a lot of time to take all these photos."

"Actually, I've never asked. She's never told me, either."

"Well, he must be a no-hoper. Otherwise, who'd have time to take pictures all day?" I'm not sure if big sis is trying to make me feel better, but it's working. "You know what we should do? Let's send a comment on Instagram, something like: *It's lucky that you've got a husband who doesn't work. He's got time to take all those photos of you.*"

I gasp. "I'm not doing that! She'll know it's me. My profile is hardly covert."

Big sis narrows her gaze conspiratorially. "I'll do it. And she'll never know it's me as I don't post any photos of myself. It's just food."

"You're on Instagram?"

"I am, lady. You're not the only one on social media these days. Look..." Big sis takes my phone and searches for her profile. "There. That's me."

"You've got an aubergine for your profile pic? And you've called yourself spicy lady?"

"Yeah, why?"

"Erm... no reason. It's fine. Anyway, let's not leave a comment, that would be trolling. It's not a nice thing to do."

"Really? Is that what trolling is? I've been doing it quite a lot."

I burst out laughing.

"I didn't think I was doing anything that bad. I thought trolls are the ones that are really mean. I just occasionally post something on the profiles of those influencer types, who are a bit too big for their boots. Like one girl, she is Bengali, and she posts all these fancy videos about Ramadan and iftar recipes. And you know what, she doesn't even fast! She mentioned in an earlier video that she can't for medical reasons.

She is married to a white guy, who doesn't look particularly religious, so I commented: *Who's eating all that stuff as you're not fasting?* That put her in her place. Flaunting her fake life with her pristine kitchen, making the rest of us feel bad."

"Did she reply to you?"

Big sis looks down. "No, I think she blocked me."

"Well, it's low-level bitchy but that's okay." Big sis truly doesn't realise how funny she is.

"You should visit Naila."

"I know. It's just that everything about her life seems so perfect. She looks amazing. I bet being a mum will be a breeze for her. Also, whenever I see her, she's a bit of a dick. She knows how to push my buttons. Right now, I don't need that. I'm not in the right frame of mind to see her and have her great new life with her gorgeous new baby rubbed in my face."

Big sis smiles. "You don't see it, do you?"

"See what?"

"You've described yourself. Apart from the looking immaculate bit. You've never been able to do your makeup properly. But you have a good life. You're married but you've got freedom. You're not having to cook all the time. No trouble from in-laws. She's probably jealous of you, if anything."

"Me? I doubt it!"

"Let's face it, you're the high-flyer with a career that nobody else has. I notice on her profile she mentioned she is a law graduate. Did she even go to uni? Even if she did, it doesn't matter what she's graduated in, if she's not using the degree now. It goes to show she cares about these things. Like most of us do. And you've got that. You've done really well for yourself. I've always been proud of you."

I smile but feel guilty at the same time. "Sorry for being, you know... a bit of a knob when you came to London for that mehendi."

"Oh lady. You don't need to apologise. We're sisters. We're allowed to be knobs with each other from time to time."

"It's so weird hearing you say that. You never swear!"

"Oh blimey, do I ever! You should hear me when I've burnt the curry!"

"You and your curries."

"I know you think I'm all about cooking fish curry these days and that we haven't got much in common but there was a time we weren't so different. You'd always come to me for advice about what subjects to choose for school and university. I even looked over your first job application."

"You did?"

"You've obviously forgotten." Big sis sighs. "Remember, there is a phase and stage for every part of life. One day you'll have kids and be annoyed that you've burnt the curry you made for dinner."

Then it comes to me. That's right, I asked big sis about my exams! I saw her as the high-flyer, the trailblazer, who worked before marriage when most girls didn't. When did things change? Was it after she got married? Or after she had kids? When did I start thinking I was better than her?

I don't bring up the other thing. I don't call her out for her part in our bust up. For her endless colourism. It's far too ingrained in her DNA and there will be no reasoning with her. There's no point. It's like telling her that making curry five days a week is unnecessary. She won't understand where I'm coming from.

"Was it hard for you, mum? When you first got married?" I ask as we prepare the makeshift floor bed.

"*Dooro*! Why you need to know such thing? That be problem with you young people. Always want to talk about feelings and things. Can't just get on with life. Have to make every small thing big."

"Was it, though? Hard?"

"Of course, yes!"

Mum says this as though I should know but how would I? She never talks to me about her life as a newlywed, or the years before I was born. I get snippets of her childhood memories. An anecdote here and there, brought on by a sudden memory. A trip to the park where the grass is overgrown reminds her of the village back home. Going to an Asian grocery shop and spotting a fruit her mother grew in their garden may trigger a conversation. She offers so little.

The door is closed. Maybe it's too much to relive. Maybe there are too many secrets she doesn't want to reveal. Maybe, no, definitely, it was harder than the hand I've been dealt. Much, much harder.

25th June, Dinner with Jam

I can't believe it. Jam can cook. How long has he been hiding this secret?

He told my husband to hurry over as dinner would be ready by nine. M, of course, duly followed instruction. We got there, precisely 10 minutes late, to find that not only was the chicken curry half cooked but Jam hadn't even put the rice on. When was he planning to feed us? Midnight? His expectation management is as bad as M's.

However, now that we are chowing down on nicely spiced chicken in a thick onion gravy, and an aubergine bhorta that is possibly the tastiest version I've tried, all is forgiven. To think, all this time he'd been eating at ours, when it really should've been the other way round.

"You're a bit of a dark horse, aren't you?" I say, grabbing another chicken leg from the pot.

Jam laughs. "What can I say? It's one of my many talents. And also a bit of consequence, as I don't have a wife to cook for me."

"Get the violins out," says M.

Jam smirks. "Seriously, I've been meaning to have you guys round for ages. I feel bad always eating at yours. Now that I've managed to snag an apartment hotel in Aldgate, it made sense to make use of all their pots and pans. Plus, I was getting bored of kebab rolls."

Typical of budget city accommodation, the pots and pans are basic as can be. The thickness of a sardine can, the nonstick peeled away. It's a miracle that Jam managed to conjure up such a feast with this cookware.

The apartment itself isn't too bad. It's all open plan, with a round table next to the window, a kitchen along the wall and reasonably sized lounge with a brown corner sofa and TV. The bedroom is sectioned off by a semi-transparent screen. It's functional. The only distinguishable feature is the canvas painting of London Bridge on the wall.

"So what's the plan, man?" asks M. "Are you going to be permanently based elsewhere?"

"For now, I'll still be in Bristol and that suits me at the moment. I've got rid of my flat and work pay for my accommodation over there, as well as when I come here for meetings." He shrugs. "I don't mind it too much but I do miss London and you guys, too. Don't get a big head."

"No chance of that, man. I've got this one keeping me humble," says M. "What else is going on with you?"

Jam spreads some aubergine across his plate. "I'm still on the dating apps. We'll see what happens with that. There aren't many Bengali girls in Bristol, so I might have to look outside, like go for a Pakistani girl or something."

"Ooh," I say, thinking of Bushra and then suddenly parking that thought, as I need to check whether she's seen Ahmed again. It's been months since we last spoke, so who knows? If she's moving at the rate I was when I was looking to get married, she may be engaged already, to Ahmed or some other lucky guy.

"What's that?" asks Jam, with hope in his eyes.

"Nothing," I reply, rubbing at a finger mark on my glass that's refusing to budge. "I was just thinking of my sister, who lives in Bristol. She comes to Manchester to get her saree and kebab fix. Anyway, will your parents be okay with you marrying a Pakistani girl?"

"I think they'll be grateful if I get married at all. You know how it is. When you're 27, they're strict about the criteria. The girl has to be from the same part of Bangladesh, the right age bracket, educated and all of that. Then, as each year goes by, they get less fussy. I'm waiting for them to be glad I'm marrying someone with a pulse and female body parts."

"Maybe that's what I should've done?" M laughs, then quickly looks at me and says: "Only joking," just in case I thought he was serious. "We're at the stage where everyone around us is getting knocked up."

"And then there's me." Jam laughs.

"And then there's us," I say.

Jam looks up at me and smiles.

All these years, I saw Jam as a third wheel. Now, he's come to be my friend, too. He's formed part of our experience in London. And I realise that in between M and Jam's heated debates about football, we all talk. We really sit down and talk. As much as I hate to say it, I miss our little party of three. If he cooks like this again, I'm more than happy to hang out. Even if his food is terribly late. I'll just have a pre-dinner dinner.

We stay for tea and I'm surprised to see that the oatmeal biscuits we bought en route are unnecessary. Jam has a selection of sweet and savoury treats to offer us. How is it that he has a better stocked cupboard when he's not living in London than when he was here?

After showing a tremendous amount of restraint, the boys fall into the conversation that they were undoubtedly dying to discuss, the Liverpool V Man United game. It's all white noise to me, so I use this opportunity to check in on Bushra.

Me: *Hey, how you doing?*

Bushra replies straight away, which is unusual, as she's often partying on the weekend. Times have changed.

Bushra: *Hey, I'm okay. How are you?*

Me: *Good.*

Would it be rude to ask her outright about Ahmed? Or even probe into her hunting status? After all, that's what I'm dying to know. Then again, she would've told me if there's anything to share.

Before I know it, my fingers are typing...

Me: *Any updates on the hunt?*

Damn me and my nosey ways.

Bushra: *I do have some news...*

Me: *Ooh! (intrigued face emoji)*

Bushra: *(cheeky monkey giggling emoji)*

Me: *Go on. Don't leave me in suspense.*

Bushra: *Okay but you can't tell no one.*

Me: *I don't know anyone who knows you! Apart from Emma, and I'm not really in touch with her so you're safe.*

Bushra: *I've been seeing someone.*

Me: *Is it Ahmed?*

Bushra: *Bloody hell! How did you know?*

Me: *Because that's the last person you were speaking to and I haven't had an update since, so… (detective's magnifying glass emoji).*

Bushra: *Alright, Sherlock. But promise me you won't say nothing.*

Me: *So I can't share it on my blog?*

Bushra: *The one that gets 10 views per month?*

Me: *Ooh burn! Maybe I will share your news, one way to go viral.*

Bushra: *You wouldn't.*

Me: *Obviously, I wouldn't!*

Bushra: *Do you think I'm mad? Or desperate?*

Me: *No! If you like him, that's all that matters.*

Bushra: *I'm not sure if I do (confused face emoji)*

Time to employ some reverse psychology.

Me: *Don't stress about it! Plenty more fish in the sea.*

Bushra doesn't reply.

"Shall we get going soon?" asks M.

"Stay for a bit longer," says Jam, looking deflated. "I'll be heading back tomorrow evening."

"We'll come round tomorrow, man," says M. "Then he quickly turns to me. "If we're free?"

"We are free," I say.

"Nah, it's okay. I can't be a third wheel all the time," says Jam, though his face suggests that he really does want to be a third wheel, for at least a little longer.

"You know what, you guys don't get to catch up that often, so you might as well meet up without me. I've got stuff to do, anyway," I say.

"You sure?" asks M, though he and Jam can't hide their delight at the prospect of having a boys' night without the real third wheel, me.

My phone pings.

Bushra: *I don't think I want to meet anyone else (red-faced emoji).*

Me: *And there it is (heart emoji).*

Who'd have thought it. Bushra has found her person, and it's the one she least expected.

12th July, Not getting excited

I won't get excited. I won't. There's no point. I'm late for my p again. At least I think I am but I can't be certain as I'm still crap at determining my cycle. I don't know why it's so complicated but all this biology goes over my head.

Anyway, I feel like I'm overdue. Was it four weeks when I last came on? Or maybe three and a half? No wonder I keep missing my fertility window. I don't even know when it is.

Must distract myself with other thoughts.

Thankfully, I've got plans today. Plans that I've been putting off for ages. I'm going to meet Naila and her new baby. In honour of the occasion, I'm armed with a gift bag full of baby grows and a cellophane-wrapped hamper that I put together with the help of a YouTube tutorial. It contains baby oil, nappy rash cream and a load of other tat that I suspect will be useful. I wish I'd recorded myself putting it all together. Surely, that would've opened the floodgates for more free stuff to come my way?

"I'm looking forward to going to your uncle's house," says M on the drive there. "I've missed your auntie's meat and potato curry."

"Me too. My attempt last weekend was pretty pitiful, wasn't it?"

"I thought it was nice. The meat just needed cooking a bit longer."

"And it needed more salt. And more oil. And more spices. Plus, new potatoes and mutton don't go together. You want the meat to be so tender that it falls apart, not the potatoes."

"Oh, yeah." M laughs. "Next time, we'll get those red potatoes."

We arrive at uncle Tariq's tower block to realise that the lift isn't working, so we climb the concrete steps to the fifth floor. I'm regretting making such an oversized care package. I can't see for the cellophane and big blue bow. I can't even pass it to M, as he's loaded with a gift bag in one hand and the obligatory carrier bag of drinks, sweets and crisps in the other.

After the fourth flight of stairs, my walk is unsteady in my uncomfortable kitten heels and my makeup feels hot and heavy on my face. I'm cursing myself for having made the extra effort of adding cream highlighter. However, I was all too aware that I'm going into the house of a makeup artist and I damn well wanted to make sure I looked half decent.

"I'm sweating through my jumper," says M.

"Why are you wearing a jumper in this heat, anyway?"

"I thought I'd smarten up. My good shirts are getting a bit snug. Hopefully I'll fit in them after doing these stairs. I wonder how your cousin gets up and down the stairs every day with a pram."

M makes a good point. What does she do? Naila doesn't drive, so I suspect she's having to get out and about on foot, pushing a pram. But how? Does she carry the baby in one hand and the pram in the other? I must take this up with her. If nothing else, it's good to get any tips for my future situation, as I also live in a high-rise tower block that requires lift access.

As we finally make it to the summit on a trek that seems as treacherous as the volcano in Bali, I see uncle Tariq already has the door open. First, I thought it's in anticipation, then I see he's having a crafty cigarette.

"She's here! She's here! My disappearing daughter!" He gestures with his hand for us to come in. "And groom! Too busy with big city job to visit!"

M chuckles nervously.

We make the walk from the square hallway into the lounge/dining room/front room. Auntie Rukhsana is laying the table with the best plates, the ones painted with dark pink roses and a gold trim.

"You're here! I thought you forgot about us." She comes over and gives me a hug. I squeeze tighter, putting my arm around her comforting, soft shoulders. I've missed them more than I realised. "Come, come... there's someone to meet you in bedroom. You can sit here." She gestures to M to sit down on the ornate sofa.

I head into Naila's room, which has changed beyond recognition since I last saw it. In the smallest of double rooms, there is the addition of a Moses basket on a wooden stand. There are packets of nappies everywhere, a pile of washing that is mostly small people's clothing, and a contraption that I assume is to do with preparing baby formula. Perched on the bed is someone equally unrecognisable. Naila is without a scrap of makeup, false eyelashes or long nails. I'm so used to seeing filtered images of her that I'd forgotten what she looks like in person. Her top lip is unnaturally puffed out, as if she's had filler injected. I never noticed that before. I assumed she overlined her lips. She is wearing a kha-ki co-ord with a white smudge on her shoulder.

"You alright?" she asks.

"I'm good. More importantly, how are you?"

"I'm not gonna lie. I'm knackered. This mum life, nothing prepares you for it." Her eyelids are heavy as if she's struggling to stay awake.

"It must be great being back at your mum's. Not having to worry about food and chores."

"Yeah, I guess." She looks down at her baby. "Anyway, here's the little man, baby Ibrahim."

She offers him to me before I have a chance to sit next to her. I bend down to scoop him up into my arms. He is heavier than I expected. Smooth skin, puffed-out cheeks and a freshly shaved head. His babygrow has the Ralph Lauren logo emblazoned on it. That's such a Naila move.

"I'll tell you what, I've done my steps for the day, getting up here. How are you managing now the lift is broken?"

"Is the lift broken? I hadn't realised. I've not been out for a while."

"Oh." I try and fail to hide my surprise.

"I sometimes take him out on the balcony on our floor but it's such a mission going downstairs with a buggy. It ain't worth it half the time."

I sit next to her with baby Ibrahim. "That's fair enough. I don't know what I'm going to do when I have a baby."

"What do you mean?" Naila furrows her fashionably thick brow. "Have you been trying?"

Oh man. This is exactly why I avoided coming here. For a brief moment, my fears were allayed by seeing Naila looking raw and vulnerable but here she comes with her seed to plant.

"Not exactly. I'm just saying, you can never assume you'll be able to have kids just because we want them."

"I know about that, man. We been trying since ages. And nothing was happening. I really wanted a boy. And he looks just like my oldest brother, don't you think?"

It's been that long since I've seen her big brother that I can't picture his face. "A little," I say.

"It's something I wanted for so long. And then you go and have one... I just feel so different." She looks at baby Ibrahim and then looks away. "I'll get used to it. I'm just tired. Mum is always banging on about breast being best but he's not having it. Formula will have to be the next best thing."

"That's not too bad, is it? We were all brought up on formula."

"Course we were! All of us were formula-fed. That's what they used to plug back in the days. Now, if you even mention you wanna feed them with a bottle, the midwife looks at you like you're the devil."

Auntie Rukhsana peers round the door. "Are you ready to come eat? I've made the meat and potato curry you like." She then looks at Naila. "Do you want to come now? Or in bit?"

"I'll come now, if you can hold the baby."

"I no be able to hold him!" Auntie Rukhsana laughs. "I need to serve the food. Put him down for a bit and put dummy in. That's what you'll have to do in your own home." She looks at me and rolls her eyes.

"He won't go down. He screams whenever I put him in the basket," says Naila. "I'll come eat in a bit."

"Or I can bring plate to you, then you can eat with spoon?"

"Whatever." Naila sweeps baby Ibrahim out of my arms before I get to have one last look at him.

"And will he come later?" I'm assuming auntie Rukhsana is referring to Naila's husband, Darren. I've never seen them all in the same room together. I've no idea how they interact.

"No, he's not coming today. He's got a day shift."

Auntie Rukhsana nods. "Okay, very good."

I guess I won't see them together today, either.

"Your auntie's meat curry doesn't disappoint," says a satisfied M on the drive back home.

"It sure doesn't. It was funny seeing Naila. She is so different in real life, compared to her social media photos."

"Isn't everyone? What were you expecting? Her to be sat in a gown, with the baby dressed as an angel?"

Okay, so I may or may not have shared Naila's photos with M.

"Not quite, but I didn't expect her to be the complete opposite of that, either. I guess those platforms are designed to make you feel like you're not good enough. That someone else has it better. The grass isn't always greener."

"We don't have any grass," says M. "None of us do. We live in flats. It's the best way."

"Fair point, though seeing her did make me think that before we have kids, we really should make the most of it. Once we're parents, we will be forever looking back at what we had before."

"No need to tell me. Have a word with yourself! I'm always saying let's enjoy the moment."

"That you are. I guess it's a lesson for me if and when it does happen."

"There's no if about it," says M, clutching my hand. "It's when."

Still not getting excited. I definitely won't tell him about my lateness until there's something to tell.

"Also, next time we're up north, do you think we could see Sophia and her baby? I'm overdue a visit," I say.

"Sounds good."

M's got that thinking face, as though he's about to say something mind blowing. "A lot of people are having babies right now, no?"

I laugh. "You're telling me."

18th July, Just another day at the office

Still not getting excited but some weird shit is going down. I'm yet to receive a visit from aunt Flo and I finally bought myself a pregnancy testing kit. I've been stopping myself from doing this a week earlier as I didn't want to get my hopes up prematurely. However, now I believe it's been long enough to justify the investment. Doctor Wong's orders and all that.

But first, work. I'm going into the office today to distract myself from wanting to piss on a stick. I've done enough of that in the last few months.

Unfortunately, punctuality is not my strong suit. I get into my shared office space at 10.30am, which means that there are very few hot desks to spare. Loren is still reeling off her usual marketing spiel.

"My name is Loren and I work for QuickTime Solutions. I'm calling to tell you about our services. We've been featured in the Financial Times, the Guardian and the Daily Express. Have you seen us in any of those?"

Hard pass. I don't fancy sitting next to her.

Jasdeep the creep is loitering near the desk of a young Asian girl I've not met before.

"I run several businesses alongside being on the board here. I'm in a rush now but if you've got time later, I'll run you through."

Another hard pass. I definitely don't fancy sitting next to the new girl and witnessing Jasdeep on the prowl. However, I am going to make sure I hop over there before close of play today, to kibosh any plans he may have with her. It's a safeguarding issue. I'm not exactly sure what the threat is but he's weird.

Benedict is his usual, affable self. I'll sit next to him. It's been a while since we've shared a desk. I've kind of been avoiding him since he teased about taking up my course, only to about-turn when he realised it wasn't free.

After a polite exchange of hellos, we return to our respective screens.

"How's business?" he asks.

"It's going good. I'm heading to a networking event in Holborn later. Keeping that pipeline flowing and all that."

That's not quite true. Yes, I'm going to a networking event but business isn't exactly booming. I would say it's coasting along. I haven't been able to replace the recruitment consultancy client I lost a few months back with any new business. There are hardly any takers for my new course that I thought would change the course of my career.

I can't say all this, can I? It would be a bit of a downer. I've got to stay chipper for Benedict. Must remain positive for any hopes of new business. Gosh, I'm sick of constantly putting my best face forward. To think I've got to do this all again, on a bigger scale, at my event in Holborn. I don't think I can face it. I'm tired of trying to fake it 'til I make it.

Plus, I feel sick and tired, literally.

"You?" I turn to him.

Benedict scratches the bald patch on his crown. "Getting there. I'm off to France next week as there is a potential client over there. And I finally bagged some investment."

"That's great."

Benedict smiles. "It's only a bit of seed funding to get this thing off the ground properly but, yeah, it's a big help right now. I'll actually have some runway to get things done."

Last year's me would be excited. Last year's me would take this as an opportunity to pitch to him. I'm not doing that anymore. I'm not getting my hopes up that Benedict moving forward with his business would involve PR and marketing. It'll only lead to disappointment.

My phone rings. I don't recognise the number, so I answer in my neutral tone, which is polite enough for a potential client and also appropriate should I need to switch to Bengali.

"I'm so glad I've caught you! I wasn't sure whether to ring or not."

Who is that?

"It's Joy, by the way."

Aha, I didn't recognise her voice without her confused fart-hunting face attached to it.

"How are you, Joy?"

"Honestly, I'm climbing the walls. I'm really not sure what to do and I appreciate you haven't really got time for this. Plus, I'm not a paying client, as you gave the refund back for the course but I'm desperate. Sorry, is now a good time to talk?"

"Yes, it's fine. I've not got a meeting until -"

"Great! Good, good. It's just, I was thinking I need to do some PR for my business. And while I didn't do all of your course, obviously I would never complete your course with the intention of getting a refund, but I watched some snippets. Erm... I remember some of the tips about pitching to a journalist... but honestly, I didn't watch all the videos, so I hope you don't think I've taken advantage."

I wish I could wind Joy up like a Jack-in-the-box to help speed up her story. "Not at all. I would never think that."

"Good, because I'm really not that type of person. I couldn't sleep at night if I felt I'd done another small business owner out of money. So... anyway, I won't keep you too long and I'll get to the point. Basically, I got in touch with a lady called Heather, she works for... hang on... she never told me which magazine she works for! Bloody hell, is she even a journalist? Do you know her? Heather? I think that's what her name was."

"Erm... there are a lot of journalists out there. Probably a lot of Heathers, too. If you could give me any more information, I could look her up."

"Thank you. Thank you, that's great." Joy breathes a sigh of relief. "I was hoping, and I appreciate this is probably overstepping, but I was hoping you could get in touch with her because I'm panicking now. I wanted to pitch the story about my work as a slimming coach and I wanted to share the example of how I've gone from a size 24 to a size 16. Show a bit of practice what I preach, that sort of thing. I figured losing all this weight within six months would be newsworthy and I was right! She loved it! Or at first I thought she did. Then she started asking more personal questions, like am I single and would I be looking for a partner? I just saw it as a nice normal conversation so I told her yes, I'm single. So... anyway... next thing, she wants to make the whole story about me and my love life. Or lack of! I don't want my private business out there."

Joy pauses, giving me a chance to interject.

"Joy, let me tell you, nothing needs to be splashed all over the papers, as you've not even been interviewed yet. Or have you?"

"No, not yet. That's why I'm calling. Heather is due to call me now."

"Now? As in right now?"

"In 10 minutes, yes. I don't know what to do. I'm all flustered. I'm scared she's going to ask me intrusive questions and expect answers on the spot... but I don't want to give out too much personal information. What if they print something I'm not happy with? I don't want my name splashed all over the papers!"

I try my best not to laugh down the phone. Joy's weight loss is commendable but not the kind of national story that would bump a government scandal off the news agenda. I don't say anything, as I know what's coming next.

"I hate to ask but would you be able to speak to her?"

It's one thing doing the donkey work for paid clients, it's quite another doing this for Joy. However, I will do this service.

Trying my best not to depict an *I told you so* tone, I say: "Sure, no worries. What's her number?"

"Hello, Heather speaking."

Her easy, breezy voice suggests this is going to be fun and games.

"Oh hi, I'm calling on behalf of Joy Anderson, who spoke to you regarding her weight loss story?"

"Oh, yes. Her story is fantastic, isn't it? Imagine shedding all those pounds! Commendable!"

"It is. She mentioned you were interested in her personal life and wanted some more information?"

"Yes, yes, that's right. I should add that I was thinking the story would be great for the women's magazines, and an angle that the readers would absolutely love is... and it's a bit out there so hear me out..."

This is going to be good.

"...As she's gone to all this effort to lose so much weight and she mentioned that she is single, I wondered whether she'd be open to meeting someone?"

It's worse than I expected. "I'm not sure, really. I could check for you. Is that something you are thinking would be part of the story?"

"Absolutely! We could position it as a looking for love piece. The angle would be that she's lost all this weight and doesn't want her amazing body going to waste. That she wants to get out there and find a man. If she's into men, that is. Is she straight?"

"I, uh... I think so. I never thought to ask."

"Well, even if she isn't, that's okay. If she's gay, that's not a major problem. We could position the story as she's looking for her dream woman. Though, I must be honest, we probably can't go too many letters into the LGBTQ, if you get what I mean? Our magazines are read by women in their late forties upwards. They're open but not that open."

"Right, I'm not sure if that's the angle she was coming from. She didn't lose weight to find love. It's really more about her doing it for her health, as she works in nutrition."

"Of course, of course." Heather sounds like she's chewing on a pen. "Oh God, yes! We could do a little plug of her business somewhere in the article. But the thing that would really get the women's mags interested is if there's a romantic angle. If not, I'm sure we can do something but the romance is the real hook as everyone loves a love story. So, could you let me know what she thinks?"

Right, it's time to get my PR hat on and earn my keep for this pro bono work. "I'll be honest, Joy isn't comfortable about bringing her personal life into the story. Of course, the human interest angle is king and she understands that. She is happy to talk about her weight loss journey but her personal boundary stopped short of whether or not she's looking for love. If that doesn't work for you, we totally understand. I just want to manage your expectations. I was going to offer the story exclusively to you, so you get first dibs. However, if it won't work for you, let me know in the next couple of days and we'll pitch elsewhere."

"No, no!" Heather's voice pierces through the phone. "I'll be happy to scrap the love life hook. It was just an idea. The story's got legs without it. Right, so if you leave it with me, I will put some points together based on what Joy mentioned and we could talk further next week?"

"That sounds good."

I can see Benedict smiling at me in the corner of my eye.

I ring Joy back straightaway. She's predictably relieved after my firefighting efforts.

"You are an absolute star! You have no idea how worried I was. The cheek of it! Trying to turn my story into a hunt for a new man! A handsome companion would be nice but I wasn't about to tell her that!"

"To be fair, Joy, she's a journalist. It's her job to look for different angles in the story. The thing to remember is, you are always in control when you're pitching. You just need clear boundaries about what you are and aren't willing to talk about. Then you don't deviate from those boundaries. Luckily, your story was interesting enough without needing to delve into your love life. Anyway, Heather said she will be in touch next week to speak to you, if that's okay?"

Joy hesitates.

"If I'm being honest, this whole experience has put me off. There seems to be a bit of an art to dealing with journalists which, frankly, I don't have time to master. That's why I couldn't continue with your course. That said, if you've got any time in your diary..."

Here it comes, the plea for free work. It doesn't matter that I have space in my diary. I plan to use that time wisely, playing tennis or something like that.

"Could I hire you on a project basis, to manage the story with Heather? And then, maybe we could see how it goes from there? I have budget," says Joy.

My half empty glass fills up. "I think I might have some time. How about I send you a draft contract?"

"Please do. Whatever it is, I'll go for it. I'm sorry if I've been pessimistic to the value of publicity before. You do something that people like me would never be able to. I see it now."

There have been times, many times, when I've doubted myself. However, the doubts are punctuated by moments like this. I feel appreciated. I know my worth.

"Just another day at the office, hey?" says Benedict, as I put the phone down.

"Yep, I'm living the dream."

"From the sounds of it, not that I was ear wigging, you're doing it pretty well." Benedict turns to me. "I've been meaning to speak to you. Sorry I got the wrong end of the stick about your PR course before. I was really interested but I just didn't have the funds. Now, I've finally got some investment and I do want to take marketing seriously. I'm probably late to the party but if there's any space on your course, I'd love to sign up."

Oh, of course I could fit you in. There's loads of space in there. It's positively roomy! I think but obviously don't say aloud. Instead, I smile and respond with: "I'm sure I could squeeze you in."

At lunchtime, I occupy the usual picnic bench that houses the curries being sold by Neetu. I admire her commitment. Once a week, she rocks up without fail, with an array of edibles, most of which are put back in her plastic pallet, unsold and untouched. Yet, she perseveres, which isn't a bad achievement, given how many startups go bust in the first few years.

Jasdeep walks in with a lady who trails behind at a respectful distance of about a metre. She's small, hunched and shrouded in her mint green salwar kameez. Her hair is in a low-slung bun like my mum would wear. She's wearing 22 carat gold hoop earrings and her head is loosely covered with a matching scarf.

To say she looks out of place in this hip and trendy office is an understatement. Jasdeep speaks furtively to her in Punjabi. He looks annoyed. She nods and looks down. Graham walks over and both men strike up a conversation, where Jasdeep offers many eye rolls in the direction of the woman. My spider sense tells me that's his wife.

He walks over to examine the hot, spicy food laid out by Neetu.

"What's all this we've got here today?" he asks. "Do you have any *chole*?"

"Sorry?" says Neetu.

"Chickpeas! Spicy chickpeas. Come on, you don't know *chole*?"

Neetu raises a hand. "My bad! You know I'm South Indian. No chickpeas but there's spinach paneer." She holds up a green, oily looking dish.

"I'll go for that, then. The Mrs loves a bit of paneer. I'm always trying to get her to try different things, but you know what they say. You can take the girl out of the Punjabi pind, but you can't take the Punjabi pind out of the girl." He laughs, revealing his gappy teeth. "How much do I owe you?"

"Just £5."

Jasdeep reaches into his pocket, and returns with a £5 note and a £1 coin. "Here's a bit more. Doing my bit to help a start-up out. Right, better get back before she starts panicking. Though first I have to try this."

Jasdeep takes the lid off the Tupperware, rips a bit of flatbread and dips it into the oily spinach. "Neetu *ji*, you don't disappoint."

"You know it." Neetu winks.

His Mrs is stood back near the door. I'm not sure why Jasdeep doesn't let her choose her own food. Why doesn't she have agency over her lunch? She must be from back home. That's what he meant about the pind. I think that means village in Punjabi.

Jasdeep's eye roll says it all. This poor lady is the simple wife he brought over through marriage. She lives in submission and walks behind her husband.

"You know, Jasdeep, I feel like we've met before," I say.

He avoids eye contact and puts the lid back on his Tupperware. "I've probably got a familiar face."

"No, we've definitely met. Not in person. Online, I think. Maybe via LinkedIn? Or somewhere like that."

He looks at me. I look straight back at him, unflinching. And there it is. He recognises me. He recognises me from my LinkedIn photo. The same one I used on the Muslim dating website. The look of horror, having been rumbled, is plastered across his face.

"It was probably one of those online networking events," says Graham. "You're big on those, aren't you, Jasdeep?"

"Speaking of networking," Neetu chimes in. "You never got back to me about that call centre in India. I might need to jack this all in and go back home at this rate. Spinach paneer isn't paying my bills."

Jasdeep laughs nervously, showing us all the piece of spinach stuck between his front teeth.

"I've definitely met you before. Was it online?" I sigh for effect. "This is going to do my head in. Right, I'm going to rifle through my emails and check."

"No need. Don't think we've met. Anyway, will leave you ladies to it."

With that, Jasdeep bolts out the door, leaving his wife slowly following, her long scarf trailing behind her.

Graham looks bemused.

Neetu laughs. "He's weird. He's always flirting with the girls. His poor wife."

"I know," I say.

This is it. I've put things off long enough. I must piss on a stick.

I've sacked off the networking event in Holborn. I fancy a night off from talking shop with strangers. There are more important things to do right now.

I haven't told M I've bought a pregnancy tester. There's no point. He'll get overexcited. He always does. Instead, I'm going it alone, sat on the toilet, foil wrapper in hand. I rip open the top to reveal the plastic stick that will decide my fate. And M's fate. But mostly mine.

I can't remember how this thing works. Let's have a look at the instructions. My God, it's like a manual! Why do the instructions have to be so lengthy? Oh, wait, it's in multiple languages. That's why it looks so onerous. Let's find the English section.

Right, here we are... again.

1. Remove the plastic cap to expose the absorbent window.

Done.

2. Point the absorbent tip directly into the urine stream.

Nasty. You can bet your bottom dollar that I'll get some splashback on my fingers. I've done so many samples that my left hand will never be the same again.

3. Hold for at least 7-10 seconds, to ensure that an adequate sample is collected by the testing device.

That's a long wee.

I don't remember having to hold it for that long last time. Is it a different brand? Let me check. Oh, never mind. I'll just crack on. Okay, here's hoping that I've drunk enough water to provide a steady stream of pee.

One... two... three... Gross, it's splashed on my hand! Four... No more trickles? That's the end? I guess that will have to do.

4. Re-cap the device and place it horizontally on a clean, flat surface.

I wouldn't really call the side of my bath clean. There is a fine layer of dust and fingermarks. Looking in the bath, there is a light brown rim along the bottom. Are we disgusting people? When was the last time it was cleaned? That's the thing when you have showers instead of baths. You neglect cleaning, as you don't have to sit in your own filth.

5. Wait 5 minutes for the test to finish processing.

This is the bit I remember. The waiting. The endless, torturous waiting.

The door opens. Damn, why is M home this early? I thought it was only the privilege of self-employed folk to get home by 5.30pm.

He pushes down on the bathroom door handle.

"Is that you, babe?" he asks.

"Who else would it be?"

"Just checking. You gonna be much longer?"

I've lost track of time. "A few minutes. Why?"

"I need to go to the poop station."

"Can you hold on?"

"I can for a bit. I might have to fart to buy some time. It might get deadly out here."

What an excellent father M will make.

"Are you okay, though?" he asks.

"Yeah, I'm fine."

"Good day?"

"I'd say so. I've just signed a new client on a small retainer."

"Excellent," M pauses. "At times like this, I wish we had a second bathroom."

"Remember when we were looking, the ensuite was way too expensive? Plus, it seems excessive to need one toilet per person."

"True that," says M. "But now it feels like a great idea. You're not gonna be much longer, are you?"

"No, but you have to be patient. Are you listening outside the door?"

"Obviously, I want to hear you plop. Just to put you off. I've got my ear to the door."

"I wouldn't bother. You won't hear anything."

"What do you mean?"

"That's not what I'm here for."

"Are you in the bath?"

"No."

"Are you shaving lady parts?"

"No!"

"Then what are you doing?"

"Nothing!"

"Are you okay?"

"Yes, I'm fine."

"Have I done something wrong?" There goes M's usual question.

"It's not always about you."

"Then what are you doing that's getting in the way of my number two?"

"I don't want to say."

"Why?"

"Because I don't want to jinx it."

I can hear M sit down outside the bathroom door. I crawl over to join him from the inside.

"Are you doing a pregnancy test?"

"Maybe."

"Do you think you might be -"

"I don't know. We've been here before. I don't want to get my hopes up, or yours."

"It's alright, you know. If we are going to have a baby, then that would be amazing. And if not, it's fine. We'll keep trying. Remember, the doctor said it's not a big deal."

"What if it *is* a big deal?" My eyes well up. "What if there is something wrong? What if we can't have kids? Would you get another wife?"

"What?"

"If I couldn't give you kids, what would you do? Could you be happy for a life of just us? I've heard of people getting other wives. Nobody in our generation, mind. According to Islam, you're allowed three more, not that I want you to take advantage of that quota. And you'd have to treat us all fairly and provide us with our own homes."

M laughs.

"It's not funny."

"It is!"

"Why?"

"You're being weird. First, I can just about keep you in house and home and fancy cupcakes. How would I feed three other wives? Second, who is to say the problem is with you? It might be me, if there is a problem. And third, haven't you heard of adoption? It's not like we'll be completely stuck if we can't have kids. And even if we didn't adopt and I was stuck with you, I'd be quite happy with that. I like being stuck with you. We spend most of the time with each other and that suits me fine. Obviously, a couple of extra small people would be nice but if it's not meant to be, it's not meant to be. There's no point stressing about it, you worrywart."

A moment passes before either of us says anything. At least it's helping count down the time.

"I suppose we could adopt," I say. "I was reading somewhere that even women who haven't had birth children can breastfeed them. I'm not sure how but the body produces milk. I wonder what people would say if we adopted? You know our lot, they can be right judgemental bastards over anything."

"I don't think anyone will say anything. And if they do, who cares?"

"I care." My voice trembles.

"You shouldn't."

"I know but it's hard. I've been brought up thinking about what people think. Everything revolves around everyone else's thoughts, not our own. It's hard to shake that shit off."

"I get it. I guess being a bloke, things are a lot easier, to be honest with ya. But you've got to remember, since when has people saying stuff ever stopped us doing anything? Think about it. Has anything really held us back?"

"No."

"There you go. We've done things our way, and we always will."

"Oh!" I was meant to gasp internally, but it just came out in excitement.

"What is it?" M shouts through the door. "Is it good news?"

"I think... I'm not sure, actually. Let me just check."

I consult the overly lengthy pamphlet to reacquaint myself with what sign I should look for on the little plastic screen.

There's no room for error here. It's a very clear plus sign.

"Oh, my life! I'm pregnant!" I shout so loud that the entire floor can probably hear.

"Right, I'm coming in. Can I?"

I move away from the door and M bursts through to give me a big hug.

Then he says: "I don't want to ruin the moment but can we celebrate in a minute? I really need the toilet."

"Oh yeah, of course. Bathroom is all yours. And no second wives, yeah? There's no need now."

I come out, positive pregnancy test in hand. I can't believe it. I can't bloody believe it. It's only when I finally stopped worrying about trying that we actually conceived.

I stare at the blue symbol. It's small, no bigger than a couple of millimetres but it's there. Undeniably there.

M is right. It doesn't matter what anyone thinks, or what other people's timetables are. Because at the end of the day, here we all are.

There's more to the story... free reads and more for you

I hope you enjoyed this story. But wait... there's more. As I mentioned, this isn't your average romcom. It's got people talking, challenged perceptions, and hopefully shown that we're not so different after all. As the series grows I'd like you to be part of my tribe, so I can share exclusive content, free reads, and get your opinion on future book covers, etc. Would you like to join my tribe? If so, sign up to my mailing list here: https://www.subscribepage.com/halimakhatun-books

Enjoy this book? Want to read more? The power is in your hands...

Firstly, thanks for taking the time to read my book. It makes my heart happy knowing that people are taking pleasure from my words. It motivates me to write more. I want my book to be read as far and wide as possible, and key to making this happen is having great reviews from readers like you.

Reviews are the most powerful tool in my arsenal when it comes to getting attention for my books. I'm not represented by a global publishing house and I don't have a huge marketing team and endless budget.

But I have something better, that money can't buy – a committed and invested readership. And I rely upon this most important asset, to spread the word.

If you've enjoyed this book, I would be grateful if you could spend just a few minutes leaving a review on the store of your choice. It can be as short or as long as you like.

Books by Halima Khatun – have you read them all?

The Secret Diary of an Arranged Marriage

Winner of the 2021 Bookbrunch Selfie Award for Best Adult Fiction...

A British-Bengali girl looking for Mr Right. A motley crew of men, some hoping it's them. A mum on a mission to match make. And an age-old tradition with a twist. Welcome to the world of the arranged marriage.

The Secret Diary of a Bengali Bridezilla

And I thought finding a husband was hard...

One couple. Three months. 600 guests (most of whom I've never met) and LOTS of opinions. Welcome to my big fat Bangladeshi wedding.

The Secret Diary of a Bengali Newlywed

I found me a man, now I just need to figure out how to live with him...

New husband. New city. New in-laws and new expectations.

Welcome to my life as a Bengali newlywed.

No One Ever Asks Mum

The side of the story you never hear...

A mum on a mission to matchmake. A daughter with ideas of her own. A suitor that threatens to tear them apart. When it comes to arranged marriages, you never hear the perspective of the mother of the 'bride'. So now it's time.

About the Author

Halima Khatun is a former journalist (having worked for ITV and the BBC), writer and PR consultant.

Since she was a child, she knew that words would be her thing. With a lifelong passion for writing, Halima wrote her first novel - a coming-of-age children's story - at the age of 12. It was politely turned down by all the major publishing houses. However, proving that writing was indeed her forte, Halima went on to study English and journalism and was one of just four people in the UK to be granted a BBC scholarship during her postgraduate studies.

She has since written for a number of publications including the HuffPost and Yahoo! Style, and has been featured in the Express, Metro and other national publications. Halima also blogs on lifestyle, food and travel and parenthood on halimabobs.com. This is where she also shares updates on her novels.

You can connect with Halima on Facebook here: www.facebook.com/HalimaKhatunAuthor/, or twitter https://twitter.com/halimabobs.

Having spent years in London, Halima has resettled in Manchester with her family.